Praise for *The Disciple*

Joseph Horowitz's captivating novel of the Gilded Age comes alive through the story of Anton Seidl, an overlooked genius of the Richard Wagner school. In *The Disciple*, Horowitz weaves the vibrant world of American classical music at the dawn of the 20th century into a compelling narrative commanding in detail. He yet again challenges our mounting cultural amnesia.

Thomas Hampson

Joseph Horowitz's knowledge of the great Wagnerian conductor Anton Seidl—one of the most charismatic figures of the Gilded Age—is second to none. He also possesses a remarkable capacity to weave factual information into a compelling fictional narrative. I learned a lot about Seidl, about the social milieu that he seduced, and about the thrilling musical life that he dominated.

Barry Millington,
chief music critic for *The London Evening Standard*
and editor of *The Wagner Journal*

The Disciple will astonish readers with its insights into an extraordinary but little-known American artistic epoch. The re-creation of Antonín Dvořák is absolutely magical—poetic, tender, funny, irresistible. It evinces Horowitz's love for the man and his music, brought to life in the most fascinating and beautiful way.

JoAnn Falletta,
Music Director, the Buffalo Philharmonic Orchestra

For several decades now, Joseph Horowitz has been our Cicerone through the delightfully vibrant scenery of classical music in Gilded Age America. Such is his love for that almost forgotten chapter of our history that he felt moved to transpose his unmatched knowledge of the era to the more easily accessible plane of fiction. Much of the attractiveness and fascination of this novel rests on the charismatic and enigmatic figure of Anton Seidl, the Hungarian-born conductor who became Richard Wagner's disciple and emissary to America. *The Disciple* moves dexterously among New York, Bayreuth, and Brooklyn, offering intriguing glimpses of a short-lived but memorable rendezvous of Wagnerism and Feminism. Those who love the cultural history of New York will come away from *The Disciple* both enriched and enlightened.

Hans Rudolf Vaget,
Shedd Professor of German Studies
and Comparative Literature Emeritus, Smith College

Praise for Joseph Horowitz's *The Marriage*

Revelatory.

Thomas Hampson

With his unparalleled knowledge of fin-de-siècle classical music in America, Joseph Horowitz [has] brought us closer to Mahler and his wife Alma than any other author I have read. ... He conjures a vivid portrait of New York society and life in the teeming city at the turn of the century. An assured portraitist, he brings his cast to life with the vibrant brush-strokes of a John Singer Sargent. ... In Gustav and Alma Mahler, Horowitz has created two of classical music's most convincing fictional portraits.

Clive Paget, *Musical America*

The 'hybrid genre' of the historical novel is subject to legitimate debate; it has often been accused of trivializing history. Joseph Horowitz is aware of the skepticism his book could encounter. He believes that historical imagination can teach us a lot ... In this case, in which history is not only retold but relived, one must agree: the project succeeds.

Günther Halle, *Die Presse* (Vienna)

Anton Seidl (1895)
Courtesy of the New York Philharmonic Archives.

The Disciple:
A Wagnerian Tale of the Gilded Age

JOSEPH HOROWITZ

A Blackwater Press book

First published in the United States of America by
Blackwater Press, LLC

Library of Congress Control Number: 2025940798

ISBN: 978-1-963614-15-2

Cover art by Francesco Dabbicco
Cover design by Martina Dabbicco

Blackwater Press
120 Capitol Street
Charleston, WV 25301
United States

blackwaterpress.com

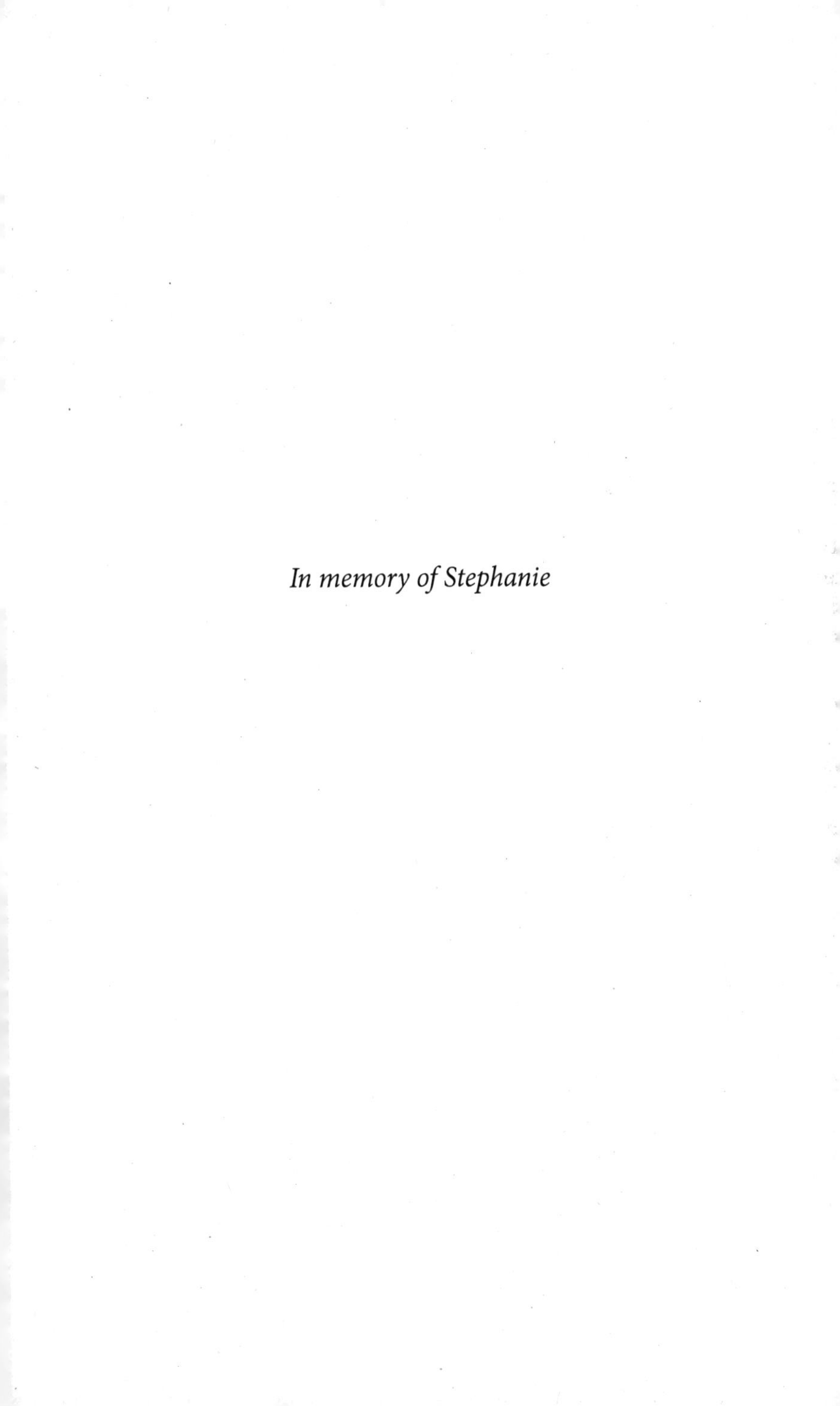

In memory of Stephanie

Contents

Preface

Some four decades ago, convinced that something had gone terribly wrong with classical music in the United States, I began to chronicle a topic barely known: its institutional history. I looked first at the glamorous interwar decades, when so many legendary Germanic and Russian artists—Heifetz, Horowitz, Rachmaninoff, Rubinstein, Schoenberg, Schnabel, Stravinsky, and on and on—became American transplants. These were also the decades of Toscanini's New York Philharmonic, Koussevitzky's Boston Symphony, and Stokowski's Philadelphia Orchestra. But the legacy of these twentieth century New World acquisitions proved shallow. By and large, their advocates and adherents sidelined American composers. Music-making in the home sharply diminished. The entire enterprise lacked sufficient New World roots.

All this became *Understanding Toscanini: How He Became an American Culture God and Helped Create a New Audience for Old Music* (1987). Meanwhile, I glimpsed something else that took me completely by surprise: a more distant, more impressive American past. Classical music in America, I would eventually discover, peaked before World War I. And nurturing a specifically American classical music was a presiding goal.

These were decades of colossal individual leadership. Judging by outcomes, the two most impactful figures were Theodore Thomas (1835-1905) and Henry Higginson (1834-1919). Thomas's itinerant Thomas Orchestra plied the "Thomas Highway," introducing symphonic music in budding metropolises and faraway hamlets alike; ultimately, in 1891, he founded what is today the Chicago Symphony Orchestra. Higginson invented, owned, and operated the Boston Symphony Orchestra and built Symphony Hall: a lightning template for proliferating orchestras in cities throughout the nation for whom a resident symphonic ensemble—an American specialty, in contradistinction to the opera house—crowned civic identity. But the hub of classical music in the United States was New York City. Never afterward would the Metropolitan Opera sustain such opulent vocal standards or demanding musical leadership. Concurrently, Oscar Hammerstein's cutting-edge Manhattan Opera was in some respects even more remarkable.

Hammerstein, who amassed a fortune in the cigar business, was also an indelible personality. Manhattan teemed with jostling musical geniuses of commanding individuality. Toscanini was already a juggernaut presence. Dvořák, Mahler, Caruso all exerted historic influence. New York was also a city of unsurpassed musical scribes, headed by James Gibbons Huneker and Henry Edward Krehbiel—cultural chroniclers with no true successors.

But mainly my inquiry into these decades yielded another name more mythic than any other. This was Anton Seidl (1850-1898), about whom Arthur Farwell—himself a composer of intrepid originality—would write in a 1944 *Musical Quarterly* essay: "For all those in any degree sensitive to the spirit of music and romance, the presence of Anton Seidl, famous alike for the depth of his silence and the height of his art, tinged the atmosphere and the consciousness of the city with a peculiarly individual and glowing quality of feeling such as it has not known before or since … Because of his known love for New York, it was downright affection, rather than admiration or awe, that New York returned to him."

Singularly among his famous contemporaries, Seidl died too young to leave recordings and in future decades was singularly forgotten even by the institutions—the Met and the New York Philharmonic—he once led. All that remained was a retrospective volume published in 1899: *Anton Seidl: A Memorial by His Friends*. Edited by the critic Henry Finck, it comprised a biographical sketch of some eighty pages, including some stories from Mrs. Seidl, tributes from colleagues, letters to Seidl from Wagner and others, and a handful of writings by Seidl himself. The documentation of Seidl's funeral, at the Metropolitan Opera, gauged the magnitude of his contribution and loss. Huneker, who was no sentimentalist, wrote: "[Seidl's] funeral was more impressive than any music drama ever seen or heard at Bayreuth. The Metropolitan Opera house was for the moment transformed into a huge mortuary chamber. It was extremely picturesque, yet sincerely solemn. The trappings of woe were not exhibited for their mere bravery. A genuine grief absorbed every person in the building," Lillian Nordica, America's leading Wagner soprano, had acquired Isolde under Seidl's tutelage; for Finck's volume she wrote: "When a man of such high purpose comes into the world he impresses an influence extending so far beyond his time that it is not given to us to estimate it."

So this was a start. But Seidl himself left no memoir, nor did his widow expand on her initial reminiscences. It was my good fortune, however, to access a pair of archives virtually unnoticed—in fact, at the time not even catalogued. One was the Seidl Archive at Columbia University, left by Mrs. Seidl upon her death in 1939—a trove of letters, scores, and assorted memorabilia dating back to Seidl's apprenticeship to Wagner. The other was the Seidl Society Archive at the Brooklyn Historical Society, documenting a story wholly forgotten: that a Brooklyn women's club, headed by Mrs. Laura Langford, became Brooklyn's major presenter of concerts, comprising a winter season led by Seidl at the Brooklyn Academy of Music and—astonishingly—fourteen weekly summertime Seidl Society concerts at Coney Island's Brighton Beach resort.

In fact, the closest thing to a Seidl shrine is the reading room of the Brooklyn Historical Society. Its Seidl materials proved a concentrated time capsule. The red leather bindings of the Seidl Society scrapbooks were crumbling non-bindings. Their thick pages, dense with pasted newspaper stories and advertisements, were yellowed and stained. The hushed rectangular reading room is itself older yet. The bookcases, tables, chairs, and flooring, the hand-carved banisters and columns are all of dark wood. The windows, with stained glass crescents, are tall but insufficient. Hanging globes in pairs cast pools of light on the long desks. A photograph taken in 1881 shows a room identical except for ornamental bunting, now gone, and an electronic EXIT sign, since added.

Langford kept everything. The tireless summertime Seidl Society orchestra commanded a repertoire of 500 works by 100 composers. Tickets cost as little as fifteen cents. At the Academy of Music, the society began with a "*Parsifal* Entertainment" on Palm Sunday, 1890. In subsequent years the winter season numbered as many as sixteen concerts. All the programs survive, their thin pages tattered and frayed: "popular" concerts, children's matinees, "Grand Wagner Concerts." The society sponsored, as well, lectures on women's suffrage and on theosophy, on the Christian meaning of *Parsifal* and on *The Ring of the Nibelung* (the last being a series of talks written by Seidl and delivered by Langford with symphonic accompaniment). The society brought working women and Black orphans to the Brooklyn seashore for swimming, dining, and Wagnerian musical recreation. It furnished special railroad cars so women could arrive unescorted from Manhattan and Brooklyn Heights. It provided bicycle rests at the Brighton Beach Hotel ("tires inflated without charge").

I might remove at random an 1890 program book and discover an advertisement for the Aeolian Parlor Orchestra, "the most wonderful and perfect of all musical instruments," combining violin, horn, flute, and cello effects; "a very useful and meritorious invention," according to Maestro Seidl. Another advertiser: the Eastern Publishing Company, Publishers and Sellers of Books Relating to THEOSOPHY, MYSTICISM, and OCCULTISM. Sunday religious services at the Music Hall feature eminent divines of the various denominations. An item: "Meyerbeer, who was an extremely cautious man when he discerned a possibility of making enemies, could never hear Wagner's name … without a disagreeable sensation, which he took no pains to conceal." "Dear Mrs. Langford! I will be happy to see you after 12 o'clock this afternoon" reads a calling card signed "Yours faithfully, Seidl." A card from Auguste Seidl-Kraus to Langford says: "My dear Mrs. Langford! Will you give me the great Pleasure, and come in my home on Sunday evening?" It is signed "With love, Your friend." A typical professional communication, from Seidl:

> Dear Mrs. Langford
> Excuse the Pencil. How is it, if you ask Mr. Joseffy to play as second number the Hungarian Fantasy by Liszt. It would be very liked by the audience. Or he may choose Piano Solos, what he want and put it in the Programme afterwards.

The intimacy of handling letters untouched and unread for a century, of eavesdropping on historic relationships both personal and professional, peaked one afternoon when I discovered a single page handwritten in pencil, with many words crossed out and rebegun. It was a Brighton Beach speech by the taciturn Herr Seidl of which no other record survives, laboriously composed in fractured English. It extolled hard-working Brooklyn women who accomplished more and spent less than their male counterparts at the Metropolitan Opera. The entire oration was a populist manifesto commending the Brighton Beach audience for favoring "good music": "the people not understand it first, but later he will whistle it with more dash and vigor, as the rich, who sits in his [opera] box and—chatter." In Henry Finck's memorial volume, the critic Albert Steinberg called Seidl an "Americamaniac": "Everything appealed to him—our democratic ways, our enthusiasm for the works of Wagner, our mixed drinks, our Welsh rarebits, our American clubs, our American scenery."

I would step outside the penumbral room and blink at the Historical Society's sunlit red terracotta façade. St. Ann's Church, next door, was by comparison dark and weathered. Seidl knew these buildings. To the east, a short walk took him to Langford's Schermerhorn Street residence. The Academy of Music was just across the street. Three blocks to the west was the Montague Street pier, from which Seidl would embark to Manhattan. The pier is long gone, as are Langford's brownstone and the Academy. But the three blocks to Montague Terrace have barely changed. A canopy of trees shades the narrow street, with its looping ornamental lamps and contiguous four- and five-story buildings of brick and stone. I would attain the long riverfront promenade Seidl would once bestride. Dour and remote, hands behind his back, he satisfied the expectations of admiring ladies and gentlemen by barely acknowledging their smiles, bows, and tipped top hats.

An elixir of memory.

* * *

And so the saga is novelistic. It begins in Bayreuth, where Anton Seidl lived for six years in Wagner's house as surrogate son and indispensable amanuensis. He toured the *Ring of the Nibelung* throughout Europe. He became Wagner's emissary in the New World. At the Metropolitan Opera, he led the American premieres of five Wagner operas, commanding six German-language seasons until the boxholders rebelled and threw the Germans out. He led the New York Philharmonic to new heights of influence and prosperity. He widely toured with the Met, and later with his "Seidl Orchestra" and "Metropolitan Orchestra." He promoted the Music of the Future in a 3,000-seat seaside pavilion on Coney Island. Turning to composition, he embarked on a Hiawatha operatic trilogy—a veritable American *Ring*. He became the high priest of American Wagnerism, a cultural avalanche generating poems and novels, paintings and plays, dominating intellectual discourse, penetrating newspapers and magazines of general circulation. A culminating crescendo of activity began in 1895 with Seidl's return to the Met. Two years later, he was conducting at Covent Garden and Bayreuth, and fielding multiple demands for his services at Europe's leading houses. In New York, a permanent Seidl Orchestra was to become the pit orchestra for the Met and Manhattan's leading concert ensemble; the concertmaster, Eugene Ysaÿe, was himself a celebrated soloist. Seidl's sudden death at the age of forty-seven was greeted as a national calamity. Bigger than the Toscanini story to come, bigger than the Bernstein story, Seidl's New World sojourn is, finally, intensified by the pathos of unconsummated promise. Its magnitude and implications challenge understanding.

Doubtless Seidl considered himself a Wagner heir truer than the composer's widow, Cosima, who inherited the Bayreuth Festival. He was also more cosmopolitan, less Germanic. His Wagner icon was more adaptable, more humanly fallible than her Wagner effigy. That is: he could have established a pedigreed Wagner mecca alternative to Bayreuth. The equation of Wagner and the Third Reich would have seemed to him no less a desecration than marauding Nazi soldiers. The Wagner of Winifred Wagner and Houston Stewart Chamberlain, of Hitler and the Holocaust, would have registered as a grotesque local aberration.

The twentieth century shadow of Hitler on Bayreuth has been a formative retroactive influence. So might have been the American Wagner shrine Anton Seidl did not live to create: an influence innocent of swastikas.

A topic for another time.

* * *

Handed a plot line so heroic and mysterious, my first impulse was to fictionalize my findings. I could, I thought, tell everything through the lens of Henry Krehbiel's probing understanding of New York's shifting musical fortunes. I knew I could impersonate the densely archaic Krehbiel style. And Krehbiel was himself a bona fide historian, able to contextualize events and actors within a grand trajectory.

But a first telling of Seidl's story, I soon realized, should be more conventionally objective. Hence *Wagner Nights: An American History* (1994). Laura Langford's story became a fifty-page chapter in *Moral Fire: Musical Portraits from America's Fin-de-Siècle* (2012). I still craved something more, and some years later wrote *The Disciple*—only to put it aside because I decided to keep going. A novel about Gustav Mahler in New York (1907-1911), I surmised, would complement and in some ways complete my Seidl narrative. So I wrote *The Marriage*, using Manhattan's post-Seidl musical affairs to test the complexities of Gustav's co-dependence with Alma. My intention at that point was to link my two novels as a single "Tale of Fin-de-Siècle New York." When *The Marriage* proved self-sufficient, I decided to publish it first: many more readers would know Mahler than Seidl. And so *The Disciple* becomes a prequel.

My story embraces a diverse cast of characters. Though today mainly forgotten, many were once influential. Carl Schurz was perhaps the most famous German-American. Robert Ingersoll, known as "The Great Agnostic," was perhaps the most prominent public orator. Both were devotees of Wagner and of Seidl. Natalie Curtis, whom we will discover in Manhattan and Bayreuth, was an important collector of Native American song. Dankmar Adler and Louis Sullivan, both of whom we will encounter when Seidl tours to Chicago, were leading American architects. Helena Blavatzky, who tutored Laura Langford, founded theosophy. Antonin Dvořák, whose "New World" Symphony Seidl premiered in New York, was Seidl's closest New York friend. Jeannette Thurber, who enticed Dvořák from Prague to New York, created America's most formidable musical conservatory. Robert Creelman, whom she engaged as a publicist, was a signature Yellow Journalist, whose sensational scoops influenced world events. Sissieretta Jones, who sang for Dvořák, was the highest paid African-American performer of her time. Cosima Wagner, who took over the Bayreuth Festival when her husband Richard died, is in my account a distant yet hovering presence who ultimately succeeded in luring Seidl back.

As with *The Marriage*, *The Disciple* includes a copious glossary of names with capsule biographies of these and twenty-eight other characters. Via Laura Langford, I have occasion to remember the Civil War, to attend a theosophical lecture, and observe Black orphans experiencing Wagner's *Tannhäuser* March. I also encounter various Wagner operas. Chapter one begins with Act III of *Tristan und Isolde* as first presented in the United States by Seidl with a pair of prodigious singers: Lilli Lehmann and Albert Niemann. As most readers will not be intimately familiar with this revolutionary interior drama, a brief synopsis is in order:

Tristan is a Cornish knight. He has fetched an Irish princess, Isolde, who is to marry his uncle, King Marke. Unbeknownst to Marke, Isolde once restored Tristan to health—and they fell in love. In Cornwall, they are discovered by Marke and his courtier, Melot, in passionate embrace. Melot draws his sword and wounds Tristan, who offers no resistance. All this precedes the third act, which begins with a heaving and sorrowful orchestral prelude. The curtain rises: at his castle in Brittany, Tristan is anxiously attended by his servant Kurwenal. He awakens from a long stupor, dazed and suicidal. In a mounting frenzy, he hallucinates Isolde's arrival ("Isolde kommt! Isolde naht!"). The moment passes. In a monologue of tortuous self-discovery, he retreats into memory and dream—and uncovers his deepest self. A second sighting ("Das Schiff! Das Schiff!") is therefore true. Isolde rushes toward him. He tears off his bandages and dies. She sings her famous "Liebestod," sinks to Tristan's side, and so unites with him in death. Wagner celebrates the turbulent human passions of the drama while at the same time absorbing the energies of a purposeless existential engine. The lovers' culminating unity proves incompatible with the daylight demands of civil society. It is an ending both sublime and unmooring.

Rather than including biographies of my three main characters within the Glossary, I position them here so they will be noticed:

Anton Seidl (1850-1898) Austro-Hungarian conductor, naturalized American. Born in Pest, he studied at the Leipzig Conservatory before moving to Bayreuth, Germany, in 1872 in order to work alongside Richard Wagner. He assisted in the production of the premiere of the *Ring of the Nibelung* in 1876. At Wagner's urging, he was named the chief conductor of Angelo Neumann's Leipzig Opera in 1879 when he was 28. Subsequently, again at Wagner's suggestion, he served as the conductor for Neumann's touring Wagner troupe, which in 1882-83 introduced the *Ring* in Holland, Belgium, Switzerland, Germany, Austria, Hungary, Italy, and England—a total of 135 stage performances and fifty-eight concerts. Seidl and Neumann next moved on to the Bremen Opera. In 1884, Seidl married the soprano Auguste Kraus. From 1885, when he arrived in the New World, until his premature death thirteen years later, Seidl was the dominant musical personality in New York City. His impact in the United States, as the central missionary and embodiment of Wagnerism, was not exceeded by that of any subsequent classical musician. Because he died before radio and recordings, his legendary presence was swiftly forgotten once those who knew and heard him were gone. He presided over six years of German-language opera at the Metropolitan Opera, introducing *Das Rheingold, Siegfried, Götterdämmerung, Die Meistersinger*, and *Tristan und Isolde* to American audiences both in New York and on tour. He maintained a world-class ensemble of German singers, exerting comprehensive artistic control over the company. Ousted in 1891 by a boxholders' revolt, he subsequently led the New York Philharmonic, where his success was scarcely less remarkable. The symphonic premieres he led included Dvořák's *New World* Symphony, in 1893. He also notably championed American symphonic music, including the Second Cello Concerto of his assistant Victor Herbert. He returned to the Met in 1895, leading *Tristan* with one of the company's biggest stars: Jean de Reszke, who was instrumental in his reinstatement. In summers, he led outdoor concerts at Coney Island's Brighton Beach resort for Laura Langford's Seidl Society. A hypnotic personality, he embodied a new type of Romantic conductor, closely modelled after Wagner. He also notably extolled democratic access to the arts.

Laura Langford (1848-1930) Brooklyn journalist and concert impresario. Born Laura Carter in Tennessee, educated at the Nashville Female Academy, she was the daughter of a prominent country gentleman whose way of life was devastated by the Civil War. In 1862 she married a ne'er-do-well Kentucky-born Union officer, Junius Holloway; like the Carters, the Holloways were slave-owning Unionists. Holloway was captured by Confederate forces, but later arrested as an accused Confederate guide; Laura successfully interceded to earn his release. Their only child, George Thomas, was born in 1864. It is impossible to know when the marriage dissolved because she subsequently kept it a secret, presenting herself as childless widow. She lived for a time at the White House, President Andrew Johnson being a relative and close family friend. While in Washington, she worked as a newspaper correspondent. She eventually settled in Brooklyn (as did George Thomas), where she initially became well known as a socialite, a clairvoyant, and an industrious journalist. Of her books, the best-known may have been *The Ladies of the White House*, a narrative of presidential wives published in 1870. The *Brooklyn Daily Eagle*, for which she served as associate editor for more than a decade before leaving the paper in 1884, testified: "What she does is done with all her might. She is not easily daunted by difficulties and ordinary obstacles have no terrors for her." Colonel E. F. Langford, whom she married in 1890, was a well-preserved Civil War hero and secretary of the Brooklyn Brighton Beach and Coney Island Railroad Company. In 1889 she founded the Seidl Society, "organized for the purpose of securing to its members and to the public increased musical culture and of promoting musical interest among women particularly. It aims to reach all classes of women and children and by its efforts in their behalf to prove the potent influence of harmony over individual life and character." Only women could join. Subsequent to presenting a "*Parsifal* Entertainment" at the Brooklyn Academy of Music in 1889, the society established a substantial annual concert season there, managed (as were all the Society's activities) by Laura Langford. It took over Anton Seidl's faltering summertime Brighton Breach concerts in 1894. Given fourteen times weekly at popular prices, and favoring music by Wagner and Liszt, the concerts continued until the destruction of the Brighton Beach Music Pavilion by a tidal wave on October 12, 1896. The Seidl Society ceased with Seidl's death in 1898. Colonel Langford died in 1902. Laura Langford's philanthropic energies subsequently revived among the celibate Shakers of Mt. Lebanon, in eastern New York State, who esteemed her clairvoyant powers. She died in obscurity.

Henry Krehbiel (1854-1923) American music critic. He was the acknowledged dean of New York music critics during his tenure with the *New York Tribune* (1880-1923). By birth (both his parents were German-born) and intellectual orientation, he was a Germanophile who honored the Classical symphonists with a purist's integrity. He completed the first English-language edition of Alexander Wheelock Thayer's *Life of Ludwig van Beethoven* and wrote a dozen books. He also translated operas from French and German, composed exercises for the violin, and edited collections of songs and arias. His *How to Listen to Music* (1896) was reprinted thirty times. *Chapter of Opera* (1908) and *More Chapters of Opera* (1919) comprise a two-volume history of opera in New York that has not been superseded. *Afro-American Folksongs* (1914) espoused the music of the Black slave as the "most beautiful and most vital in our folk song." He influentially championed Dvořák's "New World" Symphony. His close friends included Anton Seidl. After the turn of the twentieth century, Krehbiel's taste grew increasingly conservative. His insistence that art serve a moral purpose was at odds with the new modernism. In a notorious obituary documenting his fierce admiration for the fin-de-siècle achievements of Seidl and Dvořák, he denounced Gustav Mahler for rescoring Beethoven, composing polyglot symphonies, and underestimating the sophistication of New York's concert and operatic culture. No subsequent music critic has played so influential a role within the city's community of artists.

* * *

Introducing *The Marriage* three years ago, I wrote a preface arguing the value of historical fiction for the cultural historian: animating my characters, composing dialogue, I felt I had learned new things about them. And so it has been with *The Disciple.*

An inscrutable sadness typified Seidl's persona. Arthur Farwell, in his 1944 *Musical Quarterly* article, revealed what he believed to be the source. It was a story told to him long before, in Bayreuth, by the widow of the composer Engelbert Humperdinck. Prior to his departure for America in fall 1885, Seidl re-encountered Cosima's daughter Daniela, whom he had known at Bayreuth when she was a child. Daniela was now 24 years old. They fell in love. But this development "could not reduce the moral fortress of this deep and noble soul. He would countenance no wrong to [his wife] Auguste. Europe would present too close quarters; he must get as far away … as opportunity would permit. And so America was immensely enriched by this hidden tragedy of love." Daniela herself married in 1886. More is known about these events—and will be found in the pages to come. But my answer to the riddle of Seidl's sadness is not quite the same as Arthur Farwell's answer.

In Orson Welles's *Citizen Kane*, the mystery of Charles Foster Kane is the meaning of "Rosebud"—the last word he uttered. In the film's final sequence, it proves to be the inscription on a sled he knew as a child—before hardship and aspiration directed his life toward a battlefield. What I think I have discovered, writing *The Disciple*, is that Daniela was but a part of Seidl's "Rosebud," a token of a greater loss.

Prologue

Bayreuth, Germany: May 1878

The children were wearing their little helmets. Isolde and Eva wore capes, Siegfried a bearskin. They were yelling for him to go faster. Daniela, Blandine, and the governess were the other horses, helping to pull the carriage round and round in front of the house. The children had inserted flowers in his long black hair. His smooth face was streaked with dirt and sweat. His short, stocky legs were working hard. He wore a peaceful smile at odds with the commotion. The carriage was a birthday present for the master, now 65 years old: a benchmark. Yesterday everyone had wheeled the master and Cosima down the street. Today it was the children's turn to ride. Their happiness pleased him. And he enjoyed Daniela's proximity.

The children were shrieking. They were attempting to drown out another voice. "Herr Seidl?" Cosima. "Herr Seidl!" He stumbled to the side. The carriage stopped. The children laughed. Hurrying, he ran his hand through his hair to sweep away the flowers. He wiped his face with his handkerchief. Cosima stood erect at the doorway. She did not move her head, but her eyes shifted to watch him rush up the steps. The house was dark. A large dog ran forward to greet him.

He burst into the music room and closed the doors. Bookcases; oil portraits of King Ludwig and Countess d'Agoult; a bust of Schröder-Devrient; souvenirs, chairs, sofas in profusion. Standing beside the piano: a small bespectacled man with a large head and sharp features. His brow was immense, his nose large, his mouth thin-lipped and sunken, his chin pointed. He was wearing a cloth jacket, knee breeches, stockings, cloth shoes: his Renaissance outfit. He bristled with whimsy and impatience. Seidl again ran his hand through his matted hair. Wagner's blue eyes flashed.

"So sorry to disturb you." He had assumed his most gnomish countenance. His voice was surprisingly deep. "Cavorting with the flower maidens?" Seidl grimaced and looked at the rug. "You will please do me the favor of joining me at the keyboard. After all, it's still my birthday week."

On the music stand the orchestral sketch for *Parsifal*, act one, was open to the scene with the dead swan. They sat down together. Seidl glanced to his right. Wagner's eyes had turned inward. Seidl inhaled deeply. Wagner's perfume. Wagner had begun playing and singing: "Is it you who killed the swan?"

"Indeed! Whatever flies I can hit in flight!"

"You did this? And it does not concern you? What harm did that swan do to you? How could you commit this crime?"

"I do not know."

"Where are you from?"

"I do not know."

"Who is your father?"

"I do not know."

"Who sent you this way?"

"I do not know."

"Your name then."

"I had many, but I know none of them any more."

They played out the scene, with Seidl singing Parsifal and

extemporizing in the bass, under Wagner's part. Wagner sang Gurnemanz—and then Kundry, informing Parsifal that his mother was dead.

Wagner stopped. Seidl's eyes were red. Wagner accosted him gaily. "And so, am I too old to turn a new trick? How do you like our Parsifal, our holy fool? Our *homeless hero*?"

Seidl turned to Wagner and said, "This is my home." His voice cracked. "Wahnfried is my home."

Wagner shut his eyes forcefully and opened them again. They were lidded and glazed. Seidl blinked heavily.

"When I'm well put away in the backyard, decently covered with dirt, you'll go out into the world at last. Already, you're twenty-*eight*, you're no longer young, my cherub. And soon enough you'll conduct *Parsifal* and conduct it properly. We reserve this work for Bayreuth. No common German opera house will ever mount it. It's no vagrant, no Jewish harlot! The Semites will have their fun with it. They'll call it Christian and mock the redeemer in good form. And the Christians will cower and shrink from it—sacrilege, they'll cry, just because it happens to glorify true Christian suffering and compassion. Even the Buddhists will have something against it, I assure you. And one hundred miserable scribes will analyze and deplore it. The ancients had true *religion*. Read Plutarch and see what he has to say about heresy and unbelief—and compare it with our simpering church fathers. How can a Highest Power dwell among us, when we're incapable of recognizing greatness? And if perchance we manage to notice greatness, our barbarian 'civilization' teaches us to hate and persecute it. Who today can venerate the sorrow of the Savior? Answer me that. Oh yes, of course, we've patched together a simulacrum of reverence, but what 'educated' person bothers with collared fatheads preaching meekness and modesty? I'd rather endure five hours of Meyerbeer …"

Wagner was prowling the cluttered room, a ranting Beelzebub. Seidl, in his head, replaced Wagner's hoarse incantatory baritone with the *Parsifal* prelude, its chant of pain and forgiveness, its summons to reckoning and redemption …

"… in the newspapers! Such lucubrations from our learned scribes! Words! Words! Words! Would that mechanical printing had never been invented. Letters, syllables, but no living belief! Why can't governments scrape together money enough to buy out the press? Everything's for sale in the end—including the wisdom that serves every tobacco-stung eye in every wretched beerhouse once the tables are strewn with specimens of German daily journalism! That we've become a nation of newspaper readers—this is what defines our ruin. And what defines my reputation, the cross I bear, with my nervous heart, my soul-sickness, my responsibilities and expenses. Oh, once I'm gone a few people will awaken to my possible importance to the Germany that might have been without the advice of our many experts …"

… and what of me? Very well, I can conduct. I can conduct *Parsifal.* And visit your grave "decently covered with dirt" behind the house …

"… that Mozart and Beethoven, Schiller and Goethe today occupy an oasis in a great national desert, displaced in our public's fickle affections by Auber and Rossini. We regenerate *abroad*—that's where the old strain of German blood runs through all the great nations. The Anglo-Saxons in *America*—that's a civilization where German music can develop in freedom, unoppressed by the burden of our melancholic 'national' history."

Wagner wheeled and faced Seidl at the piano. "Daydreaming?!" The sudden affection in his eyes as suddenly dimmed to a Faustian gaze. He thought aloud: "My better half." Their eyes met. Neither man looked away.

Chapter One

Manhattan: December 1886

Henry Edward Krehbiel proceeded down the aisle to his accustomed seat in row L. He maneuvered his massive torso into place and had a look around the vast horseshoe: its sullen gilded décor, its darkly upholstered boxes, the bare metal railings of its three looming balconies, the steep Valhalla of its most distant seats. Normally he socialized during the intermissions and greeted Finck along the way, but tonight he was not in the mood. In fact, no one was: never had he observed a Metropolitan Opera House audience so quickly or quietly reseated. The shushing started as soon as the chandeliers began to dim. The disciplinarians were women, and not to be trifled with. More than three-fifths of the house, Krehbiel estimated, was female.

The applause began high overhead; laced with thunderous bravos and piercing cheers, it quickly spread: Seidl had entered the pit. He had the orchestra rise. His bow was curt and expressionless. He turned his back, and all sound ceased. Krehbiel's shoulders clenched.

The sweeping rise and fall of Seidl's baton produced a tidal symphonic sequence, the string choir heaving and receding in waves of pain. An oceanic sorrow gripped 3,600 enslaved auditors. Krehbiel closed his eyes. The violins traced a dissipating ascent. The curtain rose. A lamenting English horn addressed the sonic void.

Even feigning sleep, Niemann was prodigious. Though Krehbiel took no notes, his forthcoming *Tribune* review arose unbidden. *He takes possession of the stage like an elemental force. The figure is colossal; the head, like "the front of Jove himself."* Robinson, as Kurwenal, circled the huge prostrate body, waving his arms, wringing his hands. Niemann opened his eyes. Strangely large and luminous, they animated his weary face with its tangled reddish mass of beard. He more spoke than sang. *Herr Niemann's treatment of Wagner's text is, like the drama itself, an exposition of the German aesthetic ideal: strength before beauty.* "Wo bin ich? Was ruft mich?" Every nuance of his deportment and dazed declamation supported an impression wholly unnatural: of awaking from the dead.

Krehbiel studied Niemann's enormous eyes as they registered Tristan's incipient awareness of the crisis to which he had unwillingly returned. He remembered Niemann's Siegmund, three weeks prior: *The voice is as weary as the exhausted body.* But Niemann's disclosure of paroxysmic clairvoyance as Tristan revisited recesses of memory and tortured slumber—there was nothing like this before.

"Isolde lebt und wacht." A keening whispered song, a demented holy vision. "Sie rief mich aus der Nacht." Not even de Reszke could deny that Niemann at fifty-five years of age could husband his tenor in the service of heightened expression. Heinrich Vogl, at Bayreuth, had achieved a cleaner legato and a purer tone, but to what avail? In any event, Bayreuth could not compare with New York. Not that Cosima would remotely care. "Isolde kommt! Isolde naht!" Niemann was pointing, quaking in frenzied expectation. Krehbiel felt his blood rush. When ideas returned, he asked himself what Niemann could possibly have left to give. Isolde's moment would not arrive for some time to come. Krehbiel's pulse subsided. He was wary now.

Seidl was guiding his musicians toward a respite of rippling quiescence, the eye of the storm. The rocking motion of a solo horn atop a murmuring bass line: Tristan's dream of his sublime beloved, far-off and afloat. "Ach, Isolde! Isolde!" Two women to his right were tightly clasping one another's hands. "Wie schön bist du!" Niemann was approaching the cataclysm: the actuality of Isolde's ship, breaking the horizon. A pulsating, hammering orchestral surge. "Das Schiff! Das Schiff! Isoldens Schiff!" Niemann tore the bandage from his wound, staggered forward. "Heia, mein Blut!" A mass of red, lurid, covering his midriff. Beyond the bounds of pleasure. Isolde's voice offstage. Alongside, one of them had swooned; no, she had fainted. Gasps. And now Isolde: the regal Lilli Lehmann. Many were weeping. Her death-song mounted relentless, naked, ecstatic, subsiding into womb-like regions of the unborn. The curtain fell. The house froze for an eternity of minutes. Krehbiel listened to his own labored breath. Next: pandemonium. Niemann and Lehmann bowing. Lehmann offstage, returning with Seidl. Screams: the women, dozens of them, standing on their chairs. Krehbiel rose and exited up the aisle. He turned once to look back, then quickened his departure.

The sudden chill of a winter night sprinkled with snow felt cleansing. Krehbiel pulled his coat tight and hailed a cab. He climbed heavily into the compartment and shut the door. Through the window, the city—the nocturnal traffic and stray pedestrians, the hulking stone and cement, the drizzled shadows cast by flickering lamps—seemed uncanny, another time and place. He was in fact experiencing an unbidden condition of existential disequilibrium, of head and heart rent asunder, of mental faculties benumbed. Influences unknown and unknowable had violated the boundaries of his being. He floated in an intoxicating narcosis. He relinquished command.

Or was he instead perturbed? Surely, I have not succumbed to any morbid netherworld. I am not Tristan, prey to a beckoning dissolution. Niemann's delivery of "O König" had been hallucinatory. "Das dunkel nächtge Land, daraus die Mutter mich entsandt." In any event, the king's monologue was much too long. Then again: in Verdi, no cuckolding could produce such a noble philosophic sorrow. But whence nobility in the hysteria of the lovers' rapture? Or in the public disclosure of swooning and fainting and hot clenched hands? Niemann's ripping of the bandage, his crazed baring of the wound—did these gestures fall within the precincts of aesthetic enjoyment? Do susceptible opera-goers emerge from the crucible of Tristan's derangement sensitized or desensitized? Only upon its enslavement by Classical principles does the Romantic become civilizing.

The towers of Newspaper Row seemed sinister tonight. Krehbiel was eager to encounter the human company of the *Tribune* newsroom. But at one in the morning the room was somnolent and desultory. He had barely an hour to file. In Vienna and Berlin, the critics took their time, lingering in their cafés, polishing exquisite calumnies and innuendos. (What had Hanslick written of *Tristan*, in Vienna? "This assassination of sense and language.") An American newspaperman worked with speed. The public curiosity, the alacrity to learn, was generously served. The profession was self-taught: there were no professors. In Krehbiel's case, school was reporting murders and baseball games for the *Cincinnati Gazette* from the age of twenty. Before that, he acquired German at home in Ann Arbor, his father having been an immigrant Methodist minister. His further learning, in a variety of fields, testified to tenacious personal application. The Metropolitan Opera, too, was American: without lineage. It had begun in 1883 as a tiara for philistine new wealth. In 1884 it was sabotaged by a German Trojan horse. The horse disgorged *Tannhäuser*, *Lohengrin*, and *Die Walküre.* Seidl arrived a year later. The future promised *Die Meistersinger*, then *Der Ring des Nibelungen.* Let Americans encounter Siegfried—a prototype of energy unspoiled, of rude impetus and new freedom.

Richard Wagner's "Tristan und Isolde" was put forward last night by the Metropolitan Opera for the first time. The interesting character of this occurrence was fully appreciated by the public. The last seat was sold four days ago, and the vast audience-room was crowded in every portion. The attention paid to the work was intense, and the pauses which permitted such demonstrations were filled with unusual scenes of delight. Resistance toward Wagner's music is much more likely to be found in communities with whom fixed tastes and prejudices are the result of a certain degree of artistic culture attained than in communities like ours where a work is listened to by unbiased hearers for its own sake.

At Bayreuth the conditions are singular. For the singers, there are long resting periods between the acts. The audiences attend in a spirit of pilgrimage, a condition of high enthusiasm and fervent endurance. In New York, half the house speaks no German: Seidl's cuts are merely judicious. And the work has its undoubted excesses and longueurs.

If anything could justify a retention of all the music of the last act it would be the performance of Herr Niemann. He carried his hearers along with restless power and wrought them up to a pitch of painful excitement. The culmination of his sufferings was in fact horrible, and one could not help wishing he had stopped short of the extremity which Wagner's lines demand. The exposure of the sword wound sent a thrill of horror through the audience. Herr Niemann reserves his powers for this culminating scene; never is he guilty of a step which retards or reverses the development of the character that is hastening to its destruction. He disregards all extravagance of gesture or utterance. His use of the resources of tone color, with a voice that has been much worn, is marvelous, and his declamation replete with vitalizing power. In every respect his Tristan was finely mated by Frl. Lehmann's Isolde. From her first note to her last she abandoned herself without reservation to a publication of the character's passionate intensity.

Let them next experience her immolation as Brünnhilde. "Alles weiss ich." Women's wisdom. That role will fit Lilli like a regal robe. It will enthrone her in the affections of our ardent lady Wagnerites.

I am constrained to believe that the significance of this performance is not so trifling and that its probable influence upon the future of the lyric drama in this country is not so small as is imagined by those whose artistic wants are satisfied with the pretty melodies of Bellini and Donizetti. Lovers of the musical drama in New York are neither few in numbers nor lukewarm in their affections. The reception accorded to "Tristan und Isolde" at its first performance in America was not such as comes from an audience gathered together by curiosity alone. It told of keen and lofty enjoyment. Never before or since has the purifying or ennobling capacity of music been so convincingly demonstrated as by Isolde's death song, which constitutes the most powerful possible plea for the adulterous lovers. An unsurpassed feature of last night's rendition of this culminating episode of the drama was Herr Seidl's mastery of climax, in which the piling of Pelion on Ossa by other men was exceeded by the most patient and reposeful accumulation of material, its proper adjust-

ment, and its firm maintenance when once it had been gained. The more furious the tempest of passion which he worked up, the more firmly did he hold the forces in rein until the moment arrived when they were loosed, so that all was swept away.

But the screaming and the horror. He must talk to Seidl about the sword wound.

* * *

Niemann had been steadily imbibing for two hours, downing cocktails from a beer glass plus an occasional shot of—a favorite beverage—brandy mixed with ginger ale and absinthe. He was also holding court, in slurred German, for Lehmann, August Lüchow, and a small group of kindred Wagnerites lingering in the restaurant long after closing time. His vast constitution and intense volubility persevered impressively, his latest topic being Anton Seidl.

"And where is our director, our presiding genius? No doubt melancholic at home, communing with his master in heaven. That man is too much in earnest. He should return to earth once in a while. My God, do you remember in seventy-six in Bayreuth—his constant instruction and advice, delivering messages from on high?"

"He is a dear man," Lehmann interjected with some heat. Of queenly bearing, indomitable energy, and forthright opinion, she alone among the Met's Wagner sopranos partook in the late-night camaraderie at Lüchow's and Lienau's. "He is a dear man and you, of all people, realize it. And what would any of us have done without him that summer, I should like to know. My Woglinde and the infernal swimming machine for the Rhinemaidens, with its straps and buckles, being wheeled about while suspended twenty feet in mid-air, I still cannot believe that I submitted to that contraption; how it wobbled when we swam across the stage. And Seidl, being in charge of my apparatus, insisted that everything be mechanically perfect, never mind that I was to perform as well. I made my Bayreuth debut being heaved and hauled about by two workmen in overalls while singing the first words of the *Ring des Nibelungen* and praying that I would again be upright when I had to sing again. Seidl was my guardian angel."

"The old man was pleased. He grumbled and complained, I apologized for all my past sins to make him happy, and he was happy enough—for him. He would have been happier had he let me sing his Siegfried. But, no, it had to be someone else because I was to sing Siegmund. He wrote himself into that role, it was all him, abandonment, exile—*persecution.* And the inevitable rant about fatherlessness, motherlessness. He had two names growing up, you know—Richard Wagner, Richard Geyer."

"But he wrote himself into *every* role. He was Wotan, too. And Fricka was Minna. Do you remember him, in seventy-six, demonstrating Sieglinde for Scheffsky? My God, she was ugly and fat. Good King Ludwig used to have her sing for him concealed behind plants and shrubbery. She was a perfect lump onstage. How Wagner acted that part—caressing your face, hugging your neck on his tiptoes. I can never forget—I modeled my own Sieglinde accordingly—how he cried 'So bleibe hier!' and slightly turned his head, as if to run after you. And next …" — Lehmann arose, and began to act the part — "… singing 'wo Unheil im Hause wohnt!' he supported himself with both hands grasping the table, his head thrown back and his eyes closed" — she closed her eyes. "Then, with eye and ear alone, not moving his head, he followed Hunding's approach." She broke her pose. "He was your best Sieglinde—no one can approach the pathos he brought to that part."

"Scheffsky. That ox! *You* should have been my Sieglinde."

"Wagner wanted me, you know that. Even at the last rehearsals. But it was too late, I already had my share of roles in *Walküre* and *Götterdämmerung*. Not that I was ever in Germany offered the three Brünnhildes. That had to wait for the New World. I gave up Berlin and all my coloratura princesses to become an American artist. So now when Seidl does *Siegfried* and *Götterdämmerung* with us next season ..."

"What grief the old man inflicted!" Niemann interrupted, tottering. "His *six*-page letter to me, correcting my Paris *Tannhäuser!* Telling me I did too much singing in the third act—that I should whisper my part! That my monologue wasn't *tired* enough."

"And he was right, absolutely. You are the living proof of that—today. You've finally grown up, that's all. In 1861 you were just a big noise."

"That's easy for you to say—since he was in love with you. All sweetness and tenderness, meanwhile lecturing the rest of us in that sarcastic singsong of his."

"When he was in a bad mood, when he was exhausted."

"And Cosima! Don't remind me of the time she objected to my table manners, the time I borrowed a slice of Jaide's ham across the table in the garden, and Cosima sulked off to the house. That woman was worse than the seven plagues of Egypt."

"Cosima is a woman of the world. We are artists."

"You never saw him conduct. That was another matter. Say what you will about his wheedling and nagging, on the podium. The face of that little man, the flame and wit of his eyes, the mobility of his features—it was unique. The Beethoven Ninth at Bayreuth, in seventy-two, when they laid the foundation stone—Seidl was there, and Nietzsche, it was such an occasion, you knew it was for the ages. He told me to sing my solo as I pleased, to attend to the words—'Froh!' 'Durch des Himmels prächt'gen Plan!' I can see him even, the way at 'Seid umschlungen, Millionen!' he softened and amplified his very being, as if what we did at Bayreuth that day would change the world."

"He wanted me for that performance. Berlin would not release me. That was the first of my disputes with Hulsen. I advised Wagner to engage my sister—and he did. Riezl told me many times about …"

She stopped to observe Niemann stagger to his feet. Bellowing into the sleepy dining room, pounding a mug for emphasis, he assayed

> Froh, wie seine Sonnen fliegen
> Durch des Himmels prächt'gen Plan,
> Laufet, Brüder, eure Bahn,
> Freudig, wie ein Held zum Siegen.

While the others sat transfixed, Lehman began to laugh. She was out the door by the time Niemann had launched his final high B-flat: a toneless shout followed by a lurching physical collapse.

* * *

The residue in his ear was sadness: the plaintive offstage song of the English horn with all else silent. Tristan's coma, Kurwenal's vigil. The tune rising, receding, languidly entrapped, as endless and old as time itself.

Seidl was nursing a cigar with his feet up. Auguste was long asleep. A portrait of Wagner dominated the study. A bust of Beethoven crowned the piano. Framed autographs and music manuscripts covered the walls. Wotan, the slumbering St. Bernard, was his only company.

He was as ever picturesque. His long raven hair was combed straight back. His sculpted Gothic features—he was said to resemble Liszt—were impassive and implacable: thought weighed upon his visage. His eyes, nearly black, were contemplative behind spectacles. No less than the Sphinx did he emanate a charged condition of stasis.

The evening's piping English horn had sung of sorrows past. Recalling *Tristan und Isolde*, Wagner would evince a cosmic ennui, world-forgetful. He would remember Schnorr von Carolsfeld, his first Tristan. For half his life he had goaded singers to attempt feats of impersonation he himself best commanded. The effort grew tedious, another of his futile labors. The tenors were the most intractable: voices without brains. And yet Schnorr von Carolsfeld was a supreme colleague, a kindred interpreter in the most taxing of all the roles he inflicted. Niemann, it is true, is an artist—but headstrong. Von Carolsfed's vulnerability was what sealed his genius and his fate. Ruefully retelling the story, Wagner would rehearse their first encounter. *Lohengrin* in Karlsruhe, 1863. Von Carolsfeld's immense girth was instantly forgotten, so plangent was his delivery, so attuned his persona. Afterward, they discovered themselves in one another. That von Carolsfeld the singer was at once a reader, a thinker, a passionately intuitive actor rendered him susceptible to the recklessness of Tristan's self-knowledge. The two months of rehearsal, which for the others drilled implausible assignments by rote, for von Carolsfeld incited ever more dangerous acts of self-excavation. Then came the premiere on the drafty Munich stage, then high fever and delirium. "Console my Richard!" were his actual last words. The newspapers gloated that Wagner had slain his favorite. Long after Munich had forgotten, long after sundry other scandals had taken the place of Schnorr von Carolsfeld's pathetic demise, Wagner's grief endured. "I drove him to the abyss! I tried to call him back only to push him over the brink, just as we kill the somnambulist when we cry out in alarm. I am not like other men: I look down and my head does not swim. And so unwittingly I sacrificed my friend."

The shepherd's lonely *alte Weise*—adrift in a void, luring Tristan to consciousness—shadowed Seidl's night-long ruminations. My American celebrity and "success": my exile and displacement. Better here than Bayreuth, with Cosima manipulating her amiable son into a counterfeit likeness of his father. We may as well transplant what we can.

He would talk of emigrating to America. Well, he would talk of many things. His itineracy. His marginality. Whoever his father was—Wagner or Geyer—he was fatherless by the age of nine. How many conducting posts were there? Würzburg, Magdeburg, Königsberg, Riga. Then came Paris, where he and Minna had to pawn their belongings. Then Dresden, hounded by creditors. Then Switzerland, pursued by police for supporting the Dresden uprising. Vienna. Italy. Munich under Ludwig's protection. But he was hated and reviled there, of course, even Ludwig had to ask him to leave. Finally, Bayreuth—a backwater, a haven, call it what you will, buried within the patchwork "Germany" he loved and despised. With interludes in Venice, for his health. No wonder he tried to reserve Bayreuth for his "patrons," banning the opera rabble.

Seidl's own trans-Atlantic odyssey was complex. In New York, the anti-Wagner faction was wondrously muted and ineffectual. There really was a new world for Wagner here. His birthplace—Hungary—was barely a memory. He owed to Wagner his inspiration, his edification, the Euripides and Shakespeare and Schiller the family would read aloud at night. Also the letters to Neumann:

> None of the other conductors has such a clear understanding of my tempi, and the harmony between the music and the action. I have coached Seidl personally, and he will conduct your Nibelungen as no other can. If my word for his is not sufficient, then I shall *never* express my opinion to you again!

"My every wish would be gratified if you would consent to appoint to your vacant position of conductor this young musician, in whom I have more confidence than in any other." And so began Neumann's *Ring* tours. The tumult in Berlin. The entire length of Unter den Linden, from the imperial palace on down, lined with people; they cheered from the trees when we drove to the theater. At the first *Rheingold*, with Scaria, Vogl, and Lieban—Wagner was amazed by Lieban's Mime, he threw his arms around him and Lieban kissed Wagner's hand—the house rose as one when the curtain fell on the entrance of the gods, scarves waving from the balconies. The brass blew a fanfare for Wagner, barely audible over the din. He finally appeared, stepped to the footlights, and gave one of those earnest little speeches he rendered with trembling emotion. "If this reception is an expression of thanks on your part" — well, what else could it have been? — "I shall accept it not for myself, but for these artists, who have journeyed from near and far to interpret my work tonight. They have so completely expressed my thoughts, and have so incorporated themselves into my style, that I can only add my thanks to yours." For the last Berlin cycle, the men of the orchestra laid a wreath on the conductor's desk to atone for their skepticism. And Wagner had fetched the children from Bayreuth. Siegfried was all of twelve years old; he couldn't scratch or sneeze without his mother's supervision. Then England, then the German provinces, Holland, Belgium, with our missionary company of one hundred thirty-four. Five freight cars full of properties and of musical instruments. London was where Scaria entered from the wrong side of the stage and proceeded to transpose all his high notes down an octave and all his low notes up an octave, staring beseechingly into the wings when he was supposed to be raging at Brünnhilde. The next day he remembered nothing. Neumann recognized the symptoms from Ander's breakdown attempting to memorize Tristan in Vienna in 1861. Later—after the Bayreuth *Parsifal*—Scaria's madness returned full force; the poor man died insane. Amsterdam: Gusterl sang in the *Meistersinger* quintet in concert. "Kindly excuse me if I make any mistakes, I found it absolutely impossible to get the music. It is not my business to go hunting for scores." I called her "a spoiled Viennese princess"—because I knew she had the piece by heart. That was—what?—mere months before I proposed to her in Bologna. We skipped Paris at Wagner's insistence; if America was the Mississippi, France was the Isle of the Dead on the River Styx. So the Parisians descended *en masse* on Brussels. Massenet and Lalo attended the banquet. Both very nice. Never before Italy were there so many encores as in Belgium, things like Mime's song that are never repeated in Germany. That was Lieban. The artists Neumann assembled: Niemann, Materna, Schott, Brandt, Gusterl of course—all of them reassembled here in New York. We hung on Wagner's letters, his anxious inquiries and excited congratulations. I was a planet; he was my sun.

We were accustomed to his chronic erysipelas, indigestion, insomnia, depression, the cardiac spasms that prevented him from conducting. And yet in Aix-la-Chapelle we were unprepared, wholly. *Richard Wagner died yesterday in Venice*. Neumann and I resolved to proceed with *Das Rheingold* that evening. Hours later, he called us into his room to open a letter addressed to him in Wagner's hand. Neumann's fingers trembled. *Geehrtester Freund und Gönner!* Did Neumann get the letter from Amsterdam? How would the company ever recuperate from its labors? Are you really contemplating Venice? It is the least progressive of all Italian cities.

> And now may all the good blessings from Heaven be with you, to which I add my warmest greetings and ask you to bestow them further as you see fit.
>
> Yours devotedly, Richard Wagner
> Venice, Palazzo Vendramin Calergi, February 11, 1883

A surge of confused feeling, as if such a letter—from "Heaven," of all places—could reverse fate. That night the Rhinemaidens' lament became a dirge, the entrance of the gods—never before had I taken it so deliberately—an apotheosis. Neumann walked onstage to read the final sentence of Wagner's letter. I led Siegfried's Funeral Music in the pit. Disbelief and silence. Neumann and I departed forthwith for Bayreuth. The coffin had already arrived at the station. It was all so poorly organized. Cosima—that was the one time she left everything unattended. In Venice, she sat with the body for twenty-five hours. Joukowski had to go crawling for her wedding rings at the Bayreuth station; they had slipped off her wasted fingers. The military band playing the "Trauermarsch" out of tune, the miserable sheet of music blowing away and needing to be fetched. The procession to Wahnfried in the snow, supporting the coffin with Niemann, Joukowski, Richter, Levi, Wolzogen and the others. The children grasping its corners. Black flags. Church bells. And then the so very professional sermon at the gravesite. "Our father who art in heaven, thy kingdom come, thy will be done …" Well,

Wagner was ever misunderstood. We left the children behind in the cold. Cosima was still in the house.

Neumann better honored Wagner in Venice that April. Gondolas by the hundreds gathered silently on the Grand Canal. The late afternoon sun cast shrouds on the huddled palaces and soothed the water with a waning radiance. From afar came a mournful flotilla of linked barges, decked in flowers, escorted by slender boats of state. They halted, bobbing, astride the Vendramin Palace, with its tall arched windows and grave facade. Neumann and sundry singers stood motionless on the long balcony. As they uncovered their heads, so were heads uncovered on rooftops and on quays. From the water, his sixty musicians in tow, Seidl led Siegfried's threnody, the dirge throbbing and dissipating in the bronze light, resounding down the broad canal, down the corridors of history. The wail of Siegmund's loneliness, waterborne, recorded the fate of the doomed twins. Niemann's tattered tenor, confessing, confiding: "Nun weiss du, fragende Frau …"

"Tony." Auguste. "Eat." A tray: rolls and butter. Jam. Wotan stirred and flapped his tail. Gusterl glanced, sighed, departed. Seidl took a roll and fed it to the dog. The sadness of the beast's intelligent eyes was consoling.

CHAPTER TWO

Chicago: April 1889

Touring the *Ring* with his Metropolitan Opera troupe of 164 was in some ways reminiscent of touring Europe with Neumann, in some ways not. The distances were greater, the landscapes emptier. Boston was of course compact and refined; it already saw itself as venerable. Then came the long train ride to the fabled Western metropolis of Chicago, a city of one million, of stockyards and skyscrapers built in a day. The Parsifal in him experienced the wonderment of traversing a gap in time and space en route to an alien destination.

To approach New York was to glimpse from afar a harbor fronting two great rivers. The beckoning landmarks were a mythic island statue bearing a Liberty torch and the world behemoth of bridges, its stone turrets and intricate webbing linking the tall island city to a horizontal land mass of wharves and steeples. The density of vessels, the massive profile of stone and cement was a spectacle aerated by water and sky, the columns of smoke crisp and white, the sea air salty and fresh.

Chicago was a locomotive thrust, a furnace of energy. A rural terrain of distant farms gathered mass. Then, suddenly: an industrial amphitheater of factories, slaughterhouses, grain elevators, iron mills, mountain heaps of slag and coal under horizons of soot and of black and gray chimney funnels. A clamor of bells announced every crossing, where cable cars and lines of freight wagons witnessed the train's express passage. A downtown of massive young office buildings, shorn of ornament, was smothered in bituminous bilge. A narrow oily river, bristling with bridges, jammed with barges and schooners, coal scows and grain boats, appeared and vanished. A titanic shed under arching steel and glass was attained to the hiss of steam and shouts of "She-caw-go!" "She-caw-go!" And all of this was but preliminary. The company regathered at another platform and proceeded north along the oceanic lake to Milwaukee, there to perform the four *Ring* operas in five days in a city he quickly experienced as a provincial version of Manhattan's Kleindeutschland. Black Chicago, a grasping machine of sullen power and furious magnetic activity, drew them back for a prolonged visit: fourteen performances in two weeks, beginning with a *Ring* cycle in four consecutive nights.

A convoy of hotel omnibuses met them at nightfall at the station's carriage court—illuminated not by gas or arc lamps but rather by electricity, celebrated as a modern marvel to set beside ten-story skyscrapers and omnipresent cable cars, which here displaced horse-drawn conveyances as the basic transportation mode. Proceeding east toward the lake under a soot canopy swept by prairie winds, through stone canyons wedged between the interminable lakefront, the foul river, and innumerable rail lines, they gaped at the melee of labor and activity, at construction pits lit for night-time hammers and rivets, at swift cable trains of three and four cars bulging with dangling standees front and aft. Overhead, locomotives on elevated tracks—New York had those as well, but within reason—split the air with the roar and rattle of steam engines, of wheels metal on metal. This clangorous music of American enterprise proclaimed a utilitarian culture of commerce and rabid self-improvement. It exerted a fascination as hypnotic as any stage drama.

Chicago, he understood, was a mecca for writers and architects. No less than Milwaukee and Cincinnati and St. Louis, he knew, it was already a musical outpost for immigrant Germans. Thomas's outdoor concerts were a summer fixture. Balatka's local orchestras and choirs amassed hundreds of instrumentalists, and thousands of singers, for communal celebrations of Bach, Handel, and Mendelssohn. The Metropolitan Opera had visited previously with German repertoire under Damrosch and Neuendorff. But the historic significance of the present tour was unmistakable. Advance sales had exceeded twenty thousand dollars, with *Tannhäuser*, *Die Walküre,* and *Fidelio* the initial favorites. This was because *Das Rheingold, Siegfried*, *Götterdämmerung*, and *Die Meistersinger* were being given in Chicago for the first time. He had trimmed these works even more than in New York so that only the stories were left, told once rather than told and retold in Wagner's layered scheme. *Das Rheingold* finished at 10:30, the other *Ring* operas no later than 11:15. In the first *Siegfried*, Alvary's forging song had excited applause silenced by reverent hisses, then a culminating storm of bravos when the anvil split, an ovation continuing through the postlude and innumerable first act curtain calls. In *Die Walküre*, the electric light for Nothung's sword handle—a Chicago novelty—was a failure. Wotan's concealed car arrived late for his confrontation with Siegmund. The new Grane neither fidgeted nor neighed. Kalisch was no Niemann, but he was now Lilli's husband. Besides, in *Götterdämmerung* he had endured the fur covers of Siegfried's bier, so full of vermin that he had been obliged to have Brünnhilde ever so discreetly scratch his blisters while lamenting his demise. Sedlmayer's Mime, Fischer's Wotan had duly amazed, the first with his whining and wheedling delivery that excited both horror and pity, the second with his nobility of bearing and voice.

But it was Lilli who presided. That pighead Hulsen, in Berlin, for years cast her as Lucia and Violetta. He barely permitted her a few *Die Walküre* Brünnhildes. But then Hulsen cared nothing for Wagner, whom he persecuted with his chicanery. Wagner himself was late to recognize that Lilli could have been his Sieglinde in seventy-six. Certainly, had he lived to produce another *Ring*, she would have earlier taken possession of the roles she was born to sing. That she brought out the father in him may in some ways have held her back; how tenderly he would hug and coddle her. Which would make us surrogate siblings. I did not teach her the Brünnhildes she first sang in New York; she had already absorbed them whole. She instructs the entire ensemble, just as she took charge of the Rhinemaidens and Valkyries in Bayreuth. Bill Henderson, in the *Times*, said it all when he wrote that her personal grandeur fit her like a royal robe when she hurled aside Gunther's retainers, seizing the haft of Hagen's spear and pealing "Helle Wehr!"

In one sense, Hulsen's shackles served her well: she was compelled to ripen slowly. And of course those same shackles ultimately forced her to leave Germany for England and America. Krehbiel had a hand in that; he told her that her New York fees would more than compensate for her lost Berlin pension. But it was Lilli who commanded the artistic discipline and self-knowledge. In London, she practiced Isolde three and four times in succession in full voice; no other soprano would have thought to do that. Here she sings six times in eight days. For that matter, Alvary will sing both Stolzing and Lohenrin next Saturday, now that Stanton has added two *Lohengrins* to the run.

The papers are full of stories and reviews. Wagner's achievement is uncontested. Siegfried is the favorite. He reminds Americans of the "frontiersman." Krehbiel wrote the same in New York—in twice as many words. And Wagner predicted it, of course. Even Cosima, in Bayreuth, has been heard from—she was quoted in yesterday's *Tribune* decreeing that Wagner "must not be misunderstood or half understood," that proper appreciation "could not fail to grow" in the Western states.

He read today that Madame Blavatsky and her theosophists were in town for a grand convention. "If human testimony is worth anything Mme. Blavatsky does possess abnormal powers; not because she is able to set natural laws at defiance, but because her knowledge of those laws exceeds that of modern science." Just as Mrs. Langford says. But he would not spend his one Sunday—his only free day—chasing spiritualists. He had consented to tour Chicago's "people's music temple," now nearing completion. The tallest building in the city. "The heaviest building in the world." A 400-room hotel in combination with a theater gargantuan in scale and democratic aspiration. He had thought that New York City—its diversity of class and race, its plenitude of spectacle, its variety of landscape and custom—embodied "America." Or was the new city of Chicago, mediating between the frontier and the settled and habituated northeast, a more concentrated New World?

* * *

The wide boulevard teemed with families enjoying the midday sun. He strolled slowly; his hands clasped behind his back. His distracted air and windswept black locks set him apart. Even in Chicago, he was recognized by a few, whose excited gratitude he courteously deflected.

The park to his left was a strip of grass and trees fronting railroad tracks and the gigantic lake whose gray aureole merged with clouds and sky. The parkland was displaced by a building interminable in length, decked in flags, its peaked facades doubling and redoubling beneath windowed domes as it seamlessly unscrolled, its ugliness held hostage by gaudy bravado. The landscape emptied again. He discerned through the haze, far down the street and on the opposite side, a campanile scraping the sky. Cautiously eyeing the traffic, blocking out the din and the odor, he crossed over behind a painted waffle wagon and proceeded onward at his slow but steady pace. The sidewalk was home to peanut vendors, sandwich men, flower girls, bootblacks, the occasional weaving bicyclist.

Crossing Van Buren, he passed the Art Institute, the Studebaker Building, and the Auditorium Building, side by side, the first a large structure with an arched entry, the second larger with two such entries, the third, larger still, with three. It was also plainer and more purely rectangular. He counted its ten stories. Turning right at Congress, he discovered that it occupied the entire length of the long city block, with the campanile itself atop a tower where the yawning main entrance beckoned under mottled terra cotta.

"Doctor Seidl. Welcome to the Auditorium Building."

A thick-set man, balding, heavily bearded, earnest in visage, speaking German.

"Herr Adler? You are German-born?"

"Stadtlengsfeld, in Thuringia. And you?"

"Pest."

"All Chicago talks only of your *Ring* performances."

"And of your Auditorium Building."

"It is nearly finished. Come."

The great interior was idle. Tarps, ladders, tools were

neatly disposed to the sides of a long lobby. Underfoot, the mosaic was nearly complete.

"Fifty million marble pieces, hand-laid," Adler said. "Seventeen million bricks. Twenty-five miles of gas and water pipes. Two hundred thirty miles of electric wire and cable. Ten thousand electric lights."

He was led into an elevator. They ascended in silence. Adler ushered him through a door from which they descended to the front of the first balcony, thrust forward over the parterre far below. The latter was fan-shaped and steeply raked. A rounded ceiling spiraled overhead, ribbed by a series of elliptical arcs beginning with that of the proscenium. The arcs bore diamond and circular shapes in gold leaf inlaid with yellow lamps, the proscenium a frieze too remote to read. A rectangle of golden squares framed the stage, with friezes to either side. The side walls bore nature paintings. A ubiquity of spiral ornaments evoked sea shells or sunbursts. The enormity of the space and its detailed metaphoric décor, its suffusion of yellow and gold, challenged past experience. Scanning further he was arrested by the singularity of …

"The boxes."

"Ah yes, they do not face the stage."

Stacked in tiers of eight and twelve, individually arched, they eyed not the stage-show but the spectacle of the hall itself.

"How much do you know about Mr. Ferdinand Peck?" Adler inquired.

"He conceived this building, I am told."

"Indeed. Mr. Peck is a man of opinions. A lover of opera but not of opera boxes. He thinks of the Auditorium as a democratic rebuke to your Metropolitan Opera House. Our house is bigger. And we truly believe—not to appear discourteous; you yourself did not build the Metropolitan Opera House—that it is better. Mr. Cady designed your opera house around the boxes. Here, the boxes are secondary. There are only forty of them. And they are not for permanent purchase. And they do not adjoin private anterooms. They face one another. The better sightlines are enjoyed by the general public."

"But is this room not too big?"

"Four thousand two hundred seats. Many more than New York. But most of your gallery seats lack a full view of the stage. Anyway, Peck's intention is to lower ticket prices in proportion to the high capacity. For the same reason, the building has many uses. It holds a recital hall, a luxury hotel, an observatory, a music conservatory, one hundred thirty offices, all revenue sources. It serves both Mammon and Art. A Chicago endeavor."

"And whence this endeavor?"

"Have you heard of Haymarket?"

"Yes, the 'Haymarket Riot.'"

"In which a bomb exploded and a dozen men died and four were hung, three of them German. There here exists the specter of German 'anarchy.' It is real enough. Your New York does not have a German editor boasting that he will blow up the Board of Trade. But Peck is a conciliator. He believes that he can defeat crime and Socialism with Culture. Many here believe in that. And others do not, they think he is a Don Quixote. But he will never stop. And he has enlisted many men of wealth in his vision. At his Grand Opera Festival, Patti drew an audience of six thousand. *Faust* ten thousand. That was four years ago in the Interstate Exposition Building—which I assure you is no opera house."

"I saw it today. In Grant Park—which is no park."

"So you understand our needs. For Peck, this is the logical next step. He says that 'Music for the People' will …"

"Good afternoon, Mr. Adler. Is that Mr. Seidl sitting

alongside you? If so, *Herzliche Grüsse.* We are honored by your presence."

Adler turned to face the faraway stage. Without raising his voice, he said, "Mr. Sullivan. I have been expecting you. Shall we join you downstairs?"

Seidl now located the tiny figure of a man whose voice, not tiny, replied: "By all means, I am at your service."

"This is Mr. Sullivan's way of demonstrating our acoustics. He wants to show you the stage. We will accommodate him."

They arose and returned to the elevator. Seidl now re-entered the Auditorium from the rear of the parterre. He observed leaves, vines, tendrils, and shoots inscribed in wood, plaster, and wrought iron. The proscenium inscription, above an enthroned winged Muse, read: "The Utterance of Life is Song, the Symphony of Nature." To either side were names of composers, ranging chronologically from Bach and Gluck to Verdi and Wagner. There were also medallions bearing portrait busts of Shakespeare, Demosthenes, Haydn, Wagner again. On closer acquaintance, Mr. Sullivan proved a youngish man with eager eyes "drunk with *Siegfried* and *Götterdämmerung.*" He was describing the Forging Song and Siegfried's nature reverie, the "goddess Lilli Lehmann" and her pillar of flame. Did Seidl not detect the influence of Bayreuth in the circular amphitheater design? True, the pit was not covered as in the *Festspielhaus*—although this had been considered.

"You have been to Bayreuth?" Seidl asked, speaking English.

"I have not. Peck went. I, however, am the resident Wagnerian here, in charge of decorating our Gesamtkunstwerk. Surely you will privilege us with an Auditorium Building *Ring des Nibelungen* next spring? Has Mr. Adler described to you the capacities of our stage? No? May I invite you to inspect the machinery?"

He was shown the cracks that partitioned the stage floor into four sections each of which could be hydraulically raised or lowered. There were also traps, centrally controlled. The stage could be "rocked," simulating waves. It could vanish, turning the entire room into a dance or convention floor, or an indoor athletic field. The pit could be enlarged to seat 120 musicians. A rotating cyclorama could simulate fog, rain, or fire. Screens and curtains could diminish the Auditorium's capacity to fewer than 1,000 seats. Seidl felt like Wotan being shown the magic of the Tarnhelm by some benign Chicago Alberich.

Had Seidl noticed the paintings? "They express allegorically the two great rhythms of life: growth and decadence," Sullivan went on. "Here to the right you see depicted an Allegro: a spring Song at dawn, a wooded meadow, a gentle stream. The joy of awakening life touches the wandering poet who sings 'O soft melodious springtime, first born of life and love!' To the left, Adagio: the natural decline of life, an Autumn Reverie in gray, subsiding autumn. The brown leaves descend, one by one, to join the dead. The winds breathe shrill funeral lamentations. Tired nature, her tasks performed, divested of her many-colored garment, withdraws a falling veil and sinks to sleep. The poet turns to descend into the valley conscious that 'a great life has passed into the tomb, and there awaits the requiem of winter's snows.' Thus do all things rise and decline. Our intention is to promote Natural Thought, primordial instinct—the vast reservoir of life's organic forces."

Seidl waited for Mr. Sullivan to subside. "Thank you for this information, yes, you have created something different, something American, for the people." He looked out upon the rows of seats with their bright red aisles. The hanging balconies, the tiered boxes. The silence grew awkward. "We have one more surprise for you, Herr Doctor," Adler interposed, switching to English. "Then you may escape. We beg you to join us atop the campanile. The view is commanding."

He discovered himself in an elevator compartment for a ride of some duration. So was this the Theater of the Future? Something could be done with the stage planks for the descent into Nibelheim. The collapse of the Gibichung Hall: it could tumble into crevices as the stage itself buckled and fractured … A gusty observation deck. Two-hundred seventy feet, Adler was saying, the tallest … the fire of 1871 … steel-frame construction …

Other cities grew—or shrank—slowly, gradually, by happenstance, by increment. Downtown Chicago looked newly hewn. Its ubiquitous trains labored, insect-like, trailing wisps of vapor. Its industrial chimneys disgorged their plumed detritus. The vastness of the shoreline, of the railroad nexus, the stockyards and steel mills, drew the eye toward far horizons blurred by fog and cloud and the combustion of commerce. He remembered his first experience of Manhattan four years before—in an open carriage, gazing upward, imbibing the city's restless quiver and mighty pulse, turning to Gusterl: "I think we shall get along well here." He stepped forward, his long hair wild in the wind. He inhaled deeply, then looked straight ahead into the ether. His afflatus had silenced his companions.

* * *

I first met Wagner in Prague in 1863. He visited with mother repeatedly and declared himself intoxicated by her fourteen-year-old daughter. He stormily kissed and embraced me. I observed that mother was more charmed and flattered than by any emperor. His eyes and voice were so devouring that

I cried and protested that I would see him no more. But he returned and insisted that I sing. He was wearing a yellow damask dressing gown, a pink cravat, and a circular black cloak lined with pink satin: Hoffmann's Kreisler in the flesh. I warbled on command. Then he foretold that he would adopt me and that I would sing all his operas for him. Mother interposed calmly. I remember every detail. "Be content, Richard," she said. "Perhaps she will sing all your operas by and by. Lilli is too young now, and you would be too youthful a father." By then his presence had wrought impressions I could not dispel. Not long after I was taken to his rehearsals. He mesmerized the men. Never since have I heard the "Ride of the Valkyries" as he conducted it. He separately rehearsed the strings and winds, emphasizing the downbeats and secondary accents. His tempo was slower than what we hear today. The effect was electric—a maelstrom of storm and stress—and at the same time Olympian. Then he led the *Tristan* Prelude, which awoke in me a desire for profound expression such as I had never glimpsed before.

Thanks to mother, who at all times kept a level head, I clearly sensed the dangers of such an encounter. Not so with Seidl in 1876. He was twenty-six years old but seemed no more than twenty—whereas I, at twenty-eight, was already a performing artist of substantial experience. Anton was Wagner's light or dark shadow, according to his master's mood. He lived for Wagner only; his past existence ceased. Wagner of course teased him for this, but with so much warmth that their bond smoldered, forged like Nothung in a furnace glow. Seidl was uplifted and yet rendered as parentless as Parsifal. His dependency was frightening to behold.

And now he suffers hidden agonies of absence. He leads the *Ring* and *Tristan* with supreme authority: he possesses Wagner as Wagner once possessed him. But Anton's world of German opera is smaller than he knows; he cannot step outside it. How often have I tried to counsel him that he cannot spend a lifetime only serving Wagner. We take the *Ring* to Boston and Milwaukee. Now we are in Chicago, next St. Louis. "THE GREATEST OPERATIC ATTRACTION IN THE WORLD." But what American mission will he serve in ten years' time? In twenty years?

Never does he talk of his father or mother, or of his brother in Budapest. Never once within my hearing on this long journey has he mentioned Gusterl—only, when he deigns to speak about himself at all, that he misses his dogs. When he is at ease among us, and in the mood, he discourses on Wagner Remembered. His topic on such occasions is not the genius but the human being. Those who fear Seidl, or to whom he merely appears remote, cannot image how he savors the child in Wagner. The stories of Richard mishandling his knife and fork so as to perturb Cosima, of his turning somersaults in the exalted company she cherished and he would not, are among his fondest. His *Götterdämmerung* score bears an inscription in Wagner's hand—"Auf der Welt is alles Seidl"—that cloaks in jest a demonic intimacy he must revisit with each enchanted revisitation of the *Nibelung's Ring*.

Brooklyn has made a Seidl Society for him. And Laura knows what to do with it. But Brooklyn is not Manhattan. Thomas and Damrosch, with their New York orchestras, are men of practical intelligence, conductors and businessmen in equal measure. Seidl is ever the *artiste*. In Boston, he left his overcoat. In Milwaukee, a suitcase with scores, which had to be retrieved.

America: it has made me a Free Artist. No longer am I beholden to kings or princes or mere intendants. Or to conductors: I sing my Brünnhildes for Thomas, for Damrosch, for London or Stockholm as I please. I have never forgotten what

I became in Prague and Danzig and Berlin, but my talent and ambition clamored for stronger recognition; I craved a dramatic *Fach*. I have never regretted that I took hold of my destiny. I owed it to myself.

Whence comes the peculiar sense of freedom that is at once felt by everyone in America? I was not a prisoner in Berlin. There is a moral element amongst the American people such that even the poorest feels himself a gentleman, desires to be treated as such, and deems it worth his while to treat others so. The most elegant man does not remain sitting if a woman is standing, no matter how humble she may be. The most elegant lady may ask a workman to take her home or to a carriage in case of storm or ice. Children are educated to independence, and do not fear that from an early age they must themselves discover how to get on in life.

America confers its freedom on those who free themselves. Seidl appreciates American freedoms; he talks about them; he esteems "the music-loving workman" and disdains the very rich. But his lonesome face does not look to me like the face of a free man, a free American. It is a curious thing that for three years—since fleeing Cosima's seduction drama in May 1886—he has not returned to Germany—or to London or to any of the cities in which he triumphed with Neumann. What fears or sorrows now detain him from even a summer's visit? The one thing I do know is that the German opera company he commands rents the Metropolitan Opera from boxholders for whom Wagner is less expensive than Bellini or Gounod. They will not support Wagner forever. And when their wealth is withdrawn, Anton Seidl will have too much time to think—and to remember.

Chapter Three
Brighton Beach: July 1890

The Seidl Society Is in Mourning

As an iridescent dream, nothing could have been lovelier than a continuous, all year-round season of Wagner, beginning at the Metropolitan; transferred to Coney Island; resumed at the Metropolitan, next autumn. Divested of their diamonds, free from the trappings of fashion, enjoying Wagner and clam fritters, Wagner and soft-shell crabs, Wagner and fish chowder, Wagner and bathing-suits, the worshipers of the Seidl cult could pass a summer of blissful harmony, and Pat Gilmore and his military band would be banished, for want of patronage, from the happy island. It was a dream worthy of the late king of Bavaria. But alas! it has not been realized. Beginning two summers ago, Herr Seidl went to Brighton Beach with his orchestra and a full score of the Master's most intricate and diabolically difficult compositions. But, except a few curious members of the Seidl Society, nobody else would come, and the concerts for a few members did not pay.

Advertise yourself! Play popular music! Appeal to the general public! This was the brusque advice of the soulless, practical spectators who put up their unaesthetical money to pay the salaries of Herr Seidl and his band. It was a bitter Seidlitz powder to swallow; but necessity and empty benches know no law.

Here is the light, airy, popular program which is expected to attract crowds to hear Seidl's concert, this evening: "1. Overture to the Flying Dutchman; 2. Waldweben;

> 3. Lohengrin Prelude; 4. Siegfried Idyll; 5. Intermission of ten minutes; 6. Overture to Tannhauser; 7. Quintet from The Meistersinger; 8. Good Friday, from Parsifal." If these selections do not bring the multitudes, nothing can. In anticipation of the result, the Iron Steamboats are running every hour; trains are starting on the Long Island, Bay Ridge, and other routes; the Brooklyn Bridge is open, and an annex boat connects Jersey City with the Coney Island lines. It is now 8 P.M. and the streets of New York seem deserted. Evidently everybody has gone to hear the triumphant Seidl's almost too trivial, amusing and blithesome concert. Yet there were rude skeptics who offer to bet that the ten-minute intermission will prove the most popular part of the affair.

Laura Holloway Langford placed *The Spirit of the Times* on her lap and peered at the ocean. Let the rude skeptics place their bets. She was a small woman, neither pretty nor plain, with large eyes and a firm chin. The set of her chin told all.

It was nearly six. The hotel veranda was full. The surf was quiet. Mrs. Langford fixed her gaze on a paved walk that separated the veranda from a broad swath of manicured lawn. The promenaders were mostly women strolling in twos and threes in colorful summer costume. The minority men, the lingering heat notwithstanding, wore dark vested suits and bowler hats. The vast turreted hotel occupied a precinct of the island remote from the beer gardens, shooting galleries, and sideshows of Surf Avenue's "Sodom by the Sea." The circular Brighton Beach Music Pavilion, its three thousand seats open to the salty air, fronted the water on a sandy outcropping.

Mrs. Langford soon spied the object of her intense expectation. It was a man in a white suit, walking with his hands clasped behind his back and his eyes downcast or upwards averted, looking neither left nor right. His deliberate tread, clean-shaven cheeks, and long black hair, disheveled by the wind where it escaped his white hat, distinguished him from the others. His approach was in fact keenly noticed by many feminine eyes. He turned toward the hotel, mounted its steps, and only then searched the occupants of the chairs.

"Good day, Mr. Seidl."

"Ah, Mrs. Langford."

He bowed, touched her hand, and sat in a closely adjacent chair. His expression was quizzical, as if they had met by accident rather than appointment. His English bore a thick but musical accentuation.

"It is very kind of you to take time in between concerts." She paused for emphasis. "Have you seen this?" Her genteel Tennessee drawl and warm vocal timbre mitigated the evident sharpness of her disposition.

He squinted at the newspaper and shook his head.

"It says that 'rude skeptics' believe that at our Wagner concert this evening the intermission will prove the most popular portion."

He looked at her without meaning.

"It says that our concert tonight is of no popular interest whatsoever."

"That cannot be so."

"Precisely. To begin with, the Seidl Society is already here in force. And we have our special railroad cars for unescorted women, many dozens of them, departing from Manhattan throughout the day. And then there is the repertoire—all favorite Wagner selections. The writer is plainly misinformed. He chooses to be misinformed. He resents us."

"We will see."

"Indeed, we shall."

The conversation lapsed for a moment. It was in Mrs. Langford's hands.

"In any event, the purpose of our meeting is not to complain but to plan. It is true that this summer's concerts are starting slowly with regard to attendance. You will however remember your first summer here at the hotel, two years ago, when you had virtually no audience whatever. Then our Society was formed, and attendance last summer was fifty per cent improved. We had five Beethoven symphonies in their entirety. We brought working girls and their families to the seashore. With your assistance we are promoting musical understanding among all the classes. And so, it is time to think of presenting a full winter season in Brooklyn as a sequel to our *Parsifal* Entertainment at the Academy of Music last March."

Seidl's quiet delivery was halting but firm. "As you know, Mrs. Langford, I do not seek the fashionable music people. My chief aim is the musical masses who wish to cultivate their taste. The American people is prepared. Wagner is popular here already. We will play only good music—and the people will relish it more than the rich who come to the opera to chatter. This is our mission. And we must present not just concerts but festivals of opera."

Mrs. Langford understood: Wagner was less honored at Cosima's Bayreuth than he could be in Brooklyn. "Everything is possible—in stages," she responded. "We shall have a full symphonic season at the Brooklyn Academy, beginning in October. You and I have already discussed this plan in some detail. We have secured the dates, including rehearsals. We shall begin with a Wagner program. The second program shall be entirely devoted to Liszt. We shall not neglect the masterworks of Beethoven, Schubert, Schumann, and Mendelssohn. I know you greatly favor Berlioz."

"And we must serve the American music."

"We shall do so. The Society has so far committed an orchestra of sixty for each concert. We have engaged Joseffy for the Liszt program. We need to know what other soloists or vocalists you will require, and of course whether any of the programs shall require hiring additional musicians."

"We must return to *Parsifal.*"

"*Parsifal.* Well, of course. This is essential if we are to end our season in the most inspirational fashion. And the need is great. Only Mr. Damrosch has defied Madame Wagner's ban, and his performances were so regrettably lackluster ..."

"Not only Cosima's. Wagner saved *Parsifal* for Bayreuth. This he told me himself."

"So we must present *Parsifal* in concert, and in stages. Our *Parsifal* Entertainment already accomplished a great deal. We presented Lehmann as Kundry, a role she has never offered at Bayreuth. We assembled a most distinguished Brooklyn audience—Mayor Chapin, ex-President Cleveland, the Reverend Abbott, Mr. Pierpont Morgan ..."

Seidl barely smiled. "And the *Parsifal* tocque was sold in our Brooklyn stores. And in our Brooklyn churches *Parsifal* was denounced for imitating the Christ story."

"The more enlightened clergy preached finding Christ through Art. More enlightened minds understood that *Parsifal* imparts Christian values without imparting Christian dogma or desecrating Christian rites."

"There were not Flower Maidens. There was not a chorus even. We must have a chorus the next time."

"You shall have a chorus. You must decide how many singers you require, and whether they must be professional singers. The Seidl Society is starting its own chorus of women and men."

Seidl stood and took his hat. "The high sopranos must be in tune. I will tomorrow give you more information about the soloists and the repertoire. You must now excuse me; I conduct some *Parsifal* tonight."

"The stars and the ocean will lift our spirits."

"We will see." Seidl took Mrs. Langford's hand, his face unfathomable. He walked into the hotel apparently oblivious that his brief hushed exchange had been observed with general curiosity, or that his departure did not go unnoticed.

* * *

Krehbiel had truly written of Seidl: "His face shows a singular combination of youth, perspicacity, calm and inflexible determination, and strength of character, a countenance which has behind it a huge reserve force." And what was it that Henry Finck had said? That Seidl lacked "Yankee push." Also true. Consider Walter Damrosch. First of all, through his wife and through his association with Carnegie he has access to the highest society and to the greatest wealth. And he is served by a gaggle of admirers whom he cultivates assiduously and who imagine him to be a great conductor because of his German accent and his dreamy eyes and his Damrosch pedigree and his way of talking about spirituality when in fact he beats time like a clock. Or consider Theodore Thomas, who looks like a banker and tours his orchestra like a general. While poor Seidl can only state his innocent desires. What he needs we can furnish. Not in any automaton capacity or as ladies of breeding in need of diversion. We shall write a new chapter in the history of women's clubs. We shall give concerts of high merit throughout the year in order to foster a national interest in music and to enable people to hear the best music amid the most congenial surroundings. Luther wrote: "Satan hates music because it drives away temptation and evil thoughts." Music excites within us the highest ecstasy and expresses the illimitable. We shall apply it as a balm to the poor and to the homeless. We shall serve needy women who desire to improve themselves and to increase their enjoyment of life. That is why the Society hosts orphans at the seashore and presents lectures in support of social progress. We do not countenance the enslavement of women to the kitchen or to the bedroom. We espouse the new woman era. Temperamentally, it is given to men to shed blood and enslave. Women evince Christian meekness and empathy. Women of all classes can work together for the betterment of all. And women can enjoy themselves alone …

"Laura is deep in thought—which is always dangerous."

It was her husband the colonel, addressing Auguste. He was a well-preserved specimen, a Civil War veteran now an officer of the Brighton Beach Railway, whose ruddy bearded cheeks and faint aroma betrayed a recent visit to the bar. She was a full-bodied artiste become Hausfrau, whose sad eyes and gentle disposition excited empathy. As his wife remained mute, the colonel continued at a higher pitch:

"Did you hear, Mrs. Seidl, what Elizabeth Cady Stanton said about Laura? She said, 'I think if you would make Mrs. Langford commissioner of streets in New York they would not be dirty for long. She could clean New York City in less than three months.'"

Mrs. Langford rolled her eyes.

The colonel felt emboldened. "Did you know that during the war Laura was arrested for spitting on a Union soldier?"

"Edward!" While her husband shrank, Mrs. Langford addressed Mrs. Seidl. "I had hoped we would have the pleasure of hearing you in tonight's *Meistersinger* Quintet."

"How kind of you. But my singing voice has still not returned. It may never. The New York climate seems not to suit me very well."

The colonel cleared his throat and indicated that he and his guest were headed for the dining room. "I will join you later," said Mrs. Langford.

How indiscreet of Edward. How little he knows or understands. Yes, he soldiered in the war. He had seen the South. But a pious Southern upbringing is another matter altogether. Our female academies prepared future wives and mothers for lives of enforced passivity. Our kind but thoughtless mothers never imagined that we might instead be taught some trade or profession. Rather, we endured the enervating Southern sun, accustomed to being served by inferiors, and educated only in those trivial accomplishments that are said to adorn the drawing room. We suffered social bondage, then the bondage of bayonet rule. The tattered clothes and cornfield hats, the dreadful food, the taunts and random arrests. "A little rebel," President Johnson called me when from the porch I spit on the Union officers we had to harbor as "guests." I was actually arrested until he interceded. Well, he knew well enough what I was.

So she had made her own way. Hardship and confusion—else how could she have married Junius Holloway in wartime and borne him a son? A man without dignity is a man without honor. I had to intervene with the President, as if I had not already asked for favors enough, to lift Junius's detention as a Confederate spy. Then I erased him from my life—leaving me with little George and my seven siblings and my parents, all of us migrating north to New York, uprooted and adrift.

Andrew Johnson. He did adore remembering when as a child I told him I wanted to be a man so I could be Governor just like himself. But he earned that governorship. How many nights must Lucy have bent over him to guide his pen so that he could acquire a refined hand? She taught him numbers as well. A tenacious man, a querulous and obstinate man, he struggled to redeem the South from Reconstruction errors. He died exhausted and misunderstood. Only those of us who witnessed the war at first hand knew the full extent of its challenges. It left the South a cripple in mind and means. It left Laura Holloway with a despicable name not her own, with a misbegotten infant son, with a sordid prospect of genteel poverty in a city ruled by thieves and thugs.

After she moved the family north, the President had helped again. Or rather, his daughter had urged her to write *Ladies of the White House* and the President had lent his hospitality and imprimatur during the weeks she lived at the executive mansion. Her history of the First Ladies was the social and professional point of entry that she required in order to find a vocation and earn a living. As an editor of the *Brooklyn Daily Eagle,* she experienced the dignity of well-directed labor and established fresh possibilities in a man's milieu. After the languors and deprivations of Nashville, Brooklyn Heights exuded an affluence bracing and invigorating to physical and intellectual wellbeing. But it was not enough. The First Ladies she extolled for sacrifice, the women of achievement whose elevating influence she praised in other hortatory volumes intended to disturb the quiescence of the parlor, in fact led disappointing lives when judged by a dawning new woman era—or by her own chronic restlessness.

Her personal quest had yielded startling spiritual powers. She had learned telepathy and earnestly applied herself to Vedanta and theosophy. Then came Madame Blavatsky herself, in London, a creature both vulgar and divine whose magnetizing eyes and copious intellect, bulging obesity and tobacco-stained robes partnered universal wisdom and petty intrigue. Laura Holloway's acknowledged clairvoyance, her adroit occult communications and astral visions, her gathering search for intensity and altruistic purpose prepared the Wagner revelations *Tristan und Isolde* and *Parsifal.* She had mounted the lovers' ecstatic union, surrendering the self. She had inhabited the Good Friday rapture, a song of compassion for all things living. And these miracles had occurred through the medium of Wagner's own priestly emissary. Seidl was a vessel pure and anointed—but scarcely self-sufficient. If Wagner was not to be trapped in the opera house, susceptible to the whims of the idle rich, if the illuminating power of Wagner was to be served and disseminated, instruments more democratic than the Metropolitan Opera were a necessity. The Greek ideal of edification and communal uplift became a Wagnerian ideal; Krehbiel's lectures wonderfully emphasized that. Wagner's message must reach the worker enslaved by habit and routine, and the mother encumbered by domestic chore and obligation.

We sin but repent with good works. What I have done I could not have done otherwise. If even Edward does not know that I am no widow, if he thinks with the rest that I was reared by plantation aristocrats of the highest lineage whose hundreds of slaves were neither whipped nor sold, the truth is not so remote from all of that. We practiced what hospitality and kindness we could. We never embraced secession.

Life is to each of us whatever we make of it ourselves.

* * *

The colonel arrived well fed with minutes to spare. The wooden Music Pavilion, lavishly embellished with palms and potted plants, was open to the elements on three sides: to the Coney Island sands left and right; to the Atlantic Ocean to the rear. More than three thousand souls crowded the red leather chairs. Some were already enthralled. Others were novices for whom the racetrack or even the Surf Avenue amusements were their principal reasons for visiting the island: they awaited the concert casually and loquaciously. Of the women in the audience—a vast majority—a fair percentage had husbands in tow. There were also pockets of chaperoned working women, with faces self-conscious and expectant. The Germans who fall and spring patronized the Metropolitan Opera were well represented, as were cultivated gentlemen for whom Wagner was not in any way a novelty.

Heading for the topmost rows, the colonel tried without success to evade supervision. Yes, he understood where the smokers were sequestered. Yes, he would endeavor to enjoy his cigar discreetly, whatever that meant. He gratefully located some Brighton Beach and Coney Island Railroad Company colleagues who had similarly deserted their spouses. There was time for a bluff hello.

The Railway Company owned the grand hotel. Its Music Pavilion was expected to compensate for the charismatic Patrick C. Gilmore down the boardwalk at Manhattan Beach. But Brighton Beach had failed to secure an eminent band to rival Gilmore's. And so, in summer 1888 the directors instead engaged Anton Seidl and his orchestra. Concerts were given twice daily. The repertoire was mainly Wagner. Lighter numbers were led by Seidl's assistant, Victor Herbert. Seidl's failure was instantaneous. Recriminations ensued, and yet he was re-engaged for 1889. By then Laura Holloway had formed her Seidl Society and formulated a plan. The Society was to secure for its members and to the public generally "increased musical culture" and "musical interest among women particularly." It further aimed "to reach all classes of women and children and by its efforts in their behalf to prove the potent influence of harmony over individual life and character." The immediate mission, however, was to rescue Seidl's failing Brighton Beach concerts. To this end, it offered tickets for only fifteen or twenty-five cents—a move counteracting the exclusivity of more fashionable venues. It furnished special railroad cars for women without escorts. It brought working women, children, and orphans to the seashore. It offered special lunches, dinners, and a menu of lectures. It widely promoted the Seidl summer concerts via leaflets and the daily press. The Wagner throng now being surveyed by Colonel Langford was one result.

A sudden and swelling burst of applause focused the colonel's wandering gaze. Herr Seidl himself, raven locks trailing his bobbing head, was rapidly and imperturbably threading his way through the violins. Barely enduring a short bow, he cued a strident primal onslaught of strings, then a biting horn call. The *Flying Dutchman* Overture, a piece the colonel knew and liked. The salty air redoubled the overture's rolling orchestral thunder. Hurricanes of sound whipped and blasted the delighted auditors. The melee subsided, replaced by plaintive woodwinds: Senta's theme, connoting the redemptive hypnosis exerted by a pitying companion faithful unto death. The colonel smiled and lit his cigar. The music of breaking ocean waves reinforced Wagner's soft timpani rolls. Then the Dutchman's horn motif returned, mounting a climax turbulent and ecstatic. The overture's ripping final chord signaled a frenzy of applause punctuated by pounding boots and canes. Herr Seidl did not wait long before encoring the entire number. The colonel drew his watch from his pocket and saw that it was only 8:30. The *Lohengrin* Prelude, coming next, commenced with a passage of celestial high strings—at which point the Colonel's digestive energies overcame his powers of attention.

He awoke to discover himself the object of excited congratulations. What wonderful work by Mrs. Langford! How skillfully Laura had enticed the new converts! The Colonel quickly arose to acknowledge half a dozen women all wearing the letter "S." Uttering expressions of gratitude, he discovered himself prey to a turmoil of pride and discomfort. At length he wandered outside into the aromatic night air. He dutifully scanned the crowd in search of his wife. She was of course a center of attention and not difficult to locate. The colonel approached, collecting what he could of his feelings and thoughts. He could not tell what was expected of him. When he caught Laura's eye, she smiled back. He drew nearer and gleaned a conversation having to do with the music he had not heard. Something to do with Wagner's son Siegfried and a birthday present for the composer's wife. And now at any moment he would be asked his opinion. It ensued from an elderly member of the Society whose cheerful features bore excessive rouge.

"And what is your opinion, Colonel Langford?"

In response, Colonel Langford sought assistance with his eyes.

"Edward prefers the more rousing numbers. Is that not so, my dear?"

"Oh yes. Flying Dutchman. Siegfried's Funeral Music. That sort of thing."

"But of course, the men always do."

"Not always," said Laura, turning the conversation in a serious direction. "Just as a woman's taste may resemble a man's."

"And what about you, Mrs. Langford? What is your taste in Wagner?"

"For me, *Parsifal* is Wagner's highest attainment. His entire oeuvre documents a process of spiritual growth and evolution. The *Flying Dutchman* preaches woman's palliative service to man. The *Siegfried Idyll* anoints the divinity in childhood. *Parsifal* contains all of that and so much more. It is a combination of masculine striving and Eastern mother-wisdom. It absorbs both the Bible and the Vedanta."

The colonel reached for a cigar but changed his mind.

"Laura's theosophical readings prepared her for Wagner," he volunteered bravely.

"They were of some pertinence. But we must also live in the world. When he was not composing, Wagner was planning his festival, building his *Festspielhaus*, seeking sponsorship, engaging artists. He led a double life."

"Did Wagner embrace theosophy?" someone asked Mrs. Langford.

"Not to my knowledge. Wagner embraced Schopenhauer, of course—a philosopher with misogynistic and nihilistic tendencies. But Wagner himself was neither a misogynist nor a nihilist. He can be so many things. We use him to our own best advantage as a supreme agent of empowerment."

The colonel smiled. He took his wife by the arm and they strolled back to the pavilion, nodding at acquaintances and well-wishers. He would join Laura for the second half of the concert. There would be no further recourse to slumber or cigars.

At close range, Herr Seidl's rapid entrance was the more galvanic. The orchestra bristled to high alert. The sudden disclosure of the conductor's famously immobile features, as suddenly withdrawn as he whipped around to face the band, was ritually intense. A moment of silence reigned. Then he slowly raised his arms and to fluid baton strokes the pilgrim's chorus began afar in the winds. The pilgrim strains swelled steadily, immutably, to a brass peroration crowned by a penumbra of strings. The sensuous *Venusberg* music, an antithesis, was a maelstrom as hedonistic as the pilgrims' chorus was pure. The two motives warred until the Venusberg was vanquished by a culminating onslaught of faith. The uncanny physical composure with which Seidl commanded his electrified players completed the spectacle.

Could not this *Tannhäuser* Overture, Wagner's most popular number, be just a tad simplistic? The Colonel surveyed transfixed faces on every side. And those—he inwardly winced—phallic lunges: were they not a little lewd? People will hear what they want to hear, will feel what they need to feel. These blasphemous opinions—a surprise even to himself—distanced him from the refulgent final cadence. He braced himself for a barrage of acclamation. It was tidal. Though he could not join in the cheering and screaming, he was swept to his feet with the rest. Seidl's begrudging acknowledgements exacerbated the excitement.

Five singers took the stage for the *Meistersinger* Quintet, sung in German. The Colonel preferred symphonic Wagner. Anyway, the piece was brief. The crowd hungrily awaited the main event. No sooner had the *Parsifal* Good Friday music commenced than Laura's eyes closed and her face streamed with tears. The motley Music Pavilion audience was transformed into a tabernacle of believers. A rippling quiescence of exaltation gripped the multitude. A song in the high strings peaked and receded. A message of suffering and compassion—a transcendent Christian message—was more potently delivered than in any church. Seidl laid down his baton and left the stage. The musicians followed. The spell they had cast precluded applause.

The colonel led his wife into the night. Laura long remained inhabited by another spirit. A canopy of stars crowned their slow return to the hotel.

Chapter Four
Manhattan: March 1891

He had gathered a bouquet with his own hands outside the hotel. He mounted the stairs, approached her room, and summoned the courage to knock. She opened the door and observed, speechless, the flowers in his hand. Absent their aura of impenetrable authority, his spectacled eyes disclosed a shyness she had long known was there. Her own large, kind face, with its round contours, grew warm. He stammered an invitation for her to become his partner in life, to share its pleasures and sorrows. She succumbed at once. Weeks later, they were wed in Frankfurt, where she was singing, and left for Bremen, where Neumann had headquartered the troupe. They discovered their apartment filled with flowers. That night, the orchestra serenaded them. The chorus sang Elsa's bridal music the following morning while they were still in bed. She lived for him. His genius commanded her. His absentmindedness and impracticality delighted her. Scanning the future, Wagner's unfulfilled dream of America became his dream—and therefore hers as well.

When Stanton offered her a Metropolitan Opera contract for fall 1884, they decided she would accept in order to appraise his prospects in the New World. She set off for New

York to sing Wagner under Leopold Damrosch. His loneliness, which she had assuaged, returned. Her letters helped but little. The pull of Wahnfried, of the Wagner children who had been his family, of the memory of Wagner himself, regathered force. Then Damrosch died at the age of fifty-two. His twenty-three-year-old son, Walter, proved an impossible replacement. At season's end Stanton came from New York to offer him the artistic leadership of the Metropolitan Opera House. He would begin in October 1885.

Auguste had by then rejoined him in Bremen. Doubtless she could tell that he was not the same. Her love was undiminished, undiminishable. What had changed in her, what took the blow, was her sweet soprano voice. It no longer obeyed her bidding. And over time they realized she could not bear children. The dogs made do. (He glanced at the omnipresent Wotan, asleep at his side.)

Manhattan had thrilled and distracted him. Its vast harbor, its deafening elevated trains, the stark verticality of its buildings, the bustle of its multi-racial multitudes spanning extremes of wealth and poverty, beckoned and impressed. Then came the discovery of Brooklyn, a haven of churches and parks fringed with grand resort hotels and incongruous amusements.

Wagner's sporadic obsession with America—was it daydream or prophecy? With every notification of a Wagner concert in New York or Chicago, America became Wagner's salvation. He was moving to "Minnesota." He would mount the *Ring* "on the banks of the Mississippi." Then Thomas commissioned the *Centennial* March for the 1876 Philadelphia Exposition and paid him royally—exorbitantly. Had Wagner actually visited America, that piece might have amounted to something. He studied American songs and complained that they irritated him. The American Revolution did not irritate him, neither did George Washington, and he thought he could musically describe Washington the war hero in Philadelphia with palm branches strewn in his honor as in a tableau. But he had no firm image, "America" might as well have been Canada or Australia. What was firm was his five-thousand-dollar fee, he was well pleased with that. And the Americans came back for more, they could not get enough of him. The American reviews of the *Centennial* March were more respectful than the Munich reviews of *Tristan* or *Die Meistersinger*. Ullman offered him an American tour so lavish that Wagner threatened to liquidate his Bayreuth assets. He was going to transplant the entire family. Never again would he set foot in German soil. The spirit of history was moving westward. Ludwig wrote to him in a panic. Wagner read the letter aloud for the family with pride and hilarity, a command performance. "All Germans would be indelibly stained were they to allow the departure of their greatest man." America was "sterile," "loveless," "selfish," the land of Mammon.

On other days Wagner was worn down by hostility and incomprehension. He had his own picture—of Wagner the American hero, and palm branches strewn in *his* honor. It became Cosima's picture as well. What was the name of his American dentist in Dresden? *Newell Jenkins*, of course. A worldly man. He outlined for Jenkins the master plan: to give *Parsifal* to America, to give the *Ring* to America, to give America his "services for all time" and rights to his operas in perpetuity. And incidentally America was to pay him one million dollars, half to settle in some "climatically suitable" part of the United States, half to invest in an American bank "at five percent." There would be an annual Wagner festival, beginning with the *Parsifal* premiere. Jenkins tried to calm him down but it was too late, the bud had sprung. America was conceived in an act of rebellion against the tyranny of tradition. America was a civilization unburdened by habit. Americans were born free. Their ancestors were Anglo-Saxons. They embraced primal Germanic virtues. They could power a world-regenerative cultural moment. *Seid umschlungen, Millionen.* I, too, was assured a brilliant American future. I was to found a Wagner Festival, a Wagner school, a Wagner movement on virgin soil. "Seidl, you will be my emissary, my missionary to the New World. You will complete our friend Neumann's historic itinerary and what is more you will settle a *new frontier* while the rot sets in among our celebrated German kings and princes."

All the while, he held a letter in his hand. His studio was crowded with fresh floral tributes. His desk was piled with envelopes, opened and not. The letter was from Lilli Lehmann in Berlin. He had read it several times. *Dearest Friend, Take courage in adversity. A new dawn will break.* Would it really? Lilli herself—who always knew best; who lectured and advised on every possible occasion—had warned that New York was not Berlin and there were New Yorkers for whom opera meant *Faust* and *Sonnambula*. Lilli had ever insisted that we give more French and Italian works. Yes, of course, but the company is German, and what are Gounod and Bellini beside Wagner! He pounded his fist and startled the dog.

Wagner had been right about one thing and wrong about another. The enemies he had in Munich, in Paris, in Vienna, the critics who lampooned him, the politicians who decried his influence—none of them existed in America. Wagner's genius was recognized. And not only in New York.

But the rich Americans Wagner had imagined flinging dollars at his feet did not exist either. In this Ludwig was correct. No Vanderbilt or Belmont was going to bankroll a Wagner festival. Even Carnegie built his Music Hall only because his wife hectored him into creating a home for their mutual friend, Mr. Damrosch, the conductor manqué. And Carnegie was now insisting that the hall pay for itself. Businessmen. As for the Metropolitan Opera: the boxholders were interested in Wagner—up to a point—because he sold tickets. And they had had their fill after seven seasons. All that time we had served at their pleasure, imagining that the house was ours. Then they decided to exile us and notified Stanton, no apologies needed. *Faust* and *Sonnambula* would return. Mrs. Astor and her party guests, tuxedoed and bejeweled, would again be at liberty to come and go. They could flirt and chatter all they pleased. They would reclaim their damned private property. Their *private enterprise*. Where was the government? Where were state subsidies for opera houses and orchestras and for the training of young artists?

Lilli cherished "sacred memories." But what now? The railway was threatening to terminate Mrs. Langford's summer concerts. Her Brooklyn Academy series depended on the heroic efforts of a few hundred women. Could he start over in New York? Could he rejoin Neumann, now in Prague? Could he return to Germany? He winced at the thought of Bayreuth. Cosima. Daniela.

The demonstrations at the Metropolitan had been heartening and heartbreaking. This evening's *Tristan* had already produced the most complicated, most conflicted ovation he could recall: part acclamation, part protest. He was to close the season—his final season—with *Die Meistersinger* this afternoon, in ten hours' time. Perhaps there would be a riot. Perhaps there should be. Perhaps like Sachs he would be left pondering the madness of all human activity. A philosophic fatigue was at last overcoming his turmoil of feelings.

* * *

That a comedy should end his New York operatic career seemed a whimsy conceived by the sardonic composer in a typical fit of mayhem. The German seasons might have ended apocalyptically, with the immolation of the gods. They might have ended with the love-annihilation of Tristan and Isolde. Conducting Wagner was all-consuming, but on this occasion—he was swiftly approaching the singing contest in the meadow: his final moments in the Metropolitan pit—he found himself fighting the distractions of personal circumstance. The two dramas intersected in unexpected ways. The second act closed with the townspeople, awakened by an altercation between a cobbler and a clerk, pummeling one another. In act three the worldly cobbler—Hans Sachs, who also happened to be an accomplished singer and composer—wearily decried human folly. The rebel singer von Stolzing disdained the rabble and its customs. But Sachs successfully counseled a sage balancing of independence and responsibility. All round rebellion was quelled.

He could sense in the roiling public behind him stirrings of incipient revolt. The events of the opera—its nihilistic crowd, its estranged artist hero, its ultimate communality—were uncannily intensified. But nothing surpassed the pertinence of the closing hymn to Sachs. Flanking Fischer, hundreds of singers—the Met's German chorus fortified by the amateur singing societies of Manhattan's Kleindeutschland—prayerfully acclaimed Nuremberg's moral fount. From his backyard grave Wagner had gleefully inflicted a crowning dislocation. Everyone in the building was earnestly thanking not Sachs, not Emil Fischer, but Anton Seidl. Even leading Siegfried's funeral music in a Venetian barge, he had not come this close to breaking down. The opera ended in a blaze of civic zeal, Nuremberg united in art and hallowed ceremony. He managed to signal the culminating C major chords, then fled the pit to a canon shot of cheers and pounding applause.

Craving refuge in the privacy of his dressing room, he shut the door and collapsed. Observing the palsy in his hands and the commotion in his heart, he poured a glass of water and gulped its contents. His breath came heavily. "Now you see what I meant about the Americans. It will take some time for them to settle down. But you cannot hide from them, my cherub. They suffer from the impression that you and I are one and the same. You are to honor my 'hallowed memory.' Nothing can prevent this: it is your arduous destiny, you are attired in my raiment, my countenance is yours. The longer you wait, the more agitated they will become. Who knows, perhaps they are already quarreling. Perhaps they are clambering into the pit, or invading the stage. Perhaps they are ripping the silk linings of those fulsomely upholstered *opera boxes*." The little man was grinning fiendishly. There was a knocking sound: a tentative invitation to arise and open the door. He dutifully succumbed. Auguste, of course.

"Tony."

...

"Tony, you cannot imagine ..."

"I know. I must."

On wobbly legs, sighing to steady his nerves, he accompanied his wife up a flight of stairs. With every step the melee increased in volume. His disobedient pulse raced faster. He felt he was approaching a debacle of unknown dimensions, that the roaring crowd was its rancorous herald. He opened a door and entered the stage-left wings. The uproar subverted thought and feeling. Fischer—the company's most avuncular, most genial member, luxuriously robed as Sachs and bearing a gigantic wreath—caught his eye and proceeded, as if on cue, toward the front of the stage. A hush galvanized the moment. Scanning the towering auditorium, its boxes and high tiers, Fischer spoke, his familiar bass a newly tremulous instrument, his English, also new to the transfixed hearers, inflected with guttural tones. "Ladies and Gentlemen: It is impossible for me to express what I feel for your kindness and love; and I hope it is not the last time …" — here an uproar interrupted the speaker for a period of minutes — "… and I hope it is not the last time that I shall sing for you on this stage, in German." The uproar resumed. Seidl watched Fischer turn toward him and approach. He felt Fischer's arm around his shoulder. Thus was he guided into view. The great room quaked. To his bewilderment, the women of the chorus were now bearing flowers with the evident intention of individually presenting them to him. He accepted as many as he could hold before striding to the lip to speak. Another deafening silence. Surrounded by the worshipful singers, addressing the massed adherents, he felt entrapped in solitude. Summoning as much volume as he could, he entrusted his chaos of feeling to his flawed English: "Believe me, ladies and gentlemen, I understand your meaning in this great demonstration. For myself, the orchestra, and other members of the company, I thank you." He felt he had endured all that he could. Let Krehbiel document the rest. He would retreat to the East Sixty-second Street brownstone where his lonely study and faithful dogs awaited his return.

* * *

The active power of the musician and the passive indifference, not to say ignorance, of the public often combine to make them allies, and the critic is, therefore, placed between two millstones, where he is vigorously rasped on both sides, and whence, being angular and hard of outer shell, he frequently requites the treatment received with complete and energetic reciprocity. It would be a simple matter for the critic to extricate himself from this predicament. He would only need to take his cue from the public, measuring his commendation by the intensity of the applause, his displease by the signs of displeasure, and all would be well. But no, in the nature of things he is the middle factor, the Ishmaelite whose hand is raised against everybody and against whom everybody's hand is raised. The first, if not the sole, office of the disinterested critic should be to guide public judgment. He has both the time and the obligation to mediate between the musician and the public, and thus to educate taste. For the new the critic should excite curiosity, arouse interest, and pave the way to popular comprehension. For the old he should not fail to encourage reverence and admiration. To do both he must know his duty to the past, the present, and the future, and adjust each duty to the other. He should be catholic in taste, outspoken in judgment, and unalterable in allegiance to his ideas. Thus, is he equally a reporter of daily affairs, an arbiter of tradition and of innovation, and, perforce, a chronicler of history. In the last of these capacities, he must command sufficient knowledge of earlier and ever earlier events to frame the larger significance of present-day success or failure. We, in America, are a new people, a vast hotch-potch of varied and contradictory elements. We are engaged in conquering a continent and employed in a mad scramble for material things. The moments which we steal from our labors we give grudgingly to relaxation, and that this relaxation may come quickly we ask that the agents which produce it shall appeal violently to the faculties which are most easily reached. Under these circumstances whence are to come the acquisition of intellect and taste necessary to foster cultural habits susceptible to healthy native growth? Somehow the widespread appreciation of the works of Wagner has answered these needs insofar as answers may already be found in a country so young and diversely constituted. What is more the informed acceptance of Wagner, so different from Wagnerian controversies abroad, has created the interesting circumstance of an enthusiasm shared by the musician, the public, and the critic in equal measure, of a harbinger of enlightenment. So much greater, therefore, are disappointments inflicted by our furious penchant for business and industry.

Henry Edward Krehbiel could neither think nor act without engaging in instruction; every mental and emotional exertion came freighted with exegesis and opinion. For him, the experience of the season's final *Die Meistersinger* taught lessons demanding grave inscription in the public record. As the performance, with its extraordinary aftermath, had been a matinee, he had time to file a detailed report. Sitting at his desk in the *Tribune* newsroom, he proceeded to disgorge a circumnavigatory torrent of vast sentences stung by outraged feeling. *After the first and second acts there were calls and recalls for the singers and for Mr. Seidl. But this was but a preparation. After the fall of the curtain on the last act the multitude remained in the audience room for over half an hour—remained, indeed, till laborers appeared on the stage to get it ready for a concert in the evening—and called for the persons who were in one way or another representative of the system that was passing away.*

He had before him lists of numbers—of expenses and receipts, painstakingly acquired in preparation for the lessons he would now teach. *To understand the story of the overthrow of German opera managed by the owners of the opera house, and the pending reversion to the system which proved disastrous at the beginning and is fated to prove disastrous again, it is necessary to recall the particular reasons for which the Metropolitan Opera House was erected some eight years ago. The stockholders, who would become the boxholders, built a five-tiered opera house furnished with 122 boxes—104 more than were to be found at the Academy of Music, whose boxes were fully subscribed and therefore inaccessible to persons craving a social cachet. Having in effect created a triple semi-circle of private seats with a public opera house constructed around them, these newly prominent custodians of culture decided to lease the premises to Henry Abbey, who was to produce opera featuring stars of rare refulgence without incurring deficits of more than modest size. Mr. Abbey began with "Faust," starring Christine Nilsson and Italo Campanini, both artists who had been heard in the thrice-familiar Gounod opera many times when their powers were greater. Nor did Mr. Abbey stint on sumptuous trappings. That a single Wagner work on his list—"Lohengrin," sung by Nilsson and Campanini in Marchesi's Italian translation—attracted the most numerous audience subsequent to the opening night was a circumstance pregnant with implication. The monumental financial fiasco of the Abbey enterprise caused no surprise among impartial observers. One needed not to be prophetically gifted to foretell that New York could not afford two such costly establishments as the Academy of Music and the Metropolitan Opera House. The world of fashion, which in the nature of things supports Italian opera, and has ever since the art form was invented, was hopelessly split in its allegiance. This was the state of affairs when, the summer days of 1884 being nearly gone and the prospect of a closed theater confronting the Metropolitan's directors, Dr. Leopold Damrosch submitted to them an inexpensive proposition to give opera in German under his management, but on their account. Either the forcefulness and plausibility of his arguments or the direfulness of their need led the directors to make the venture. Dr. Damrosch went to Germany toward the end of August; toward the end of September he was back in New York, ready to announce a season of opera in German, with a completely organized company and a promising list of operas. Few persons knew what was coming, and the information brought with it a shock of surprise.*

Dr. Damrosch's first German season enacted revolutionary reform; both the company's repertoire and the manner of presentation were new. The price of tickets was so substantially reduced that a Family Circle seat could be obtained for as little as fifty cents. Instead of Abbey's expensive and wasteful star system, a German ensemble was set in place. As the singers were also actors, and the repertoire stressed tragic works of large dimension, unusual attention was paid to the mounting of the operas, the first performance being of *Tannhäuser*. No doubt to a large portion of the audience, it must have seemed an inexplicable departure from the hurdy-gurdy Italian list, at times little short of monstrous. The season's pièce de résistance was *Die Walküre*, which had earlier been given in New York in a production at the Academy both painful and amusing in memory. Damrosch's untimely death marked the advent of Anton Seidl, who from the first was looked upon as a prophet, priest, and paladin of Wagner's art. The new operas included "Das Rheingold," "Siegfried," "Götterdämmerung," "Tristan und Isolde," and *Die Meistersinger.*

Memories. The history of opera in New York disclosed an earlier farewell performance of enduring import: Albert Niemann's final *Tristan und Isolde* on February 7, 1887. Although out of doors the night was dismal, the house was crowded in every part. There were delegations from Boston, Philadelphia, and Cincinnati. After two recalls had followed the second fall of the curtain a third round was swelled by a fanfare from the orchestra. Niemann came forward alone, and a laurel wreath, bearing on one of its ribbons the line from *Tannhäuser*, "*O kehr zurück, du kühner Sänger,*" was handed up to him. The third act wrought the enthusiasm to a climax. After the curtain had been raised over and over again, Niemann came forward once again and said, in German: "I regret exceedingly that I am not able to tell you in your own language how sincerely I appreciate your kindness toward me. I thank you heartily, and would like to say 'Auf Wiedersehen.'"

That season's other operas, all given in German, included such titles as *Fidelio, Tannhäuser*, *Lohengrin*, *Die Walküre,* and *Die Meistersinger*. A new era was attained, not the least beneficial aspect of which was the increased prospect of a native tradition of opera in English. The popular taste had once found complete satisfaction in the tuneful Italian composers. The spectacle presented by the lyric stage in Germany seems now to show indubitably what course opera as an art form must take if it is to live. Gluck, Weber, and Wagner have pointed the way. Granted that the German seasons now past have featured foreign artists singing foreign works in a foreign tongue. But the change in repertory has promoted an appreciation of truthful expression in whatever tongue.

The growing restlessness of the boxholders was such that for the 1890-1891 season Italian novelties by Franchetti and Smareglia had been scheduled (albeit necessarily sung in German by the German artists at hand). Then, in January, the directors announced that they had again concluded a contract with Mr. Henry Abbey under which opera was to be given in the next season in Italian and French only. The alleged reason was that Mr. Abbey was willing to assume all risk of financial failure; the real reason was that the stockholders, or a majority of them, were weary of German opera, and especially of the dramas of Wagner. So far as the subscribers to the opera and the majority of its patrons were concerned, this action of the directors seemed a conspiracy to set back the clock of musical progress in New York a quarter of a century at least. The stockholders had in fact never unitedly been in favor of German opera or the principles of art which it represented. Throughout the German period there had been a hankering for the fleshpots of Egypt. Mr. Abbey's announced Italian and French company would include such expensive names as Patti, Campanini, and the brothers de Reszke. Ticket prices would increase commensurately. No sooner had this termination of German opera been decreed than the directors conceded that financially Wagner must save the present season from shipwreck, and "Die

Walküre," "Siegfried," "Götterdämmerung," "Tristan und Isolde," and "Die Meistersinger" were substituted for scheduled works by other composers.

Let the record show that the sum total of seven German seasons comprised 599 staged performances, including 155 on tour, of which 320 were of works by Wagner. How much Wagner did to keep the Metropolitan Opera House alive can be proved by statistics of the last five German seasons. The average Wagnerian receipts for the season now past totaled $3,209.46, versus $3,056.71 for non-Wagnerian fare. The operatic diversions preferred by the stockholders, and now to be reinstated, mark not only artistic retrogression, but a fresh financial burden that they will soon resent. And yet many a sumptuous Fifth Avenue dinner party costs more than a seasonal contribution to the Metropolitan Opera House. The fickleness of public taste, the popular craving for sensation, the egotism and rapacity of the artists, the lack of high purpose in the promoters, the domination of fashion instead of love for art, the lack of real artistic culture—all these things have stood from the beginning, as they still stand, in the way of a permanent foundation for opera in New York. The stockholders of the Metropolitan Opera House created an art spirit which was big with promise and rich in fulfillment, and then killed it because its manifestation bored them.

So there would be no German opera at the Metropolitan the coming fall. German works sung in German, Krehbiel felt certain, would return in some guise sooner or later. He equally believed that the zeal of the German seasons now concluded would ever be remembered as a high-water mark in the history of America's fitful relationship to the parent musical culture abroad.

Chapter Five
Brighton Beach and Brooklyn Heights: August and September 1891

They marched toward the turreted hotel, hair glistening wet in the mid-day sun. They were returning from the beach, had showered and changed. They were happy and they were hungry. The spectacle of more than one hundred Black boys did not escape the notice of the promenaders. Some peered quizzically from under parasols. Other smiled in response to smiling faces.

The hotel's large dining room was set for one hundred and thirty eaters. Flags, bunting, and plants with trailing vines decorated the space under a banner bearing the initials "S. S." Tables with fruits, cakes, and flowers bore representations of the goddesses Pomona, Flora, and Ceres. A four-foot-high letter "S," centrally located, was fashioned from cut flowers in red and white against a backdrop of greenery. Awaiting the guests were dozens of women wearing white aprons over dresses of silk. The children wasted no time taking their seats. Soon they were devouring roast chicken smothered in gravy. To the side, a pert, middle-aged woman conversed with a Black clergyman large in body and voice. The Seidl Society had been preparing for three days. "We engaged three professional cooks. But the cakes and pastries were made wholly by ourselves."

"The color line has been blotted out," the reverend observed in round tones. "Even the Society's Thanksgiving dinners in Brooklyn Heights cannot compare to these seashore excursions."

"Fresh air," said Mrs. Langford in her low, honeyed voice. "It is essential to leading truly Christian lives. These children, especially, require sunlight and grass and ocean salt breezes. The beach is a therapy. You know, Reverend Johnson, I happen to understand the experience of displacement. As a child of the south, I am myself an orphan of a sort. We Carters lost everything we had in the war. I had to restart anew here in Brooklyn. And with the Lord's help I have managed."

"Oh, I know that Mrs. Langford. And I appreciate your friendship with General Howard, long before the Howard Orphan Asylum was established in his name. For a southerner such as yourself to cast her lot with the former commissioner of the Freedman's Bureau, with the founder of Howard University—it is a blessed act of generosity."

"We are all God's children. 'When man to man united/ And every wrong thing righted/The whole world should be lighted/As Eden was of old.' Your orphans are among the best behaved and most grateful of our listeners. We do look forward to serving and inspiring them."

"With music. That is the chief thing. These children are musical. The opportunity to hear your great orchestra is one that they seize with all their hearts."

"And with their souls, Reverend Johnson. Music ignites higher feelings and higher thoughts. Do you by chance know my brother-in-law, William Henderson, the music critic of the *Times*?"

"I don't believe I do."

"He is an apostle for the folk songs of the Negro. And so is Mr. Krehbiel in the *Tribune*. They share a great notion—that the wonderful Negro melodies of the south are in fact our national music of sorrow and redemption."

"Well, you have heard our asylum chorus sing those very songs. We are not yet the Fisk Jubilee Singers. But we are getting there."

"Mr. Seidl adores conducting children at our children's symphonic concerts, both here and at the Academy. He has even composed several choral numbers for them. Perhaps we can enlist you …"

"Oh, not yet. Not yet. We will want to make a splendid impression."

"Reverend Johnson, your young gentlemen at all times make a splendid impression."

They mutually surveyed a room of puffed urchin cheeks, milk moustaches, and ice cream smudges. Involuntarily, she remembered other Black faces, once familiar Tennessee faces. Yes, it was a penance, she could not deny it. These children were agents of her own redemption.

She took her leave of Reverend Johnson and walked outside to the veranda. She surveyed the lawn fronting the hotel. The photographer was already in place. He waved an acknowledgement. Eleven servants, who all unwittingly pre-empted our possible instruction as home-makers. Loyal, pitiful beings, submissive to the auction block, submissive to plantation rule, submissive to "freedom" and "Reconstruction." "Wooly-haired cannibals," father used to say. Another world, best forgotten. But these boys are incubated in a missionary environment. The evil of the plantation, the evil of the city are not visited upon them. Let us see what can be done.

They poured onto the great lawn, then dutifully formed lines by the flagpole according to height. The photographs were taken while they sang. It was "Jesus Loves Me," led by the Reverend. And now they are heading to the pavilion for the 3:30 concert, with neither expectation nor complaint. A race whose long sad history, pregnant with song, yields no definite future.

She sat to the rear so she could relish their response. The pavilion was half full, with very few men. The orphans were conspicuous, not least to the ushers with their "S" badges, all of them keenly solicitous. Seidl wore white: matinee attire. Although the program was not a designated Childrens Concert, he had chosen selections with the orphans in mind. Would he smile for them? Of course not. A whip of the baton summoned a fanfare for trumpets and drums embellished by excited strings: the *Tannhäuser* March. The boys snapped to attention. The march entered softly in the woodwinds, then with broad ceremonial stride—a royal processional in the low strings. Next: the courtiers, tramp tramp tramp. She could hear happy feet tapping the wooden floor. Stentorian trombones—berobed counselors of state—after which a triangle chimed the beat for trilling, tripping violins: ladies-in-waiting. The whole sequence was reprised, culminating in a tornado of drums and cymbals. The orphans joined in the clamor. Seidl repeated the entire number. A fragrant pizzicato by Delibes was followed by selections from *Carmen*, of which the Toreador Song was obviously the boys' favorite. A pause in the program allowed them to leave. She followed as they trooped toward the train station in the late afternoon sun. Packets of nuts and chocolates were distributed. She shook hands with the reverend and waved as they departed.

Maybe they could be invited to sing with the Seidl Society Children's Chorus. Seidl had taken a shine to "America." Imagine that beautiful song with a mixed choir of piping young voices, Black and white: a national benediction. "God shed his Grace on thee." Dvořák and Mrs. Thurber might do that sort of thing at the National Conservatory. Brooklyn was more conservative, of course. But possibly.

* * *

Colonel Olcott arrived, as ever, in white Asiatic attire, abundantly bearded, bespectacled. He had aged—or was merely tired by the journey from India. It was his first visit to the ample Schermerhorn Street brownstone she shared with Edward. Olcott was a man embattled by theosophical schisms—his break with Blavatsky years ago; his current altercations with Judge and with the upstart Annie Besant. Laura knew it all and too well. In London, Blavatsky had denounced Laura as a fraud. Sinnett had taken her side. The Masters Morya and Hoot Koomi, their letters precipitated from remote Himalayan realms, had shifted allegiance many times. "Henry, it is over for me," she told Olcott once they had settled in the drawing room.

His eyes grew wide. "You have left theosophy?"

"I regard it as a private matter. Anyway, I have lost my gift for prophecy."

"I cannot believe it."

"I am preoccupied with other matters entirely."

"You mean your Seidl Society."

"Yes, of course."

"And it bears no relationship?"

"Yes and no. People here do not realize that I became a chela. My studies with Blavatsky, my collaboration with Chatterjee, my astral visitations with Koot Hoomi were never reported in Brooklyn. It was said that I went abroad to recuperate from an illness, and that my interest in theosophy was journalistic."

"But I feel certain your spiritual quest is continuous. I can sense it even now."

She paused, then arose to get a paper from a drawer. She resumed her seat and read aloud:

To Herr Anton Seidl

Rhineland gods, 'tis said no more
Disport themselves on sylvan shore.
The muses all their silence keep,
The fairies and the elfins sleep.

Echoes only fill the air,
Mute that voice of power rare,
Which sang of Odin and his band,
Mystic King of Valhal land.

Singers many lisp his song,
For his mantle myriads long,
Yet but one has come to be
True teacher of his minstrelsy.

Only one with kindling heart
Can his secrets deep impart,
But for him in western world
Wagner's banner would be furled.

Master loved this pupil well,
Leads him now by magic spell;
For, last night, in 'Siegfried Idyl,'
He was incarnate in thee, Seidl.

"So Seidl is a chela," Olcott surmised. "And you have discovered in Wagner a member of the Brotherhood."

"His lineage is long. The knowledge came to him in stages. He was planning a Hindu ceremonial work, a sacred rite for the ages, when he died. And of course there is *Parsifal*, in which he divined many higher truths."

"I have read what our friend Ashton Ellis has written—that Parsifal amalgamates Christ and Buddha; that he preaches our virtues of universal brotherhood, and compassion, and renunciation of desire."

"Ashton Ellis also writes that the Knights of the Grail are occultists, that their knowledge and ceremonies had migrated from the Himalayas, and that they would ultimately return East with the Grail and Spear that Titurel had obtained from Chohans."

"Blavatsky called Parsifal an 'idiot' …"

"That was ever her way with what she could not fathom. In Brooklyn, many have denounced *Parsifal* as a blasphemy because it appropriates Christian myth and ritual. But of course *Parsifal* appropriates many things: Christ as a Master who loveth God and loveth his brother also; the Buddha as a Master for whom all life is holy. Surely when Parsifal is rebuked for killing the swan Wagner recalls the bleeding swan that aroused the Buddha's compassion. Surely when Parsifal says that he has many names Wagner acknowledges the passage of the spirit from one physical body to the next. And surely the ideal of Nirvana is Wagner's spiritual ideal."

"So Parsifal attains Nirvana."

"Parsifal and Kundry both. She is the very embodiment of entrapped womanhood, enslaved to man. Klingsor dominates her through hypnosis: her unbridled sexuality renders her a debased carnal instrument. For the Knights of the Grail, she is a mute servant, driven and employed."

"There are those who say Sinnett hypnotized you in London."

"There are those who say much worse about Sinnett and myself. In any event, women must ever struggle toward freedom. It is a part of the evolution of humankind toward higher states of being. Toward asexual states of enlightenment."

"And this is what you preach at your Seidl Society *Parsifal* concerts?"

"Of course not. We emphasize Christian meanings. It was through seeking a higher form of music drama that Wagner found the Son of God. But you must not underestimate the interest in the occult here in Brooklyn. Brooklyn abounds with spiritualists of every variety. Seances are altogether common. There are some who know that I commune with the dead. Also, there is a growing curiosity about Buddhism, even about Hinduism. I am not a stranger here."

"Are there factions?"

"You would ask that. Strife and scandal—allegations, "investigations"—will ever afflict the Theosophical Society. That was part of Blavatsky's nature: to be confrontational, to be controversial, to be supreme. She could not tolerate rival sources of authority. Actually, her intellectual potential was of far greater significance than her psychic powers and claims. But all that is behind me now. And you should cease your hostilities with Judge—you are far too harsh on him. If you remain in New York, by all means come to our Wagner concerts. They will pacify your combative side. After all, you have no such opportunities in India or Ceylon—unless, that is, you can perform quite unprecedented feats of astral transmission."

Colonel Olcott could not tell whether Mrs. Langford was in earnest, or had acquired a sense of humor he had never before experienced. He decided not to ask.

* * *

Olcott did not appear at the Seidl Society meeting the following day at the Groves mansion. In his place his sister, Mrs. Mitchell, read his scheduled lecture on "The Relationship of

Music to Psychical Development." Mrs. Langford explained that, having last been in the United States more than two years previous, the colonel was preoccupied with pressing business matters. The lecture proved short. Its nondescript delivery vitiated the novelty of its contents. Music is vital to all religious rites, Mrs. Mitchell began in soft, level tones. Conditions of religious trance and convulsion may be traced to the mesmeric agency of tones. If a violin can shatter glass, so might it produce more subtle effects akin to materialization of the spirit. Professor Cook's list of aethrobats—or persons who fly through the air—includes instances of musical nuns and monks whose diminished specific gravity facilitates feats of levitation. Just as soldiers are known to become more courageous under the spell of martial strains, the Algerians at the Paris exhibit were rendered insensible to pain by their own war chants. In Japan, the rhythmic beating of drums aggregates astral atoms, making visible the effects of sonorous vibration.

Mrs. Mitchell invited questions. The author being absent, none were asked. Mrs. Langford thanked Mrs. Mitchell, whose departure removed a source of awkwardness. The business meeting now commenced. Only Society members—on this occasion, more than one hundred—were in attendance, spouses being barred. Interest and attention were keen.

The Brighton Beach season had started slowly—the weather was inclement—but was ultimately successful, Mrs. Langford reported. As the membership appreciated, the Society had been created in response to Herr Seidl's initial Brighton Beach season of 1888, which the Hotel and Railroad Association had not promoted suitably and effectively. In particular, no provision had been made so that women without escorts could travel to the resort hotel without compromising their reputations. With the advent of the society, special railroad cars were furnished for this purpose and many additional efforts were undertaken to attract concert patrons. In summer 1889, attendance more than doubled. In 1890, in collaboration with Colonel Langford, the Society undertook a de facto management role for the summer concert season and the attendance levels secured in 1889 were maintained. During the nine-week summer season just past attendance and revenues again held steady. About $34,000 was disbursed versus ticket income totaling slightly more than $33,000. The Hotel and Railroad Association had made up the difference, but might not do so again. The artistic highlights of the season included five symphonies by Beethoven given in their entirety, as well as three by Haydn, two by Mozart, and one by Schubert. The one hundred and thirty-four concerts included one hundred and seventy-one Wagner selections. The second most performed composer was Franz Liszt, with fifty-two selections. The final two concerts, just weeks ago, drew capacity audiences and epitomized the felicitous balance of serious and popular numbers—of elevation and diversion—that Herr Seidl strove to maintain. Individual movements from Beethoven's Third, Fifth, and Seventh Symphonies were given, as were Wagner's *Kaiser* March, "Ride of the Valkyries," and *Die Meistersinger* prelude. The Victor Herbert numbers included his "American Fantasia." Herr Seidl's arrangements of "Swanee River" and "Yankee Doodle," the latter with its delectable piccolo and bass drum preamble, were also heard. The summer's philanthropies included children's matinees and the recent luncheon hosting the Howard Orphan Asylum. On multiple occasions, special provision was made for working mothers and their children, for whom tents were erected and cots provided for afternoon naps. The summer lecturers had included Mr. Krehbiel and Mr. Henderson.

The Entertainment Committee was laying plans for the October 27 benefit dinner honoring Herr Seidl and Auguste at the Groves Mansion. More than 1,500 invitations would be mailed. The event would be the social highlight of the Brooklyn season. For the reception. Mr. Pouch would make available the large parlor, the art and music rooms, and the first-floor library. The second floor would be reserved exclusively for women, the third exclusively for men. Mrs. Abbott was charged with supervising both the musical portion of the evening and the meal. Her report would follow presently.

The Society's season at the Academy of Music would comprise six Grand Concerts commencing November 11, with a program for which Herr Seidl had scheduled an important novelty: "The Inferno" from Liszt's *Dante* Symphony. Mr. Friedheim would solo in Liszt's E-flat Concerto. Madame Fursch-Madl would sing Beethoven's "Ah, Perfido!" and the "Liebestod." The other selections would be Beethoven's *Leonora* Overture No. 3 and *Siegfried*'s "Rhine Journey." The season's other soloists would include the much beloved Emil Fischer as well as Frau Lilli Lehmann and her gifted husband, Herr Kalisch. If all members were to purchase two season tickets, financial success would be assured, and the Society freed from the anxiety and hard work of selling tickets from concert to concert. Season subscriptions cost $3, $4.50, $5, $6, $7.50, $10.50, and $12. Good seats could be found in all parts of the house. The Academy's Family Circle would again be reserved for working women. Members of the Society were to designate suitable candidates. A Thanksgiving dinner for the Howard orphans would again be planned by the Philanthropic Committee, chaired by Mrs. Fraser. A variety of lectures would be scheduled on women's issues, and on religious and musical topics. A Seidl Society chorus was planned for the near future.

Mrs. Langford's report was received with fervent or merely diligent applause, but also with a scattering of perplexed faces. Questions were asked and accumulated momentum. What exactly is the Seidl Society? Is it an arm of the Theosophical Society? Are we to consider ourselves suffragettes? Is the Society a precinct of Brooklyn Heights high society, or a philanthropic enterprise serving disadvantaged members and guests? Or is it a music club devoted to Herr Seidl and to Wagner? Or is it not finally and actually a "Langford Society"?

Mrs. Langford was no stranger to adversity. She throttled her consternation and delivered a speech partly practiced and partly improvised. "The Seidl Society is a new departure in the history of women's music clubs," she began serenely. "According to our published constitutions and bylaws, we aspire to secure to our members and to the wider public increased musical culture, and to promote musical interest among women generally. We aspire to reach all classes of women and children, independent of sect or social clique, and in their behalf to prove the potent influence of harmony over individual life and character. There is no other place in the world where concerts approaching in artistic merit and decorative accessories those given in Brooklyn by Anton Seidl and his Orchestra may be heard at the nominal cost of fifteen or twenty-five cents. They have raised the standard of musical culture for an entire city of 800,000. They have also spread the name and fame of the Seidl Society over every city in the Union."

Mrs. Langford paused and scanned the room. She then continued in a less inflationary tone:

"That we sometimes engage speakers in theosophy does not mean that we are all theosophists. That we have engaged to speak Mrs. Susan B. Anthony and Mrs. Elizabeth Cady

Stanton does not mean that we necessarily embrace their cause. I am not unaware that there are some Society members who blanch—let us be frank—at the response sometimes elicited by the orphans and working women whom we host, both here in Brooklyn Heights and at the seashore. And in fact, we are short of chaperones for our less fortunate guests. I will even acknowledge that our guests do not always conduct themselves with proper circumspection. Nor can they invariably be expected to do so—it is in the nature of our calling to risk not embarrassment, of which there is no need, but a degree of disappointment. Finally, I do realize that for some of you Mrs. Anthony's admonition that 'a woman's object in life is not to help a man' appears applicable to our own relationship to Herr Seidl and his mission. But we are capacious enough to endure our own reservations and doubts. Let us say that our ideal of usefulness, as women, is to set a high example for practical work and for public enterprise."

In the wake of Mrs. Langford's remarks, the room grew calmer. No member possessed the temerity to inquire further into the purposes of the Society. Instead, Mrs. Lyman Abbott (whose husband was of course Brooklyn's most eminent clergyman) offered an incongruously perfunctory Entertainment Committee report. Signor Maresi would cater the October 27 dinner in honor of the Seidls. Due care would be taken that the food would not run out, as it once did—as all recalled—at the *Parsifal* Entertainment. Ten musicians would be engaged. The decorations would include the usual floral arrangements as well as a bust of Herr Seidl, laurel crowned. The doors would open at 7 p.m., with presentations to the guests at 8:30 and dinner at 11.

There being no further business, a move to adjourn was seconded and passed. The members departed gradually. A few felt chastened and had fallen silent. Others chatted gratefully or beamed with exhilaration. Most were visibly buoyed by their coming activities and responsibilities.

* * *

But the questions do nag. Like Kundry, I have led many lives, past and present, more lives than anyone could possibly know or grasp or assemble into a whole. I am a mother, a remnant of a premature marriage, a relic of the Old South. I was a journalist, an interloper in a newsroom world of men, a superficial chronicler of eminent people and random events. I was and am a clairvoyant, seduced by Blavatsky's bulging magnetic azure eyes, disgusted by her tobacco odor and loose sweaty skin, estranged by the self-indulgence of quarrelsome occult sects. Then there is Edward, my spouse of—what?—some sixteen months, pleasant enough to live with, invaluable for his railway and Heights connections. And he keeps to his own bed.

Celibacy—Christ teaches that divinity is sexless. In heaven there is no marrying—we enter His kingdom by transmuting sexual energy through the alchemy of divine love. Transcending the tyranny of sexual energies frees us to seek higher orbits of experience. Not that my union with Edward will ever be spiritual. But I am not subordinate. When I recall my *Ladies of the White House* with their sweet simplicities, their faith in their important husbands … Or my *Mothers of Great Men and Women*, paragons of propriety, hospitality, and Christian motherhood, guardian angels to men of genius … All this is no longer for me, I trade submission for activism.

Another fraternity I will not join is the shrieking sisterhood of the suffragettes. Susan is a grand lady, a noble lady, and she is correct that women are more spiritually inclined, more naturally judicious. But the ballot is not the remedy for our condition of suppression. So long as a man is hampered by the indulgence of any weakness, above all when he is guilty of subjugating another human being to sexual selfishness, of interfering with liberty of person and conscience—so long will it be wholly impossible for him to attain true wisdom or actual freedom.

And do spare me the cosmetics and fantastic dress of the social elite. How Mrs. Peabody fretted over the *Parsifal* Entertainment. But my dear, I cannot wear a low-cut dress for a 5 p.m. event. And the dinner interlude does not permit me time enough to change for the evening component and reception. Would it not be possible to start with the dinner and shorten the *Parsifal* excerpts? No one will know the difference, at least I won't. And of course, Alfred wishes to wear tails for such an important occasion, and yet 5 p.m. is nearly a matinee, you see. The kind of people Wagner had hoped to exclude from Bayreuth. Certainly, from *Parsifal*. The *Eagle* lampooned us, and viciously. One supposes that they had their reasons. Lilli said we had secured a cathedral ambience. In the hall itself. The trappings were the problem. Not the lobby rugs and easy chairs and palms, the mass of palms in the pit, everyone applauded that, we canceled the everyday aspect of the Academy. It was the dinner that was ill-considered. The rush upstairs, the congestion outside the Assembly room; we had to call the police. And it was snowing, so the neighborhood restaurants were a difficult option. If Mr. Ford had not insisted on two hundred dollars for the Art Rooms, then Maresi would have had twice the space for his six-course meal. Some gentlemen drank too much. Many couples arrived only at dinner time. Anyway, our boxholders are nothing like Mrs. Astor and her Metropolitan Opera House, reeking of wealth. The *Parsifal* Entertainment was our first spring concert, our first production of any kind; the Grand *Parsifal* Concert last year did not repeat the previous mistakes.

Music is the thing. Music of the Spheres, securing an alignment of souls, linking to vibrations from other realms, knitting the material and the spiritual. How Wagner understands the layering of time and space, layers conjoined by the ethereal. I invited Seidl to read the Vedas. He finds them "interesting." But his is an intuitive faculty—not analytical; "not an empiric," as Krehbiel says. Wagner commanded a conscious understanding of illumination, an instinctive understanding, every kind of understanding. A Master.

"What is the Seidl Society?" Well, it is a quest. For harmony. For a degree of independence. For a modicum of personal authority. A woman must live for something.

Chapter Six
Manhattan: December 1893

Threading his way through the mid-day bustle of Stuyvesant Square, sidestepping puddles of ice and snow, Krehbiel found himself auditioning the speech of bundled immigrant mothers and grandmothers: the Yiddish guttural and excited, the Irish euphonious and laced with felicities of expression, the Slavic thick with glutinous consonants. St. George's Episcopal—J. P. Morgan's church—lent a welcome if incongruous formality to the multifarious human spectacle. If this was one face of America, so much the better; it bristled with animation and expectation. His breath lingering in the chill air, he navigated northeast towards Seventeenth Street between First and Second Avenues, descended a short stone staircase, and knocked. A man in shirtsleeves opened the door. He was swarthy and broad-nosed, with wild red whiskers and deep-set black eyes: a countenance at once lined, livid, and dignified.

"Dr. Dvořák."

"Herr Krehbiel. *Bitte.*"

The bird cages were open; he could both hear and inhale the thrushes. Having visited before, he understood that he was expected to ignore them, and also the children underfoot. There would be no greetings, no small talk. The little room he entered smelled of tobacco, which was better. They proceeded to converse in German.

"I must thank you again for this opportunity."

Dvořák pointed to a chair astride a table.

"Having already heard your new symphony in rehearsal under Herr Seidl, I am certain that it is a landmark achievement. I hope to publish certain excerpts from the score with commentary. With your permission."

Krehbiel laboriously removed his overcoat and fumbled with a worn briefcase from which he extracted a notebook and two pages of music paper, neatly inscribed. He placed these on the table and waited while Dvořák sat. Krehbiel settled himself opposite; the chair creaked in protest.

"Would you be so kind as to look at these with me and offer some remarks I can share with our musical public? This first example, the main subject of the first movement ..."

Dvořák's gaze remained remote.

"Could we suggest something racial here? The Scotch snap? The pentatonic scale?"

Dvořák raised his eyebrows and shrugged his shoulders.

"These are folk music traits, are they not?" Krehbiel persisted. "They color, shall we say, the Negro melodies of our friend Mr. Burleigh? Certain Indian chants? Could we call this theme 'American'"?

"If you wish. These features are common to many forms of folk music, of course."

Krehbiel pointed to the next musical example. He had labeled it "Movement One: Third Principal Subject."

"And this beautiful and poignant theme, Dr. Dvořák, is it not influenced by our slave songs? Does it not evoke some of the specimens I have shared with you? Does it not in fact specifically resemble 'Swing Low, Sweet Chariot'?"

Dvořák gestured a kind of assent by opening his hands.

Krehbiel's plump index finger moved downward to an example marked "Movement Two Principal Subject." "And surely this tune, the one introduced by the English horn, is flavored by plantation song. Or could we perhaps say that it suggests the loneliness of a night on the prairie?"

"The American prairie is a lonely place. Empty. Sad."

"Thank you, Doctor. And here we have your trills, your birdcalls—animal life on the prairie scene."

"Birds. Of course."

"And the Scherzo? What are its national characteristics? Something Indian?"

Dvořák lifted his chin in a quizzical way. "The scherzo also has its birdcalls. I don't see them here."

"Yes, of course, the flutes in the Trio section. Could you possibly write those out? I would be very grateful."

Dvořák took a sheet of music paper and patiently set to work. Krehbiel admired the efficiency of Dvořák's hand. The passages materialized gradually on two staves, fully harmonized. What kind of a man kept birds in his home uncaged? A rustic man, one who himself felt caged in a tall island city teeming with inhabitants. One who rarely set foot on the city's hard pavement without the companionship of his eager amanuensis Kovářík. An imbibing man who best enjoyed simple conversation and company, or the organ loft of an unprepossessing country church. A man whose fascination with the city's departing railroad trains and ocean vessels—from Grand Central Depot; from the great downtown harbors—told of restlessness, loneliness, homesickness …

"My birds modulate from E minor to E major." Dvořák was still writing. "You must not underestimate the musicianship of birds."

Krehbiel's own musical examples included one more specimen, labeled "Movement Four—Violas." It showed a three-note tune chasing its tail. "Could I trouble you with a final inquiry, Dr. Dvořák? Forgive my possible effrontery, but to all American ears this" — he pointed — "will sound like … 'Yankee Doodle.'"

Dvořák actually smiled—like a grizzled pirate; he only lacks a bandana across his forehead emblazoned with a skull and crossbones. A daunting man, not unfriendly, never frosty, but externally a tough kernel of a man.

"A more general question, please, Dr. Dvořák." Krehbiel cleared his throat. "You have hinted at a relationship between your symphony and Henry Wadsworth Longfellow's poem 'The Song of Hiawatha'."

"The story of Hiawatha's wooing is a favorite of mine. I read it first in Czech, later in English. Probably when I composed the slow movement this was somewhere in my mind."

Krehbiel scribbled in his notebook, then continued:

"You have titled your symphony 'From the New World.' All of my readers appreciate that Mrs. Thurber, when she engaged you to direct the National Conservatory of Music, entertained the hope that you could inspire American composers to cultivate their own native school based upon native sounds and impressions. Has this not been your method in composing your symphony?"

"A composer must listen to his surroundings. This is only natural."

"His surroundings, yes. Do you not agree that music in its highest form springs from the surrounding dialects or idioms, dialects or idioms that are national or racial in origin and structure?"

"Every composer has a people."

"As you have been true to your own Czech people and have bequeathed a new musical voice to that people with your *Slavonic Dances* and kindred works inspired by the peasantry, its customs and folk dances. You were yourself raised among peasants, were you not?"

"My father was a butcher and kept an inn. I played the violin there as a child. These were my musical beginnings and remain deep inside me. And I keep my faith in the poor. They work hard and seriously."

"In America, we call such men as yourself 'self-made.' This is an American ideal."

"Is it your ideal, Herr Krehbiel? Are you yourself 'self-made'?"

"I would in general say so. I have no degrees. I have instructed myself in many fields."

The conversation halted. Krehbiel began again.

"May I offer my own opinion? What I observe is that you have discovered in our 'Negro melodies' the music that is most vital in our own folk-song. It originated with the Negro slaves of the south partly because those slaves lived in the period of emotional, intellectual, and social development which produces folk-song, partly because they lived a life that prompted utterance in song, and partly because as a race the Negroes are musical by nature. Being musical and living a life that had in it romantic elements of passing pleasure as well as of great hardship and suffering, they gave expression to those elements in songs which reflected their roots in Africa as modified in the American environment. The result is a folk-music that touches the American heart. That it also touches your heart is manifest in your new symphony—and especially, I would say, in the slow movement."

"Your Negroes, and also your Indians, have suffered. Suffering yields self-expression."

"And may I venture a further surmise? New directions in musical development today have come from the Slavonic school—from yourself and from Smetana, and from

Tchaikovsky. The new Slavonic school is fearless in the face of convention. Could one say that it preserves the barbaric virtue of truthfulness?"

Dvořák's black eyes darted to the side. "You must excuse me," he said, rising from his seat and lifting a watch from his pocket. "I have another appointment this afternoon."

"But of course." Krehbiel hastily gathered his things and repacked his briefcase. He glanced at the thrushes on his way out. The meeting, if very brief, *sans* amenities, had been highly productive. He would incorporate the musical examples alongside Dvořák's commentary, preparing the reception that Dvořák's symphony deserved. He swelled with importance.

* * *

"Good day, Professor."

He was long well-known to the drivers and brakemen of the Fourth Avenue streetcar. Today he was bundled in a thick coat, the fur collar of which hugged his neck against the cold. Invariably he rode in silence, mounting the car on East Sixty-second, absent-minded, self-absorbed. As often as not, his vacant gaze less masked thought than music, vigorous or pathetic, on this occasion the bracing horn call of Dvořák's new symphony, a declamation of New World energy and purpose. Its forging progress accompanied the car's more labored progress uptown, bell clanging in the cold amidst sundry horse-drawn vehicles and busy pedestrians. The screaming elevated railroad an avenue away made far quicker time; but its grinding wheels, soot and cinders, and flames of steam deafened the music of the mind. Dvořák's horn motif now billowed and churned through a series of developmental modulations. Last season—the first of Dvořák's directorship of the National Conservatory—he had included half a dozen Dvořák works on his Philharmonic programs, alongside formidable samplings of *Lohengrin*, *Tristan*, and *Parsifal*. He had also premiered a Wagnerian American symphony—the hour-long *Sintram* by George Templeton Strong. He had even led the hymn "America" as sung by Fischer. Thomas's Philharmonic programs, by comparison, had more featured older music. Though Thomas's departure for Chicago had opened new concert possibilities, he remained exiled from the Metropolitan: *Lohengrin*, and *Meistersinger* were being given in Italian under Mancinelli. The tickets were expensive, the audiences restless and gaudy. His own weekly Saturday night concerts at the Opera House, with their German overtures, tone poems, and opera excerpts, were a bitter sop, painful remembrances of better times.

His mood now found solace in the sad English horn of Dvořák's Andante—which he had slowed to a Largo at Tuesday's rehearsal. It ached for places quieter, older, rooted in custom. Dvořák's Prague. Bayreuth. The English horn sang sorrowfully of Daniela.

"That English horn, my boy—it's first cousin to my shepherd's song in *Tristan*." The familiar specter, in the shadows of the chilly streetcar, gabbling on. "Forget your absolute music; it's already seven decades since Beethoven cast his anchor on newfound shores—and his anchor was the *word*, a steadfast haven for the wandering heart. *Freude*! *Seid umschlungen!* And the word, this human archangel, foretold the Artwork of the Future, redeeming music into drama. Your Dvořák Andante or Largo, call it what you will, is not 'symphonic' but a *tone poem*, a paean to prairie hardship and waste, a portrait of vacant physical space, of far horizons and parched bones. Harken to its *words*. Render Burleigh's slave songs, yearning for a new birth over Jordan waters. Render Hiawatha's cries for his dying Minnehaha, his intimations of extinction on your barren Western plains." The tapering English horn yielded a frigid winter dirge, the ceremony of Minnehaha's wrapped corpse borne through the prairie snow. The sadness of the lingering Indian, a stranger to progress, streaked the wintry New World spectacle of entitled rich and embattled poor, of the striving masses he now glimpsed astride the avenue.

"Union Square, Professor."

His accustomed stop. He preferred to walk the rest of the way, his stolid black presence mocked by the enveloping public spectacle. Though he permitted himself courteous acknowledgement of the many who recognized him, he otherwise enjoyed a condition of ironic anonymity. A daily dose of the teeming square was a reliable tonic. The city's eclecticism of class, race, and fashion, so foreign to Budapest or Berlin, here attained a crossroads merging the Ladies' Mile, the entertainment district, and the immigrant melee; stores and theaters of every caste densely commingled. Sleek mares, manes braided, jostled with gray nags, doughty carts with liveried maroon carriages in a chaos of traffic. The horsecars and streetcars, the harness bells and gongs and rattling metallic wheels, crisp in the wintry air, competed with the cavorting children and barking dogs of the slushy park. He promenaded serenely past baby carriages and nannies, bowlered businessmen and fashionable ladies in billowing hats and high–button shoes, past the towering equestrian statue of Washington and down Broadway toward McCreary's huge cast-iron dry goods emporium, toward the Gothic spire of Grace Church, finally to his invariable destination: the second-floor roundtable of Fleischmann's Vienna Model Bakery.

A good thing Huneker was absent; Seidl was not in the mood to contribute his droll frugality of speech to an avalanche of purple Huneker repartee. Neither in evidence were

Neilson, Herbert, or Scharwenka, any one of whom would have invited a gregarious camaraderie. Instead, Dvořák sat alone, puffing one of his thin cigars. A raft of German and Czech newspapers lay on the table. He and Seidl were a fabled pair; they communed wordlessly while others kept their distance. Dvořák was taciturn but legible, Seidl formidably inscrutable; "Der grosse Schweiger," Huneker dubbed him. Seidl removed his coat and became quizzically attentive. Dvořák downed the remainder of his beer with pronounced aggravation. He fixed bleary eyes on his tacit interlocutor. They conferred in German.

"Krehbiel visited this morning to 'interview' me. About the symphony."

"What did you tell him?"

"Enough."

Dvořák signaled for another beer.

"'From the New World,'" Seidl continued in a low, steady voice. "Isn't that what Mrs. Thurber wanted?"

"Composers do not speak of such things."

"'Composers do not speak of such things.' Please don't parrot Hanslick to me. Composers have pictures and thoughts. Look at Tchaikovsky."

"I do not choose to write such symphonies. I do not parade my nightmares."

"But you disclose your pictures. Did you not tell Creelman that the 'Negro melodies' would foster a 'great and noble school of music'?"

"Creelman invented that interview. To sell newspapers."

"You don't believe that Negro melodies—mainly invented by white men, I am told, but never mind—are the proper ingredients for an 'American' symphony? I have been living with your particular symphony for weeks now. I have put it into rehearsal. And I think the slow movement is one of the most important things you have done. I have decided that it is a Largo, by the way."

Dvořák registered surprise. Seidl's dark eyes surveyed the ceiling. His puckered lips conveyed a scathing or ingratiating irony.

"*Innerlichkeit*—a quality unknown to your friend Doctor Brahms—it cannot be rushed. That movement is full of sadness, of loneliness. Do you know why?"

Silence.

"Because of some Indians? Because of 'Negro melodies'? It is full of sadness for you and for me because it expresses *Heimweh*—homesickness."

They lapsed into their private sorrows, secret sorrows, feeling both alone and together. There were sorrows of which they were mutually aware and would never mention. There were other sorrows they barely acknowledged to themselves. Seidl felt the existential shudder that New York kept at bay when he was busiest, when there were operas to prepare and superintend.

"You should be writing tone poems," he suddenly told Dvořák. "You should be composing operas."

"I intend to compose an opera about Hiawatha—another thing I do not have to tell you. I await a libretto."

"Ask Neilson."

"This is in Mrs. Thurber's hands."

"It would be a service to the Americans. They have no operas. Their symphonies sound like Schumann and Brahms. But there is talent here. Victor Herbert. MacDowell. Chadwick."

"Everyone one of whom studied in *Germany*," Dvořák responded in his thick and distorted German. "I have gifted pupils of my own. But nothing will happen in this country. Private wealth, it is everything. Who pays for Mrs. Thurber's conservatory? Her husband. Who built our new Music

Hall? Carnegie. Who finances the Metropolitan Opera? The boxholders, with their Fifth Avenue mansions and Newport Beach summer castles. The other day I offered a scholarship to a young man who could not accept it. He would have lost his bookkeeping job; he must spend six days a week in Brooklyn. In my own youth I was supported for *five* years by the Ministry of Public Education. The situation with American publishers is also impossible. Americans must publish their music in Germany."

But Seidl was an immigrant, not like Dvořák a visitor. "Mrs. Langford's Society does not depend on great private wealth," he said with some emphasis. "The New York Philharmonic is a cooperative enterprise. It supports itself."

"Mrs. Langford's Seidl Society presents a handful of concerts at the Brooklyn Academy of Music. The entire New York Philharmonic season consists of six concerts and six public rehearsals. In Boston, Higginson's Boston Symphony gives one hundred concerts a year—that is a real orchestra. Higginson is a banker. He pays for the conductor, the soloists, the musicians. I am in Boston in a few weeks. Paur will conduct my symphony."

"Paur will mis-conduct your symphony. Are you coming to Friday's matinee? Are you not curious to hear your Largo?"

"I will come Saturday night."

"And the Seidl Society performance in January? Mrs. Langford has invited you. You have not written back. She has asked me to help obtain your kind attention."

"I am a composer. That I have to teach as well is enough."

"Mrs. Thurber pays you a lavish salary. Mrs. Langford is an indefatigable force. Where in Europe would you find such women? They are democratic missionaries. Mrs. Thurber gives full scholarships to your Negro pupils. Mrs. Langford charges twenty-five cents, even fifteen cents for tickets to her concerts. She merely requests your presence, with your family."

But Dvořák's head was elsewhere. He wanted to be home. Home was Prague. No, it was 327 East Seventeenth Street, with his wife and children. And his birds. Perhaps Seidl would accompany him. He was not in the mood to walk three blocks by himself.

* * *

"Ottie! Aloisia! Maggie! Anna, where are the girls?"

"Any moment, Papa."

"The carriage is waiting!"

Dvořák's wife and three oldest children would accompany him. They had endured the week's crescendo of anxiety. The day before, Papa had decided not to attend the "public rehearsal" of his new symphony—its actual premiere. In the sitting room, a copy of the *Tribune* lay open to page five—three columns of tiny print including no fewer than fourteen musical examples and headed "Dr. Dvořák 's American Symphony" and signed "H.E.K." Dvořák had gotten no further than the massive preamble: "The production of a new symphony by the eminent Bohemian composer would be a matter of profound interest under any circumstances, but to this occasion is given a unique and special value by the fact that in the new work Dr. Dvořák has exemplified his theories touching the possibility of founding a National school of composition on the folk-song of America. His belief on this point, put forth in an incomplete and bumbling manner through newspaper publications last spring" — Krehbiel was here challenging Creelman, in the latter's capacity as publicist for Mrs. Thurber — "created a great deal of comment at the time, the bulk of which was distinguished by flippancy and a misconception of the composer's meaning and purposes."

Though Dvořák had trimmed his beard, a top hat and tails ill-suited his rustic mien. The private carriage—it had been ordered by Mrs. Thurber—was equally an incongruous novelty for the family. The children piled on board eagerly, Anna dutifully, Dvořák hastily. The concert would begin in forty-five minutes.

Prague slept at night. New York was inextinguishable, the ubiquitous trolleys festooned with colored lamps, the hotels stacked with gleaming windows. Fire signs blazed the night's amusements. Broadway was illuminated by arc lights mounted on twenty-foot cast-iron posts. Madison Square, at Twenty-third Street, brandished its sun tower stop a 160-foot mast. To Dvořák's consternation, the driver here headed up Fifth Avenue with its Vanderbilt Row mansions, their fairy-tale gables and turrets. This face of New York invariably incited his disapproval and discomfort: he could no more deflect its hauteur than he could enjoy the careful attire tonight's occasion demanded. The carriage turned west and proceeded in heavy traffic. The entrance of Carnegie's new Music Hall was thronged. As with the Metropolitan Opera House (which Dvořák had only once visited), both its external plainness and gargantuan scale contradicted every European hall he knew.

The family negotiated a short flight of steps to attain a cramped vestibule thronged with well-wishers. The massed bodies parted amid salutations and gleaming smiles. Dvořák hurried his brood upstairs to the second ring of boxes. No sooner was the family sited than number ten was unlocked. A second door opened, and the vast burgundy auditorium burst into view. "Aha, at last the good Doctor, whose miracles we await. What reports 'From the New World' have you in store for us this evening? Something negroid, perhaps? Or a bow and arrow from Master Longfellow's quill?"

Fat Jim Huneker was shaking his hand, with the Thurbers alongside. The adjoining boxes were packed with prying eyes: he glimpsed Joseffy, Scharwenka, Stanton. Downstairs, heads were upturned. "The man of the hour," Francis Thurber was calling him. He mumbled his gratitude, bowing, nodding, indicating Anna and the girls. Creelman was going on about "prophesies in the wilderness." Mrs. Thurber was beaming, hers was a languid dark-eyed allure, no doubt about it …

A burst of applause: Seidl's quick, featureless entrance. What was on the first half? Mendelssohn and Brahms?! The one dismissed by Wagner as a Jewish imposter, the other by Seidl as lesser than MacDowell. The gossamer stirrings of *A Midsummer Night's Dream* were a momentary distraction. Shakespeare music. Dvořák himself had composed an *Othello* Overture. He had conducted it in New York, with Damrosch's orchestra. Seidl had conducted it with the Philharmonic. It better suited Seidl than Mendelssohn—this reading was getting heavy.

It now became possible to look around—no one would notice. The hall was handsome in an American way—huge but gracefully proportioned, with simple boxes and amenities. It did not glower, like the cavernous and encrusted Metropolitan Opera, in which a mere Bohemian visitor could lose his way. Acoustics: clear and warm. Orchestra: attentive, efficient. The winds reasonably in tune. How old was Mendelssohn when he composed this overture? *Seventeen*? At that age I had not nearly mastered form. If I developed more slowly, I am in fact still developing. My music here is different, much different than before. Because America is different. Burleigh's slave songs—let Creelman publicize my "prophesies" all he wants—the pain and ecstasy of those songs will one day inspire music rooted in American soil, in American experience … Mendelssohn's overture is sounding terribly fastidious. Now I'm beginning to talk like Wagner. Like Seidl.

Polite applause. Here comes young Master Marteau, for the Brahms concerto. He's about as old as Mendelssohn was … My God, how turgid Brahms can be, how padded and learned. But then Seidl detests this music; he's conducting mechanically. My own violin concerto is not without its longueurs. A cumbersome genre …

Dvořák's body and mind were mutually estranged. His busy thoughts could not subdue his trembling heart. He had not yet had a heard a note of his "New World" symphony, except at the piano. Never had he composed music so intently awaited. Krehbiel's gargantuan article was one of a dozen already published in the New York press—and there would shortly be a dozen reviews. In Vienna, a new symphony by Brahms, by Bruckner, by Dvořák was nothing urgent: these New Yorkers were looking to him—a Bohemian peasant born and bred—to point the way to a promised land. Warding off Brahms's concerto, he eased himself into a predilection for anesthetic slumber …

Anna's tap on the shoulder signaled that intermission had arrived and it would not become him to be observed asleep. The main thing was that Huneker was gone. So were the Thurbers. No, he would prefer not to join Anna and the girls in the lobby. Anna rolled her eyes and departed. He shifted his weight and warily surveyed his surroundings. Strangers smiled or nodded or escaped his gaze. His symphony came next—the tremors resumed, and with them feelings of solitude and displacement. He turned around—there was a noise—and gratefully discovered Kovařík, who for some reason chose to address him in English:

"And now for the *main event.*"

Dvořák muttered something in Czech—it sounded like "Hlavní událostí"—only to find himself suddenly joined by his students, emboldened by Kovářík's visit to the august box. Burleigh and Arnold, whose black attire nearly matched their dark skin; Goldmark, Fisher, Shelley, all of them thoughtfully attempting to restrain their excitement. Dvořák felt the need to rise and say hello. "Don't get up, Master." "Please, don't bother yourself." "We don't want to disturb you." "We will see you later. "We'll be on our way." Kovářík sat down beside him. Dvořák was breathing rapidly.

At church that morning, Dvořák had prayed that his capacity for public composure would not desert him. Perhaps it had been a mistake to skip the rehearsals. He had not imagined that it would be this difficult. But the Lord watches over all. Certainly, his American adventure had so far proved a blessing. It had achieved financial security for the family. It had refreshed his artistic calling. He was esteemed and appreciated. How petty, how selfish to focus on himself, his comforts and discomforts. And he had attended dozens of first performances of his symphonies and operas and quartets, sober baptisms of his musical offspring. But the stakes … Was it not presumptuous to guide another nation's musical destiny? The Negro melodies he adored—who was to say that they would speak to all Americans? Krehbiel. Mrs. Thurber. Burleigh, of course. *Creelman*, in his role as paid "publicist" for the conservatory. But what did Huneker think? What did Huneker *really* think?

"Deep in thought, Doctor? How did you enjoy Brahms's Hungarian finale? Even our Hungarian friend Seidl seemed aroused, his notorious aversions notwithstanding."

The devil in person.

"The national in music is ever present, at least in this our era of national ferment abroad. Will there already be a native American music, racy of the soil? Are we yet equipped, do you think? Or must we wait another generation, or even two?

Perhaps you can help us to ascertain our prospects. Perhaps even this evening help is on the way."

Huneker's loquacity allowed Dvořák time to fabricate a response. "Your friend Krehbiel is an expert in such matters. Ask him."

"But Henry's views are well-known. We read them daily, encrusted with fulsome detail, filling the long columns of the *Tribune*. But enough, the main thing tonight is your beautiful symphony, to which we now eagerly attend."

Is he done? Apparently. But where are Anna and the girls?

"Where are Anna and the girls?"

"I will fetch them," said Kovářík.

"Never mind."

All four looked guilty and worried. Next came the Thurbers. Jeannette's eyes were as ever a jolt to the system. A burst of applause, intense but brief, announced Seidl. He commanded an unbearable stillness, then suddenly, with an elegant gesture of the baton, a sorrow song in the cellos. Dvořák closed his eyes. Then a ripping of strings, a clarion alarm in the winds, a fathomless undercurrent of mystery, a surge of pregnant drama, a quick but mighty crescendo, a timpani roll, a slashing violin tremolo, my God how Seidl had mastered the symphony and made its preamble his own, with every event choreographed and consummated, a music drama infinite in detail. Now he swiftly propelled the main theme in the horns—the Wagnerian method: extremes of tempo, of plasticity, of expression. The movement's accumulated energy and force attained a broad climactic plateau, then receded, retarded, softened to the Indian flute theme with its odd accents and primal accompaniment. Where Dvořák repeated the simple tune, triple-piano, Seidl thinned his forces to a whisper, the melody in the second violins no louder than the pizzicato drone in the cellos. Dvořák's eyes clenched tighter: Seidl had seized a barren moment of prairie sadness. The moment mobilized, modulated to the major, escaped into sunlight, toward flowered Bohemian meadows succumbing in turn to plantation languors. At the slowest possible tempo, Seidl delivered the Negro melody Burleigh insisted was "Swing Low." Well, it was a kindred benediction, sweeping through the orchestra, swelling heroically, trailing trumpets. Seidl pressed forward, accelerating into a migratory episode of churning adventure. His orchestra, so methodical in its Mendelssohn and Brahms, was now a thing possessed, bows flying, bodies rapidly swaying in thrall to a shared irresistible impulse. Dvořák was listening as if to music not his own. The two subsidiary themes duly returned in new keys, shifting the harmonic plan toward the home E minor. Seidl now whipped harder and harder, attaining maximum velocity, maximum intensity, driving the movement to a series of clipped and stuttering final chords. And it was over. The hall erupted. Dvořák wiped his brow and discovered it drenched, wiped his cheeks, sighed and sighed again to settle his pounding chest, could not subdue his trembling hands. Seidl stood immobile and waited.

Now the Largo. The opening brass chorale, which Dvořák had imagined purveyed in two human breaths, at Seidl's new tempo traversed a Wagnerian vastness of time and space. And the English horn tune, which Dvořák had heard shaped by Burleigh's firm baritone, conveyed impersonal sorrows, excavated Biblical sorrows. The passage for church organ—the chill wind of its violin tremolos, the soft footfall of its pizzicato double basses—was for him the stoic forest funeral of Minnehaha, struck down by a winter famine, verses he knew by heart:

Then they buried Minnehaha;
In the snow a grave they made her,
Underneath the moaning hemlocks;
And at night a fire was lighted,
From his doorway Hiawatha
Saw it burning in the forest,
From his sleepless bed uprising,
From the bed of Minnehaha,
Stood and watched it at the doorway
That it might not be extinguished,
Might not leave her in the darkness.
"Farewell!" said he, "Minnehaha!
Farewell, O my Laughing Water!
All my heart is buried with you."

Otakar, Josephine, Rozaka. Dvořák's three first-born. Dead. Dead. Dead.

Seidl's double basses stroked the softest, most consoling D-flat major chords ever conceived. A trance enveloped the hall. As it gently lifted, scattered applause commenced. Then, feeding on itself, an ovation thundered and echoed through the chamber. Seidl turned and gestured. A reflex action caused Dvořák's legs to straighten and his body to rise. Voices from below, voices from on high murmured "Dvořák!" "Dvořák!" He saluted the players with quavering hand; even his legs were shaking. He carefully collapsed into his chair. Seidl turned and raised his arms. The Philharmonic split the silence with a pair of tingling chords. A rapid drumbeat in the strings ignited a taut Indian dance, its stealthy, tip-toe tread swelling to fierce poundings of the earth.

To the sound of flutes and singing
To the sound of drums and voices,
Rose the handsome Pau-Puk-Keewis.
First he danced a solemn measure,
Very slow in step and gesture,
Then more swiftly and still swifter,
Whirling, spinning round in circles,
Leaping o'er the guests assembled,
Eddying round and round the wigwam,
Till the leaves went whirling with him,
Till the dust and wind together
Stamped upon the sand and tossed it
Wildly in the air around him;
Till the wind became a whirlwind,
Till the sand was blown and sifted
Like great snowdrifts o'er the landscape.

Am I not a man in borrowed clothes, masquerading as a primal Indian, as an indentured Negro? As if on cue, a lilting Bohemian dance, an interlude for colorful couples in high boots, a village vignette sweetly embroidered with chirping birdcalls, answered Dvořák's perplexity with the aroma of Nelahozeves, of poignant homeward longings. Well, his Scherzo was many things. The opening mimicked Beethoven. The tapered ending—the Indian dance receding offstage—sounded like one of Wotan's storm-tossed exits in *Die Walküre*. More applause, but Seidl pressed forward with the finale. "You should write tone poems and operas." In the final pages, themes from all four movements interlocked. The skittish rhythm of Pau-Puk Keewis's dance transmuted into muffled timpani taps for a dirge: a ghost image of the leaping warrior, drifting sadly into legend. The threnody's apotheosis, the final E major chord fading to elegiac silence were in Seidl's monumental reading epochal, a vanishing of the noble savage.

> Thus departed Hiawatha,
> In the purple mists of evening
> To the regions of the home-wind
> To the land of the Hereafter!

When it was over, amidst the shouting and cheering and clapping, every eye accosted his. The musicians were waving their instruments. Even Seidl was applauding. Dvořák stood and stood again. Then he led the family to the coatrack, thence to the lobby only to discover it deserted. They could hear that the ovation continued unabated. "Papa!" He relented and they returned to box number ten. He tipped his top hat, and again, and again. To his amazement, Krehbiel entered the box, followed by Steinberg and Finck. They came with fervent handshakes and congratulations. Then it was Henderson of the *Times*, with his sister-in-law Mrs. Langford (whom he still owed the courtesy of a response). And Creelman and his "fulfilled prophecies" (but no sign of Huneker). Would he like to visit Herr Seidl in his dressing room? Mrs. Thurber wanted to know. Thank you, too tired, must go home.

Dvořák waited for the commotion to subside. Papa would sit silently in the vast auditorium until it emptied. Ana and the children felt vigilant, Kovářík diligent. Finally, all six arose to leave. Kovářík led the way downstairs to the stage door on Fifty-sixth Street—which was discovered to be thronged with grateful well-wishers. Kovářík found a carriage. The Dvořáks piled on board. It slowly maneuvered downtown in late-night traffic.

The new world.

Chapter Seven

Boston and Manhattan: December 1893 and January 1894

The mountebank Creelman has delivered his Dvořák sermons, and now the pot is boiling precisely as he wished it to boil. It was not enough for him to fashion Dvořák speeches extolling the capacity of "Negro melodies" to transform the musical fortunes of a foreign land. He equally made certain that those least likely to understand such a prophecy would have every opportunity to denounce it. Only a practiced Yellow Journalist would have thought to accost an innocent church musician like Anton Bruckner with leading questions about Afro-American folk-songs. And so now we have Bruckner in newspapers on both sides of the ocean expounding that "the basis of all music must be found in the Classical works of the past," that however sweet may be Dvořák's aforesaid Negro melodies, they can never form a groundwork for American symphonies. I trust Mrs. Thurber finds that an enlightening insight, courtesy of her press specialist. But canvassing Boston's composers was by far the more damaging strategy—Creelman has aroused all Boston against Dvořák, he has engendered a false discourse on musical styles and sources. Mr. Paine has apprised us that "individuality of style is not the result of imitation of Negro melodies or 'heathen' Chinese tunes." Mr. Chadwick has publicly opined that he would be very sorry were such Negro melodies as he has heard to become the basis for an American school. Mrs. Beach does not desire to question the beauty of Negro melodies, but cannot help feeling justified in her belief that they are not exceptionally typical of America because most Americans are not Negro. Well, one supposes that it could not have been otherwise, Creelman or no Creelman. When Dvořák conducted his Requiem here Apthorp called it "barbarous," which is to say scientifically inferior to the Anglo-Saxon. But the worst of the Boston lot is the supercilious epicene Philip Hale, who delights in insisting that "all careful observers have determined that the Negro is not inherently musical," that their plantation songs originated in white throats at campground meetings, that our former slaves are best consigned to African jungles from whence they came with spears and cannibal chants.

Krehbiel was lumbering in a dense maze of Boston streets and traffic wholly inimical to Manhattan's expansive grid. He blamed his failure to yet locate the Music Hall on its poor location and insignificant brick façade.

Hale has already ascertained that "the Negroes encountered by Mr. Dvořák have a singular habit of whistling Scotch and Bohemian tunes." And what Negroes has Mr. Hale encountered, one would like to know. Slandered Boston Negroes. That learned imbecile Agassiz should have been returned to Switzerland the moment he embarked on his theory that Blacks were a separate species, that "polygenetics" were willed by the Creator. How his tender sensibilities were affronted by the characteristic features of Black men, by their degraded speech and degenerate songs. Incredible that he was not laughed out the door at Harvard instead of being crowned emperor of Natural History. The problem with this place is its Harvard comforts: they sedate the mind with "tradition." As if Europe were not ten centuries older. The Mayflower and Plymouth Rock harden and retard New England intellects. America is about din and bustle, a vigorous hotch-potch of peoples, not a venerable central bloodline of Lowells and Cabots and Adamses … oh, here at last: the august "Music Hall."

Slowly but relentlessly, he made his way into the auditorium and refreshed his memory. Yes, it was as garishly spare as Carnegie's new Music Hall was quietly elegant, a severe rectangle with two shallow balconies to the back and sides, no boxes, plain chairs. Even the starkest of Massachusetts churches possessed more charm. Over the stage Higginson had imposed a giant sounding board at a slant—his "woodshed roof." Crawford's gargantuan Beethoven sculpture, on its high pedestal, looked down upon the players from behind—only Boston would think to situate a consecrating icon on the stage itself. A single additional ornament of consequence, the Apollo Belvedere, stood in a high alcove at the opposite end of the huge room. And, notoriously, the air was stale.

He greeted Colonel Higginson, whom he liked for his bluntness and honesty, in conversation with Mrs. Gardner, whom he abhorred for her aura of eccentric aesthetic indulgence. He did not acknowledge Hale, whose trim figure and loose black silk tie bragged of Exeter and Yale. But there was no gainsaying the caliber of the crowd—New York had no such symphonic constituency as this. On a bitter cold night every seat was taken, and by serious people who had come to listen to an orchestra already justly famous for its polish and dedication. A pity Nikisch no longer conducted it; he had seemed "theatrical." Instead, there was Paur, a musician unworthy of tuning Seidl's piano.

Dvořák's symphony came first, with Beethoven's violin

concerto and Tchaikovsky's 1812 Overture after the interval—a program as lopsided and impulsive as Paur's interpretive propensities. The band's smooth execution was never in doubt—Paur was conscientious in rehearsal. But the first movement of the symphony was too moderate and the second much too fast—it reminded one of the dinner at which everything was cold except the ice cream. One might say that Paur, new to America, conferred a certificate of national character to the work in showing so convincingly his inability to grasp its spirit: Dvořák's poetic evocations of slave song and Indian dance, of prairie desolation and the noble savage, went for naught. Doubtless Hale and his brethren will lecture us on Dvořák's immunity to whatever they may imagine to manifest the authentic America. They will furnish assurances that a Bohemian peasant of genius cannot be other than Bohemian. That there are creative possibilities latent in the folk-songs of America as in the folk-songs of other peoples, and that Dvořák has demonstrated as much, will evade detection. And yet those songs are accomplished facts, a trove not to be squandered. They will not be added to for the reason that their creators have outgrown the conditions which alone made them possible. Modern civilization is as great an obstacle to the creation of folk-song as it is to the creation of legends and mythologies. The faculty which brings them forth has atrophied. It ought to be looked upon as a privilege, if not a duty, to save them, and the best-equipped man to do this, and afterward to utilize the material in the manner suggested by Dvořák, ought to be the American composer. Musicians have never been so conscious as now of the value of folk-song elements. We have our own folk-song field and it is rich. Why sneer at the only such material which lies at hand? What matters if the man who points out the way be a Bohemian scarcely two years in this country? The peripatetic gypsy is the universal musician, and he makes Hungarian music in Hungary and Spanish music in Spain. It is characteristic of the vagueness which haunts the musical mind of Boston that the stamp of Dvořák's individuality on his symphony will be cited as proof that it is not American. It would be a pity if so pronounced a personality as Dvořák should conceal himself in a composition, but it would be a greater pity if the idea should prevail that in order to be American a composer must foreswear himself.

Kneisel's account of Beethoven's concerto was the evening's chief satisfaction. The vulgarity of Tchaikovsky's overture was surpassed by that of Paur's reading. Higginson is far too shrewd to retain such a man; doubtless he is already scouting Germany and Austria for a suitable replacement.

Boston is ever an interesting place to visit. So long as one does not have to live here.

* * *

Mrs. Thurber rose from her desk to greet Dvořák. Creelman, looking conspicuously dapper, his beard and long twirled mustaches as trim as Dvořák's forest growth was entangled, also offered his hand. An angel, disturbingly radiant. And her shadow, merely disturbing.

"How was the Brooklyn performance of your symphony?" she asked. "Were you satisfied?" Her honest interest challenged Dvořák's composure.

"Oh yes, Seidl has mastered the work. He knows it better than I do."

"And you have heard the Kneisels perform your quartet and quintet from Iowa."

"Indeed. A pleasure."

"And Boston, too, has already heard all three of those

wonderful American compositions. Well, you are certainly a busy man, Dr. Dvořák. We will not detain you long. I have asked Mr. Creelman to report to us about Madison Square Garden."

Creelman now became the incongruous object of her lovely gaze. He cleared his throat. "We live in a moment of industrial unrest. Businesses gone bankrupt, personal fortunes overturned, millions out of work. Armies of men without jobs, without food, without proper clothing or shelter. We have scheduled a special concert in support of the *Herald's* Free Clothing Fund. At the Madison Square Garden Concert Hall, which holds about fifteen hundred." He handed Dvořák a paper that read:

January 23, 1894

The National Conservatory of Music Orchestra
St. Philips Colored Choir

Miss Bertha Visanska, piano
Mme. Sissieretta Jones, soprano
Harry T. Burleigh, baritone

Dr. Antonin Dvořák, conductor

Mendelssohn: Overture to *A Midsummer Night's Dream*

Rossini: "Inflammatus" from *Stabat Mater* for Soprano, Chorus, and Orchestra

Liszt: *Hungarian Fantasy* for Piano and Orchestra

Volkmann: *Serenade* for String Orchestra

Foster: "Old Folks at Home"—arrangement by Dr. Dvořák for soprano, baritone, chorus, and orchestra

World Premiere

Dvořák scanned the page and looked up, first at Creelman, then at Mrs. Thurber. Creelman handed him a second sheet. Dvořák read it slowly and with care. Mrs. Thurber was quiescent. Creelman rustled papers and checked his watch.

> To the Herald:
>
> The Herald's Free Clothing Fund is the best and most practical movement that has been organized since the beginning of this terrible period of suffering. It gives every man, woman and child in this City an opportunity to do something toward clothing the hapless thousands pressing us on all sides for help. As Director of the National Conservatory of Music I am authorized to arrange and conduct a public concert in aid of this great charity. I will be most happy to do all in my power to make the concert a success.
>
> Dr. Antonin Dvořák

"Is the letter acceptable?" asked Mrs. Thurber. "Are you comfortable with the program?"

"I am happy to arrange Foster's folk song. It is a favorite of mine. I am happy to have Mr. Burleigh sing it."

"The chorus will comprise one hundred thirty Negro singers," Creelman continued. "The ladies will wear white and pink, the men dark suits. Our orchestra, of course, includes many players of color. The inter-racial aspect of our event is a novelty. New York has never seen anything like this before."

Dvořák decided to be entertained. "Our event—is it for the poor, or for the Conservatory?"

"It is for both, Dr. Dvořák," Creelman quickly began.

"It is our American way of doing things," Mrs. Thurber smoothly interrupted, her eyes gleaming. "Mr. Creelman is an agent for good causes and equally an agent for good business. With us, it is one and the same. We call his line of endeavor

Yellow Journalism, never mind why. It signifies that as a journalist he is never neutral. He ever engages with a mission. Mr. Creelman has pursued many interesting missions. He was once arrested by the British Marines for placing an imitation torpedo on a warship—to prove that such a thing was possible. In Russia, he interviewed Count Tolstoy about his infamous views on marriage. For us, he has promoted the cause of Negro melodies and of course the Dvořák cause."

"He has also asked Bruckner and Richter and Rubinstein about the cause of Negro melodies."

"Well, not directly. But he did ensure that your prophecy was known to the most eminent musicians of Europe. We are all of us serving the larger goal of a 'great and noble school of music.'"

Dvořák had to smile in recognition of the phrase that Creelman had minted in his behalf. He began reviewing what he would conduct. "Sissieretta Jones?"

"Why, she is the Black Patti," Creelman answered.

"Sissiereta Jones is known as the Black *version* of Adelina Patti," Mrs. Thurber explained. "She is our most important Black soprano."

"She sings two high C's in the 'Inflammatus,'" Creelman added.

"She does not sing at the Metropolitan?"

"She has never been invited to sing by any of our opera companies." Creelman was now in his element. "Purely because of the color of her skin. It is our accursed legacy of slavery, Doctor. She knows the operas, of course. She is a great artist condemned to perform mere extracts from the masterpieces. She has sung at the White House. She has sung at Carnegie's Music Hall. She was a featured artist at the World's Columbian Exposition. She sings Verdi. She sings Gounod. All the great composers."

"I have a Black composition student named Maurice Arnold," Dvořák said. "He has just finished a set of Plantation Dances. I would like these included on the Madison Square Garden program."

"Capital!" Creelman exclaimed.

"And I would like Mr. Arnold to conduct them."

"Done, Doctor!" Creelman slapped his knee.

Mrs. Thurber observed with delight that a common agenda was in play. "Very well then it is all settled," she said. "And what can we next expect of your own, Dr. Dvořák?"

"Perhaps next some piano works in the American style. I know you desire a Hiawatha opera. I await a suitable libretto. Seidl says maybe Francis Neilson …"

Mrs. Thurber knew something about English language librettos. She had once created an American Opera Company. "Mr. Neilson is a very pleasant and intelligent British gentleman but a mere fledgling in the theatre. Someday, perhaps, he will become an important actor or playwright. But we will keep looking. As you know, I have secured the permission of Miss Longfellow to adapt her father's poem, which you so admire. We must visit the Buffalo Bill Wild West when it is next at Madison Square Garden—not the concert hall, of course, but the large arena. This may help you—the Indian chants and dances."

"And will Mr. Creelman be put in charge of my Hiawatha opera?"

"But of course," replied Mrs. Thurber with such a combination of humor and sincerity that both gentlemen could only marvel at her fabled capacity to charm.

* * *

"'According to the New York Herald Mr. Dvořák began to study native music after his arrival in New York. Unfortunately for the future historian we are not told how he studied it, or whether he disguised himself in his exploration so that the music would not become suspicious, frightened, and then escape. It would be a pleasure to read of his wanderings in the jungles of the Bowery and in the deserts of Central Park. It would be interesting to know precisely his first thought on seeing the Harlem goat, an animal now rare.'"

"'Goat'?"

"The German is 'Ziege,' I believe."

"Goat."

"Goat. Hale goes on: 'Then I read in other New York City newspapers statements about Dvořák and his symphony, which convinced me that the work could only be appreciated properly by an audience composed exclusively of intelligent Negroes and combed and washed Indians.'"

"'Intelligent Negroes and combed and washed Indians.' Natürlich. And what himself did Mr. Hale think of our symphony?"

"'Dvořák has written delightful music, music that can be enjoyed by men and women, and by children of any or every land, and without indulging himself in musical Americanisms. The composer has the simple faith of a healthy child.'"

"A child. A healthy primitive Slav. Our friend Krehbiel must like that."

"Here is Krehbiel, in the *Tribune*: Dr. Dvořák's symphony, From the New World, was performed in Boston on Saturday night at a concert by the Symphony Orchestra. Its success with the public, while pronounced, was not so emphatic as it was in New York, for which fact an explanation might be found in the circumstance that it was not so well played. The newspaper critics in their reviews are unanimous in praising the beauty of the music and denying its right to be called American. Much of this kind of talk is merely quibbling. The sarcastic and scintillant Mr. Philip Hale of the Boston Journal does not deny that Dr. Dvořák's melodies reflect the characteristics of the songs of the Negroes in the South, and that the symphony is beautifully and consistently made. If so, why should it not be called American? Those songs are the product of American institutions: of the social, political ... And so on and so on and so on."

Francis Neilson was a heavy-set, square-jawed Briton seventeen years Seidl's junior. Seidl was in the habit of having Neilson read reviews to him, with Auguste knitting in the corner and Wotan snoozing underfoot. Chiefly, he enjoyed Neilson's company, which at times reminded him of his own discipleship in Bayreuth. Also, the ritual improved his English. Least important was its informational aspect: his interest in what others thought was circumscribed by impervious self-regard. That he was esteemed as redoubtable or resisted as arrogant were for him tedious facts. That he was now an American citizen was of greater personal interest. He had determined that New York was capacious and eventful: a world city. Its inhabitants were intriguingly varied and formidably free-spirited. Its aggregation of skilled instrumentalists exceeded that of any city abroad. Its musical schools and institutions of performance were incongruously dependent on private wealth: a problem solved by a Mrs. Langford or Mrs. Thurber, otherwise insufficiently attended. The part-time Philharmonic, administered by the players themselves, utterly lacked the services of a Colonel Higginson: its membership shifted from rehearsal to performance; its programs were infrequent. The Metropolitan he regarded with undisguised bitterness and contempt; he had not conducted opera there since his expulsion more than two years ago. Of the city's conductors, Damrosch was a dilettante bathed in admiration and dollars by a coterie of misguided socialites. Mancinelli, at the Metropolitan, was a skilled Italian transgressing on Germanic property deservedly his. Thomas he respected as an anachronistic Kapellmeister, a human metronome nonetheless adroit and prepossessing.

To a man, the New York critics understood him and his mission: a situation unthinkable in any European capital. They partied with him in restaurants and clubs; they feted him at banquets which Thomas refused to attend. Krehbiel was pompous but sincere. His trove of folk-song—the transcribed Indian chants and Negro melodies that he would eagerly circulate—was actually invaluable. For Seidl, the verbose German pedant in Krehbiel induced subliminal homeward longings (Wagner's prose was hardly a model of concision). Huneker: another mountain of unfathomable verbiage and as frivolous a personality as Krehbiel was dogged; but a personality with which to reckon. He would tell Seidl that he could "hear him thinking," that he exuded "the magnetism of the Sphinx," that he was an "incarnated baton." Finck: his two-volume Wagner biography—he had dedicated it to Seidl with a facetious threat that he would otherwise choose Damrosch—could be read without a dictionary. Henderson was Krehbiel recast in crisp American prose; he called Wagner's luxurious taste in fabrics and perfumes "unmanly" and his extremities of depression "pathetic." That was the Princeton part of him, that even now served the naval militia. But Henderson submitted wholly to the music dramas. They were acolytes all.

The critics' views of Dvořák mattered to Seidl more than their views of Wagner. Wagner was a closed book. Dvořák opened a new chapter in American music, a chapter of which Seidl was part. Was the "New World" Symphony American?

"Huneker—what does he write? He with Krehbiel disagrees, yes?"

"Oh, most assuredly. Just a moment. 'Dr. Dvořák's so-called "American Symphony" will be an enormous favorite with the public, and will doubtless be played all over the world. It has that unmistakable ring of the folk song which will endear it to all nationalities. Yet the American symphony, like the American novel, has yet to be written. And when it is, it will have been composed by an American. This is said with all due deference to the commanding genius of Dr. Dvořák.'"

"The American novel has yet to be written?"

"What he means is that American novels, like American symphonies, are still essentially European in idiom."

"So an American symphony sounds like what?"

"We don't know yet. Not European."

"And your opinion?"

"My opinion is that Henderson's review in the *Times* makes the most eloquent case for Dvořák's symphony as an American work. Listen to this, on the Largo: 'It is an idealized slave song made to fit the impressive quiet of night on the prairie. When the star of empire took its way over those mighty Western plains blood and sweat and agony and bleaching human bones marked its course. Something of this awful buried sorrow of the prairie must have forced itself upon Dr. Dvořák's mind when he saw the plains.' And here's another bit: 'In spite of all assertions to the contrary, the plantation songs of the American Negro possess a striking individuality. No matter whence their germs came, they have in their growth been subjected to local influences which have made of them a new species. That species is the direct result of causes climatic and political, but never anything else than America. From the canebrake and the cotton field arose the spontaneous musical utterance of a people. That folk-music struck an answering note in the American heart. If those songs are not national, then there is no such thing as national music.' I think that answers Hale."

"We must find our own American musical art. The first step is American operas. Wagner—not symphonies—is the future of music. And, of course, our operas must speak English. And Dvořák's Hiawatha opera?"

"I don't know that there will ever be a Hiawatha opera by Dvořák. Mrs. Thurber says she is attempting to find a librettist for him. But I feel she is misguided, that Longfellow's story is the wrong starting point. I've been thinking about your aspiration to undertake a Hiawatha opera of your own. Longfellow mistakenly believed that Hiawatha and Manabozo were the same deity, whereas they're actually quite distinct. Manabozo is the illegitimate son of the West Wind. He's a practiced magician but purposeless as a leader. Hiawatha teaches peaceful arts and pursues noble aims. My libretto treats Manabozo and Hiawatha in sequence. An epic evolutionary narrative. It will celebrate the primal and castigate the vandals of civilization. And you, not Dvořák, will compose the music."

"Is that what you think? We will see. We will see if I have become an American to move Wagner to New York. When the spring season ends you must join us in the Catskills. That is where we can work without disturbings. And I will talk with Wagner about it."

"Talk with Wagner?"

"Natürlich. All the time."

Auguste ceased knitting. Wotan detected suppressed excitement in his master's tone. Neilson realized that he had been chosen to ameliorate the Seidl melancholia. Seidl recognized that his American fate would demand creative tasks he had not previously envisioned.

* * *

Aha, my boy, so you're now a composer! Bravo! Bravissimo! And what, may I ask, qualifies you for this splendid endeavor? Oh yes, I had quite forgotten, your prodigy years in Budapest—you took harmony and counterpoint with Nicolitsch, did you not? And, of course, thoroughbass with Paul and Richter in Leipzig. Ample preparation. And afterward your gift sat dormant these many decades.

What's that you say? *Improvisations*? You mean your extemporaneous ramblings at the keyboard so admired by Auguste, your flashes of spontaneous genius neither recorded nor remembered? Perhaps your transcriptions for Brighton Beach are more to the point. Your symphonic incarnations of Liszt's keyboard pyrotechnics? Not so bad, actually. And, of course, there are the excepts from the *Ring* and other operas of my close acquaintance, sewn together with your own needle and thread. The *Siegfried* act two I find a bit much, pounding my fragrant Waldweben with the bombast (also mine) of Fafner's fight with young master Siegfried.

But it all takes time and patience—witness my own pathetic delayed development. Have you looked at *Die Feen*? *Das Liebesverbot*? Granted, I showed a modicum of early talent—or at least of early artistic temperament. But no authentic craftsmanship to speak of. I was a cocky youth, imbued with revolutionary ideals. I did not condescend to learn the old ways of doing things, and had not yet glimpsed the new ways I would someday find. What? You think I've done your work for you!? All right, I bequeath a template of some substance to posterity. As for your contention that conducting is a form of study, I concede your knowledge of the orchestra and of the singers' art, even your notion that to activate a musical composition in performance may be tantamount to the conservatory habit of copying orchestral scores as a pedagogical exercise. And you yourself of course copied *Parsifal* for me, making good sense of my scribbled pencil sketches, a job indeed well done. And you added the missing trombone parts to my Symphony—a youthful indiscretion, I know, but not without intimations—when it was exhumed for belated performance. Those were wonderful years together, times never to be forgotten.

I furthermore confess that it did occur to me that your musical gift might one day yield a truly creative outcome. A man needs a mission in life, calibrated bravely to his maximum capacity. My mission was to save German art—to rescue a legacy, to fortify and perpetuate a lineage, to rehabilitate and preserve an endangered cultural community soiled by princes and politicians, by petty journalists and Jewish money-lenders. You're an American now, a Yankee Doodle; you don't so much as think about Bayreuth except to castigate my poor widow. Your mission has become one of enlightened service to American art, counteracting the Wall Street barbarians and also those mercenary "pioneers" desecrating your virgin West. Importing high-quality German goods is a useful starting point, to be sure, but only that. Rejoice that in America there is no need to prostrate, as I all my life had to and did. No American Bismarck to beseech for state favors, no Munich cabal to decry your "meddling," no Hanslicks to denounce your old friend and colleague RW. Above all else: you sense the creative urge. Seize it! Not even our lady friends with their myriad charms offer satisfactions more prolonged. Chin up, lad. Look to the future!

Chapter Eight

Brooklyn and Manhattan: April 1894

Victor Herbert sat in a drab Brooklyn Academy dressing room with the intention of fingering some of the trickier passages of his Second Cello Concerto. He was a cheerful-looking man with a large round head and a smart curled mustache. He enjoyed a substantial name as a solo cellist and a growing reputation as a composer. He had premiered the concerto with Seidl and his Philharmonic weeks before. But Herbert's big head was consumed by a nascent operetta he was rapidly confecting to a libretto by Francis Neilson, a young British actor whose enthusiasm for *The Mikado* and *H. M. S. Pinafore* had inspired such lines as:

> Oh my specification
> I herewith unfold,
> On the list you will find virtues many.
> The personification
> Of morals of gold,
> When most people are born without any.
> My head is all brain, on top you will find
> Intellectual bumps without number;
> You never could guess the size of my mind
> Phrenologically I'm a wonder.

And this became the jolly song Herbert's vagrant cello was singing. To his fingers, to his heart, the concerto, however new, seemed a remnant of his strict Stuttgart musical education. The operetta, as yet unborn, connected to his Irish homeland and to his maternal grandfather Samuel Lover, who famously sang Irish songs in a voice sweet and true.

Dvořák's project for an American school, abetted by the fetching Mrs. Thurber and by the ubiquitous Henry Krehbiel, seemed stifling. A New World Symphony was well and good, up to a point. But Jim Huneker was correct: it remained a symphony, a product of Old World lineage and training. It had been Herbert's good fortune, a year before, to inherit Pat Gilmore's 22nd Regimental Band. He had just toured it, with Campanini—one of Seidl's favorite artists—singing opera: the "Toreador Song" and Figaro's patter aria. The *Tannhäuser* Overture sans strings was as ever a favorite selection—and so was the "Anvil Chorus" from *Trovatore* à la Gilmore, with half a dozen anvils pounding the beat. Herbert sustained his popularity as an instrumentalist by regularly casting himself as solo cellist with the band. He also composed American marches and potpourris for it. He was even taking his uniformed winds and brass to Manhattan Beach—since Gilmore's death, the province of Gilmore's redoubtable rival John Philip Sousa. Compared to orchestras, bands were the more American, the more patriotic. They were native to circuses. Every municipal park of size wanted one. Sousa used to complain that Gilmore was too much the showman. And the high-toned musical journals had rebuked Herbert for abandoning art. Hypocrites. A light opera imposed the same demands on a composer as *Carmen* or *The Barber of Seville*. He had known Strauss and Suppé abroad: craftsmen. He could write a proper fugue. He understood the mechanics of sonata form. Didn't the finale of his cello concerto ingeniously combine the themes of the previous two movements? It was hardly different, in that regard, from Dvořák's thematic machinations in "From the New World."

At the same time, Seidl remained Herbert's lodestar—his mentor and advocate. As Seidl's principal cellist and assistant conductor, as Seidl's frequent soloist, as one of sundry American composers Seidl championed, he was instructed and transfixed. For one of Creelman's *New York Herald* Clothing Fund extravaganzas, Seidl had even conducted Herbert's regimental band in tandem with the Seidl Orchestra in the *Tristan* Prelude and Liebestod—and then handed the baton to his protégé. And Herbert taught alongside Seidl at Mrs. Thurber's conservatory under the bulldog gaze of Dvořák (who so execrably led the conservatory orchestra). Dvořák was today in the house, awaiting the Victor Herbert Cello Concerto No. 2 in E minor. What would he think? That it was not a proper concerto, most likely. But no one could deny that the solo part was skillfully and inventively conceived. Or that the composer had cleverly—even very cleverly—enabled the cello to sing without fear of being submerged, and had invited the orchestra to add luster and mass without seeming restraint.

There was a knock, and the door opened a crack. "Ten minutes, Mr. Herbert." He decided to try the passage in rapid arpeggios that drove the finale to its climax. But there was no need, really; it had gone well enough at Carnegie Hall. The reception had been warm. Seidl had programmed his concerto with the *Euryanthe* Overture, Beethoven's Fourth, and a novelty: Nicode's *Symphonic Variations.* A sensible program of sensible length. Not so in Brooklyn with the Seidl Society ladies. Seidl had begun with the "New World" Symphony—all of it, encored from the Brooklyn premiere performance months before. Well, nothing wrong with that, I suppose. But the Society craved Wagner and Liszt—and so after the Dvořák had come the *Parsifal* Prelude and Siegfried's Funeral March. And *then* Liszt's *Hungarian Fantasy*—the pyrotechnics of which Mr. Courtland Palmer was at present doubtless negotiating. Then my concerto, its twenty minutes forestalling the closing Wagner salvo: the inescapable Prelude and Liebestod. What kind of program was this? Did Seidl imagine my concerto was a species of New World equivalent to Liszt's piano showpiece, bookended front and back by Wagnerian tumult?

A second knock: time to go. He briskly grabbed his instrument and strode backstage. As soon as he glimpsed Seidl, his body bristled. Seidl's poker face confided a wink, and Herbert's neck and spine bristled again. They proceeded onstage. The ovation was loud: a full house. Flowers and palms everywhere, courtesy of Mrs. Langford. Bowing, he looked up at her box: Dvořák and Kovářík. He briefly tuned to the oboe's A, shifted his weight, and signaled his readiness. Seidl flicked his baton and a surging theme in octaves erupted from the band. Herbert joined the fray with a flourish of his bow arm and a piercing attack. This was as earnest and strenuously vehement as any music he had ever composed. And it remained so, forging and thrusting … to what end? He knew—now—that this angry first movement lacked variety, that its effortful affect disclosed effortful origins. Surely the concerto's singular gestation was self-evident. When he had tired of these E minor exertions, Herbert had abandoned all pretentions and sought respite in a happier realm. Seidl guided his men through a calming transitional interlude. Musically, the symphonic stage was reset with trees, an amber spotlight, a paper moon. The second movement now commenced with a love song Samuel Lover might have crooned, an intimate cello melody casual and yet sincere. Herbert absorbed the crowd's rapt attention. His whispered song waxed rhapsodic. Passages of fervent declamation animated a faster episode. Then the tryst resumed. To round the vignette, the love serenade rode an aerial carpet of high strings, adorned by the cello's caressing obbligato.

Now came the coup. Recalling the angry motto with which the work began, Seidl's orchestra inflicted a storm. But it proved make-believe: a foil. The cello argued for a softer, friendlier tone. Taking charge with ricocheting arpeggios and double stops, it orbited its love song above becalmed remnants of the furious first movement. There ensued a delirious series of combinations and sleight-of-hand recombinations of the two tunes. The orchestra's breathless dash toward closure was prodded by increasingly brilliant cello figurations. The concerto's jubilant ending banished its anguished Germanic beginning. The audience responded in kind. Herbert bowed deeply, beaming his pleasure. Seidl stood stone-faced, nodding his head.

Herbert elected to remain backstage for the concert's Wagnerian finale. Having performed the Prelude and Liebestod countless times under Seidl's baton, he seized this unencumbered opportunity to study the conductor at work. Upon remounting the podium, Seidl was transformed, his countenance drained of its accustomed ironies, consumed by a gravitas that gripped every member of the waiting ensemble. He fixed the winds with a steely glance and the music commenced as from a void. An erotic languor surged fitfully toward arousal, mounting in volume and inexorable largesse; Seidl's chiseled ivory pallor began to redden. The restrained deployment of his arms and hands concealed from all but the musicians an encroaching nakedness of visage; barely moving his head, he commanded every man with his black eyes alone. The Prelude subsided to a tense existential hush. Isolde's Liebestod arose trembling at the threshold of audibility. Its ocean of sound mounted, receded, orgasmically regathered.

The conductor was now visibly at the mercy of tidal forces. His autocratic gaze had blurred. Orchestra and leader succumbed to a fate imposed both within and without. Wagner's climaxes pummeled and repummeled them. Sailors in a tempest, they strained to right the vessel and persevere. Finally, the sea grew calm and still calmer until the very water of the womb was attained. Seidl closed his eyes and willfully reset his mask while torrents of amazed acclamation assaulted him from behind. He had the men rise, then turned to perform the curtest of bows. He was recalled again and again. Women bearing flowers rushed to the lip of the stage. At last, he was permitted to retire, blind to all about him.

Victor Herbert had not moved. His cello lay resting against a chair. He picked it up and left the scene. Later, in his dressing room, he was joined by his wife and by Auguste—both of whom happened to be Wagner sopranos early retired from the Metropolitan Opera. Suddenly Dvořák appeared, bright-eyed and bristling, grasping his hand. "*Ganz famos!*" he exclaimed and disappeared. Mrs. Langford and the colonel offered their congratulations, as did ladies with Seidl Society pins. Robert Ingersoll informed him that he must take part in a musicale. Would he not? Seidl would be there. Yes, happily, thank you very much. Then they left, all of them. He was packing his cello when he noticed Seidl alongside. They spoke in German.

"Did Dvořák say anything?"

"'*Ganz famos.*'"

"That's all?"

"Two words."

"He told me more than that."

"Yes?"

"He told me he was going home to compose a cello concerto."

Herbert was still processing the evening's events; he found himself without words.

"You should feel flattered," Seidl added tonelessly, and was gone.

***

Victor Herbert heard the Pilgrims' Chorus from *Tannhäuser* being played on a piano. Carrying his cello, accompanied by his wife, he was being ushered toward the salon. The pianist, he assumed, was Seidl. Instead, he discovered a wiry, eagle-eyed man, gray-haired and densely grizzled, whom he recognized as the nation's most prominent German-American. Colonel Ingersoll robustly shook his hand and kissed Theresa's. "Do you know General Schurz?"

Schurz nodded and continued playing.

"Yes. Not well, but … "

"And Francis Neilson? Oh, of course, your own *librettist*! Herr Seidl. Miss Bartlett, for our musicale. Dr. and Mrs. Curtis. Their daughter Natalie. How old are you now, my dear?"

"Eighteen."

"Eighteen. And she has already studied with Friedheim and Busoni. And has been to Bayreuth. Will you play for us later?"

"Perhaps not."

"Perhaps not. Dr. Curtis and I have been discussing the latest remarkable developments at the Pullman Car Works. Have you heard? Debs's railway union has voted a national boycott of all Pullman sleeping cars in support of the strike."

"A boycott which your friend Debs wisely attempted to resist," Dr. Curtis opined.

Having greeted the Herberts, Ingersoll turned his full attention to the conversation. His fame rested upon strong opinions strongly voiced. His causes included agnosticism, women's suffrage, and Wagner. The irrepressible buoyancy of his presence mitigated the ultimatums lacing his oratory. "Debs also said: 'When a man surrenders his honest convictions, his loyalty to principle, he ceases to be a man!'"

"Oh, come now, Colonel, this is no time for messiahs. Those workers have families to support. They will not regain their jobs. They are being misled, misdirected."

"Dr. Curtis—the Pullman Car Works is an affront to human dignity. Yes, Pullman houses and feeds those men, furnishes their churches and cemeteries—which are one and the same. And he deducts from their wages accordingly. Now he has reduced those wages as much as fifty per cent. He cannot be allowed to play at being God Almighty."

"That is easily said. But this strike will certainly backfire. The attorney general will side with the railroads. So will the President. There may be violence."

Schurz abruptly stopped playing and wheeled toward the room. "And this there must not be! Another Haymarket is not what is needed. The Pullman workers will have fallen into a trap. They will be pilloried as 'anarchists,' like the Germans in Chicago. You will see. It is already happening. I know the President, he is a cautious man. He will fail to restrain the backlash. And Mr. Debs will have blood on his hands." The cessation of the *Tannhäuser* hymn inflicted a loud silence.

"Eugene Debs has been a guest in this house more than once, you know," Ingersoll said without heat.

"He has been a guest in this house, and I have many times been a guest in the White House, where I assure you Mr. Debs is not likely to be invited. And I say this without prejudice against Grover Cleveland, who endeavors to be a fair-minded man, a considered man. Imagine if *Blaine* were President now. There would already be federal troops at the Pullman works."

The mention of Damrosch's father-in-law piqued Seidl's interest. "Federal troops? What for federal troops?"

"What for?!" Schurz rose from the piano bench, whiskers taut. "Because, my dear Seidl, whose head is ever aloft in the realm of pure art ..." — Schurz waved his bony right hand toward the ceiling — "... because the United States government cannot allow a work stoppage of this scale. Do you realize what a railway strike could mean? How do you suppose Colonel Higginson's orchestra manages to get from Boston to New York City?"

"Could these be the trepidations of our former German insurrectionist who took up arms in 1848? Who consorted with Karl Marx in Cologne and with Richard Wagner in exile in Switzerland? Who risked his life returning to Berlin to rescue a comrade from a Prussian prison?"

With his round face, big belly, and orotund delivery, Ingersoll was as ample as Schurz was tall, lean, and acerbic. The latter, eyes aflame, fast replied: "That, Colonel, was another time and place. A monarchy—a Prussian *tyranny*—governed the affairs of men. I thank the Lord that I was evicted by that evil regime and here washed ashore to find my freedom. Our government needs adjustment to be sure. But our government does not need Mr. Debs. We have had our revolution. We have also had a bloody civil war in which both of us served the Union cause, the cause of justice. Now is not a moment for recrimination. Ours should be an era of reconciliation and stability."

"Reconciliation or capitulation? You and your political colleagues, General Schurz, defectors from the Republican Party of Abraham Lincoln, are too much enamored of Southern traditions. We must remain vigilant against the slavery party. 'Stability' may breed complacency. It becomes a contagion of old age."

"The *slavery party*! And what might that be? The liberals among whom I cast my lot as a lifelong advocate of personal tolerance and manly independence? Not even Mr. Nast in his most vicious caricatures has impugned my wartime credentials as a major general of the United States Army. I had thought to have helped to free the plantation slaves."

"'Anger is a wind which blows out the lamp of the mind.'" The familiar Ingersoll aphorism, uttered in level but reverberant sermon tones, chilled the room. Dr. Curtis appended a lame "Hear, hear." His daughter keenly sat forward. His wife sank abashed. The butler serving drinks and sandwiches ceased all movement.

But Seidl and the Herberts—and also Mr. Neilson, the lantern-jawed young Briton who had become Seidl's daily companion as well as the lyricist for Herbert's new operetta—were impervious observers throughout this mounting exchange between the two famous orators. Victor Herbert's considered response was to casually unpack his cello and with methodical strokes to apply resin to his bow. Quickly resuming his role of host, Colonel Ingersoll announced: "I see that our promised musical refreshment will shortly commence." Seidl bestirred himself to take his place at the keyboard. Herbert sat and tuned. He cleared his throat and assumed a benign expression. "For those not already tired of it, we will perform the slow movement of my Second Cello Concerto," he said, and proceeded to play it. The tender serenade, previously heard at Carnegie Hall and the Brooklyn Academy, made a different impression in Colonel Ingersoll's charged music room. Herbert himself experienced the music as a sweet antidote to confrontation, administering American cheer. For Natalie Curtis, it fueled hopes and worries concerning America's musical future. For Schurz, it seemed a banal non sequitur to his speeches of self-defense.

The music cadenced in a stratosphere of harmony. Herbert released his bow and smiled. The performers arose and acknowledged fervent or polite applause. Seidl retired to the back of the room. Herbert remained standing and spoke. Irish origins and German training alike inflected his friendly baritone.

"Thank you. Thank you. And now with your indulgence: a little encore. As some of you know I have been working on my second operetta with our friend Mr. Neilson." Herbert and Neilson nodded to one another. "We call it *Prince Ananias*, never mind why. The story concerns a certain monarch who has lost a most vital ability—the ability to laugh. There is also a company of traveling players, including two pairs of star-crossed lovers. Mr. Neilson has fit it all together so that it ends happily for all. I would like to share with you a number. Miss Bartlett has kindly consented to sing it for us, with Mr. Carson at the piano."

A willowy young lady emerged from the small audience and also a gangly young man. They sang and played:

A ray of golden sunlight fell
Across my life when you passed by,
I felt my heart with rapture swell –
A glance —'twas all, and love came nigh;
And love came nigh and fluttered round,
All through the hours till spring made bright,
The dearth with myriad flowers was crowned
For thee, my love, my heart's delight.

In beauteous garb was nature clad,
When heart to heart we pledged our troth;
The birds with joyous song made glad,
And clearest heaven smiled on both.

For love is spring and ne'er grows old,
When once the light shines clear and bright;
What though the earth is crowned with gold?
Love flowers for thee, my heart's delight.

Herbert reappeared at the front of the room to share the applause. He also had Neilson rise to receive his share. It was too much for Schurz. As soon as the clapping ceased, he loudly inquired, "And when, Mr. Herbert, might you favor us with a bona fide opera? Americans could use a good one, don't you think? How else can we truly transplant this grand European artform to our shores?"

Herbert remained standing while Miss Barlett and Mr. Carson resumed their places on a corner sofa. "Great art need not at all times be in earnest, General Schurz," he said. "I share your passion for Wagner, you must know that. But no American Wagner will appear among us. He is a product—a great product—of Germany, of Europe. His musical speech—its breadth, its complexity—is Germanic and opera is his mother tongue. America will create its own musical theater, in English—I am sure of it. And American youth and vigor will be part of this endeavor."

Colonel Ingersoll turned in his chair to address Herbert, Schurz, and the others, sweeping his gaze as he spoke. "And what of Dr. Dvořák's magnificent new symphony? Is it not couched in a European genre, a veritably Germanic genre? And yet does it not speak to us as Americans? Is it not pregnant with the Negro melodies of our old plantations, with the arid vastness of our Western plains, with the elegiac fate of our Indians?"

Schurz could hardly believe the adversarial posture that the evening's events had thrust upon him. Had he not long discovered America through the eyes and ears of a grateful immigrant necessarily attuned to nuances of culture, politics, and government? Had he not prominently served his new homeland in war and peace? Had he not personally counseled Lincoln to emancipate the slaves? As President Hayes's interior secretary, had he not grappled with the Indian question at close quarters—not, like these drawing room New Yorkers, as sentimental observers of mythic Hiawathas two thousand miles distant? Had he not at the same time maintained his allegiance to German language and art, and so understood as others could not the complexities of patriotic sentiment and expression in a nation of intermingled and intertwined European races? The urge to instruct, so native to his passionate disposition, was ever alert.

"Colonel Ingersoll, the 'elegiac' Indian of whom you speak—have you ever conferred with such an individual?" Schurz began, and the room grew taut. "I have not. I have however enjoyed the privilege of knowing Chief Ouray of the Utes—as vigorous a man as I have ever met, and a fair and resourceful negotiator for his people. The most humane Indian policy is of course one of pacification and *assimilation*—what our Indian schools in Virginia, Pennsylvania, and Oregon are undertaking, however belatedly. What you term 'our' Indians are nothing of the kind. Not yet, in any event. We can look forward to their integration in our national fabric. For the present time, however, the Indian remains an exotic. For the purposes of our composers, he is at best what the Hungarian gypsies were for Schubert or for Brahms—a purveyor of color. An *epiphenomenon*."

Now it was the turn of Miss Curtis. Pert, self-possessed, she was no stranger to the gathering or its issues of contention. She sang in Seidl's Manhattan chorus. She had long known General Schurz through her late uncle George William Curtis, Schurz's celebrated predecessor at *Harper's*

Weekly. At Bayreuth in 1891 she had gratefully submitted to Schurz's Wagner lectures between acts of *Parsifal* and the *Ring of the Nibelung*. But the mentor whose aura of omniscience had far trumped Schurz's had been Busoni—and Busoni revered the Red Man. "Dr. Dvořák's symphony was for me a supreme inspiration," she interjected. "I heard it in New York and again in Brooklyn. As a young American musician, I experience it as a challenge I cannot and must not escape. No one claims—certainly not Dr. Dvořák—that this music represents actual Indians or actual Indian music. Of course, Dr. Dvořák's 'elegiac' Indians are mythic. That myth is part of our national inheritance. And there is more. Dr. Dvořák is a devout man. He recognizes that Indian music and Indian religion are one. This unity of life and art stirs his musical imagination as it stirs his soul. We have all heard that he intends a Hiawatha opera or cantata, and seeks a proper libretto. Mr. Neilson—you have yourself been enlisted in this search, have you not?"

Neilson blushed and muttered that this was a matter for Mrs. Thurber to decide.

"Dr. Seidl—are you not knowledgeable about Dr. Dvořák's plans?" Miss Curtis persisted. "Should he not embrace a Hiawatha project, in your opinion?"

Seidl stirred to life. Scanning the ceiling, he volunteered: "It is a good thing that Mr. Krehbiel is not tonight here among us. We would a lecture performance have on this topic."

"Well, we must do better," Miss Curtis concluded. "When my teacher Busoni toured the American West, he sought out the Indians and studied their ceremonies. And Busoni is a very wise man. I am sure we can learn from our Indian brethren."

Seidl pursed his lips. Dr. and Mrs. Curtis beamed. Colonel Ingersoll stared at General Schurz. The latter strode to the piano and began to play Elsa's Dream. "Would anyone like to sing from *Lohengrin*?" he inquired, sustaining a tremolo high in the treble. "Frau Förster Herbert? Nein?" The Frau politely demurred. The General commenced Elsa's stately song, a miracle of lyric ecstasy. The future identity of American music was left unattended.

* * *

Wenonah! Once my wife
A vision, shorn of life,
And now fore'er departed.
No more your face will light my eyes
Your charms will not my spirit thrill.
I would not your being
Here relinquish 'neath unholy sod.
Rather a sepulcre I create
Hidden and inviolate to man.
A vault eternal I transform
Into a haven bound by storm.

It was past midnight. Neilson sat at his desk pondering the evening's conversation: the ambiguous response to *Prince Ananias;* the enthusiasm for Dvořák's new symphony; his embarrassment when asked about the libretto for Dvořák. Mrs. Thurber had rejected his preliminary draft out of hand. But she little knew that he and Seidl had since secretly embarked on a Hiawatha project of their own. That Dvořák had shared Longfellow's poem with Seidl and set him afire.

Seidl recognized that *Hiawatha* was no opera plot, that he required a compact libretto with calibrated dramatic incident. And Longfellow had mangled the tribal legends he appropriated. But by distinguishing Manabozo from Hiawatha they could create an epic structure—an American operatic trilogy—narrating a trajectory of Indian legend and lore climaxing with Hiawatha's advent. An homage to a majestic race now nearly extinct, an elemental tapestry of Ojibways and Dakotas well-nigh swept aside by the vandals of civilization.

Seidl had already reviewed his first attempt at the West-Wind's opening monolog. It could not yet readily be sung, he said. It too much resembled speech. Use Wagner as a model. Excising, revising, Neilson now wrote:

Wenonah, mother of my boy,
The pain of life was not your due!
No more your charms will thrill the god
You made your slave. Beneath the sod
You shall not lie!
This sepulcher I now transform
Into a haven bound by storm.

Wind-Wind summons a gale. At length, the wind abates.

O love sublime, unequal strife,
Ineffable the joy now lost,
My sun is set, and hopes decline,
Long years my grief will not console!
Your glorious youth was all my life,
And made a carnal love divine,
Whose heavenly ecstasies have cost
The light of my immortal soul!

He rises.

But our love-child lives!

He is thrilled by a great idea.

Our son,
Wenonah, he will be
Of all men most exalted
His name I now immortalize!
Hiawatha!

Groggy with sleep, Neilsen attempted to imagine his words rendered in declamatory song. A Wotan voice. Certainly, he had managed a feat of prosody remote from his *Prince Ananias* rhymes.

Remote—remote from his own upbringing, from the Liverpool Institute for Boys, from his early New York days on the docks. In twenty-seven years, he had migrated from Birkenhead to *Manabozo*, to Henry George and to Victor Herbert and now to Anton Seidl. His actor's life was fresh; the whole city hummed with personality. But nothing on Broadway had so stirred him as Lehmann and Niemann in *Tristan* and *Götterdämmerung*. They brought to the stage dimension and depth previously unknown, unthought of. Except in Shakespeare—to whom Seidl was always comparing Wagner. *Macbeth*: Wagner had used that play for *Götterdämmerung*: the vacillating Gunther; his scheming half-brother, whispering murder in his ear; the ravens; the chanting Norns, foretelling doom.

Double, double toil and trouble.
Fire burn, and caldron bubble.

Tales of sound and fury …

Duse. She possessed something like the magnetism of the great Wagnerians. A presence shorn of excess. *La Dame aux Camélias*—'twas caviar to the general in New York and so

La signora departed. No, it's on the German opera stage that acting is properly appreciated here. And at Conried's Irving Place Theatre, where Goethe is given in German to German audiences. No wonder that Schurz was impatient with *Prince Ananias*. No wonder that Seidl avoids the Broadway plays. "VINDmills!" he calls the actors. Fischer delivering Sachs's monologue in *Meistersinger*: how vast was his range from external to interior expression; from rage to practical resolve; from exclamations of worldly ennui to the quiescent absorption of a sudden inspiration. And all of it rendered while sitting in a chair. That was Wagner.

> O love sublime, unequal strife,
> Ineffable the joy now lost,
> My sun is set, and hopes decline,
> Long years my grief will not console!

Neilson winced. Immeasurably easier to emulate Mr. W. S. Gilbert.

Chapter Nine

The Catskill Mountains and Brighton Beach: May and June 1894

Only two passengers—an older and a younger man, both beardless—alighted from the train at the little station. The former, dressed in white linen with a soft alpine hat, was plainly artistic or professorial, with long raven hair, spectacles, and a puckered gaze. The latter, wearing a vested brown suit, was heavy-set and square-jawed, probably yet in his twenties. They consigned their bags to a porter with a wagon and proceeded on foot toward a nearby hill. The air was fragrant with mountain pine. The path was heavily wooded on either side. The setting sun cast a glow on the horse and wagon overtaking the travelers on the winding incline. A descending cloud of dust, aloud with barking in several registers, disclosed no fewer than eight dogs, of which seven were dachshunds running and leaping on short, crooked legs and the last was a lordly St. Bernard robed in white and golden fur. The yipping dachshunds, their collars decorated with ribbons and small flags, encircled the older man, who stopped to greet each individually by name: Mime, Tik, Tak, Tek, Froh, Freia, Erda. The St. Bernard crowded forward and placed both forepaws on the man's stocky shoulders. The man staggered from the weight and laughingly scolded: "Wotan, hinab!" The ascent resumed with the small dogs running up and down the hill while Wotan strode abreast.

A handsome wooden house bedecked with flowers and leaves was eventually attained. A woman with fading blonde hair, buxom and soft, stood in a vegetable garden wiping her hands on an apron. Ignoring the importunate animals, she gave her husband a warm peck on the cheek and shook hands with his companion.

"Mr. Neilson, how nice of you to come! Welcome to our Seidl-berg."

Neilson thanked her in turn while Seidl attempted to calm the menagerie. Auguste took Neilson by the hand and led him inside. "They haven't seen Tony for months. They will stop eventually, once he has fed them their crackers and asked them to do their tricks. They are his Catskills symphony, you see. He conducts them. Come, I will show you the house."

They ascended four wooden steps to a large porch commanding a mountain view, its columns wrapped with colored ribbons. Directly inside was a drawing room. Neilson surveyed a bust of Beethoven, wreathed portraits of Bach, Schubert, and Mozart, autograph scores under glass, medallions, floral garlands—all subordinate to the imperious oversight of Wagner above the piano. Upstairs, Mrs. Seidl had him poke his head into the master bedroom so he could observe Mime's basket and Wotan's blankets. His bags were already resting in the guest room. Dinner would be served in fifteen minutes. He washed the dust off his face and hands and unpacked his *Manazobo* libretto, which he and Seidl had discussed during the train ride. He admired the view and inhaled the air, both foreign to his Liverpool childhood. When he returned downstairs, he discovered the table set for dining on the porch, called by Seidl the "piazza." Bertha served the Leberknödelsuppe. All eight dogs were in attendance. Neilson had dined with Seidl and Auguste before, but the Catskills mood was different. Seidl's layered countenance, which he had learned to read, disclosed both fatigue and elation. In deference to Neilson, the conversation was in English.

"Everyone is asking for you, Tony. And Fleischmann is giving a big dinner tomorrow night."

"A dinner—and will there also be a costume party?"

Mrs. Seidl turned to Neilson. "Last summer Tony was a *Mädchen*, with curled hair. He wore an apron and a straw hat with flowers and ribbons."

"I was believable, I think. Not possible to recognize."

"Tony forgets the Metropolitan Opera House when he is here."

"How can I forget the Metropolitan Opera House when I have my dozen Sunday nights conducting the 'popular concerts' with one rehearsal?"

"And how was Juch last Sunday?" Mrs. Seidl asked with a soprano's professional curiosity.

"As always. Passabel."

"And you played some Dvořák?"

"The slow movement of 'Aus der neuen Welt.' The *Carnival* Overtüre."

"Did he attend?"

"You know very well, Gusterl, that Dvořák never goes into that building."

"I though perhaps he had …"

"He is a man who does not change his mind. A Bohemian *Maultier*. And who can blame him? Why I myself lead these concerts when they give *I maestri cantori di Norimberga* with *Luigi Mancinelli* is the question to ask."

Neilson felt summoned. "But you are at least 'in the door,'" he said. "And the public adores you."

"Not that public—not Mr. McAllister's *Social Register*."

"But Tony, the critics—they are always writing about the unfairness of it all—your Vertreibung in 1891, the German operas being given in Italian …"

"While Damrosch, and his dollars, rents the house and conducts his *Ring* with Fisher, Alvary, Gadski. And invites me to conduct *Lohengrin*, *Tristan*, *Rheingold*, *Götterdämmerung* and nothing else as his 'guest.'"

"You could have said yes, dear."

"I could have my own German opera season and invite maestro Damrosch as a 'guest.' In *four days* Mrs. Langford raised fifteen thousand dollars. But this is America, where Walter Damrosch becomes Hans Richter—or Anton Seidl. And where he has Steinway and Carnegie inside his pockets."

"You will succeed in Brooklyn, Tony."

"That is seventy thousand at least—for a proper season of German and French opera, staged, sixteen performances minimum. This must be. I have told Mrs. Langford. She is never tiring. But she is not Mrs. Carnegie."

The trout was a distraction. The diners busied themselves paring the meat from the bones. The dogs sniffed and stirred.

"Francis and I must do the lectures for Mrs. Langford."

"And work on your opera."

"Our opera. He is still explaining his libretto. What was that you now explained?"

"'And made a carnal love divine/Whose heavenly ecstasies have cost/The light of my immortal soul.'"

"'And made a carnal love divine.' With my English I am supposed to do this."

"This is the Monologue of the West-Wind, at the beginning of act one," Neilson told Mrs. Seidl. "His beloved wife, Wenonah, has just expired. He mourns her. But then he divines that their infant son will be 'of all men most exalted.' He sings: 'Your name I now immortalize! HIAWATHA!"

Auguste was startled by Neilson's exclamation.

"But this is not Longfellow's Hiawatha," Neilson continued. "At least, our story is not Longfellow's. You see, Longfellow confused Hiawatha and Manabozo. Manabozo is an illegitimate son of the West Wind. Hiawatha is the West Wind's true son and heir, whose mission it is to lead the tribes to noble aims and ends. Hiawatha never appears in our opera. But we end with the *prediction* of Hiawatha, fulfilling his father's prophecy."

"So, he is Wotan and Hiawatha is Siegfried," Mrs. Seidl inferred.

"Of course, the model of Wagner is to some degree inescapable," Neilson hurriedly added. "Ours is a music drama, an epic national legend. But it is in no sense Germanic."

"Correct," said Seidl. "It is British and Hungarian, obviously."

"The music will incorporate Indian motives," Neilson continued. "Naturally, a leitmotiv method similar to Wagner's will doubtless be employed. But all contemporary composers will now absorb this methodology, it will become universal. I am sure our composer will speak in his own voice."

"Tony is a wonderful composer—if he ever will write down all the music in his head. Which he sometimes shares at thc piano."

Seidl was meanwhile carefully dividing his Apfelstrudel into eight equal parts. Mime was made to walk on his hind legs and got the first piece. Wotan was fed last. This dessert ceremony pre-empted all further conversation until it was time for cigars. Auguste joined Bertha in the kitchen. Mime awaited his turn to flick the ashes from Seidl's cigar with his paw.

"Come Francis, with your West Wind Monologue. But now to bed for tomorrow's fresh labors. As our Meister would say: 'A morning without work is a day spent in hell.'"

They arose and went inside, Mime preceding.

* * *

"Hello, Mr. Wilson. Please come in. Can I offer you some refreshment?"

"Thank you, Mrs. Langford, I am sufficiently refreshed already. A little pressed for time, in fact."

"Then we can dispense with formalities. Do have a seat. I am always happy to talk about the Seidl Society for the *Daily Eagle.*"

"I am sure you are. And many in the office remember you vividly. You were a 'tornado of energy' I am told."

She smiled grimly. He shifted his body and produced a reporter's pad. "Your coming to the Brighton Beach season—a new departure, is it not? There were no concerts last summer or the summer before. And now the Society takes over from the railway as sponsor."

"Yes, it does feel momentous. As you know, the troubled national economy has greatly stressed the Brighton Beach Railway, and they reluctantly decided to abandon the Brighton Beach concert season in 1892 and again in 1893. But we are confident we can obtain a robust audience."

"And your husband Colonel Langford, who is an officer of the railway company—has he not facilitated this new arrangement?"

"That, Mr. Wilson, is between Colonel Langford and myself."

"Yes, of course, of course."

"You can please apprise your readers that the subscriptions are obtainable in booklets at Bradbury's, or at the Abraham & Strauss dry goods store, or, once the season opens, at the Brighton Music Pavilion. It will cost them only twenty-five cents per concert—forty-eight tickets for twelve dollars—to hear Mr. Seidl and his splendid orchestra of 50 men. Discounted round-trip railway tickets are also available. The season begins *June 30* and ends *September 3*. There are two concerts daily, at 3 and 8 p.m. Every Saturday and Sunday we will feature vocalists. Fridays we have "Symphony" nights, beginning with Dvořák's "From the New World" and then, on successive Fridays, Beethoven's symphonies numbers one through eight in sequence. Am I speaking too fast?"

"Oh no, I use shorthand, please continue."

"So we have all the Beethoven symphonies this summer, excepting the Ninth—which is of course annually a specialty of our winter season. And then there are the Classic masters: Bach, whom Mr. Seidl so adores, and also Mozart. And the Romantics, including Weber, Schubert, Schumann, Berlioz, Liszt, Saint-Saëns. Our American list this summer includes Mr. MacDowell, as always, and also Mr. Shelley, who has studied with Dvořák in New York."

"And there is Wagner."

"Yes, excerpts from all his gigantic works remain the core of our repertoire and mission."

"What may we specifically expect on your inaugural weekend?"

"We are featuring solos and duets from a new opera that is already a sensation abroad: *Pagliacci* by Leoncavallo. That is P-A-G-L-I-A-C-C-I. Have you yet heard the Prologo for solo baritone?"

Mr. Johnson had not.

"Well, it is a truly remarkable number, in which the singer appears before the curtain and tells the audience what they are about to see and hear. As in Shakespeare. The Society has engaged Giuseppe Campanari from the Metropolitan Opera to sing it for us. And—let me see—our first Saturday includes the *Tannhäuser* Overture, which I would say is the single favorite number with our patrons, it is always cheered to the rafters. It is often encored, in fact. And there is Mr. Seidl's popular symphonic arrangement of Liszt's Spanish Rhapsody. And popular numbers from *Carmen* and *Coppélia*, which Mr. Seidl infuses with such grace and charm. A balance of serious and popular, quite different from, say, Mr. Thomas's Central Park Garden Concerts, which are fundamentally popular in flavor. Our first Saturday—June 30, in three days' time—is also the day of the Society's Brighton Beach dinner, which presents Mr. Seidl as a dinner speaker."

"Speaking in English?"

"Speaking in English, which I know he is looking forward to. He has insisted on preparing his remarks without assistance. We will discover if his grammar is improving or not. I know he intends to locate his verbs properly."

"And your philanthropic and educational work this summer?"

"Thank you so much for asking. We will again host orphans and working women. We will present half a dozen Children's Matinees. Mr. Krehbiel and Mr. Henderson will be among our lecturers. But the greatest educational feature of this summer will be Mr. Seidl's lectures on the *Ring of the Nibelung*—the first instance, we believe, that lectures have been delivered to the accompaniment of a full orchestra. I had urged upon Mr. Seidl his personal obligation to Wagner to write such lectures himself and impart as Wagner's own pupil the knowledge that he so abundantly commands. At first, we both of us envisioned a single lecture with a piano accompaniment. But we soon realized that this would not prove as artistic or informative as several with orchestra."

"And you yourself will read the lectures, will you not?"

"It will be my very great privilege to do so."

"This feature of the season has been commented upon with some anxiety. The size and openness of the Music Pavilion may prove too much for the vocal powers of even a man."

"No, the acoustic properties of the pavilion are well-nigh perfect."

"But what if the wind and tide are against you?"

"Wind and tide will not affect the music at the beach this summer. Precautions will be made so as to enable a speaker to be heard with clearness and distinctness. Already a new bulkhead is in place, and a new lawn between the pavilion and the surf. And the wall of the building on the ocean side will be newly padded."

"Will not that be a costly and difficult thing to do?"

"We women, who are going to do with it with the help of a man and a ladder and sufficient material, have not considered it a difficult matter."

"And do you fear the possibility of insufficient attendance? Of inclement weather?"

"The season will succeed as a natural result of persistent hard work, combined with the allied factors of public interest in orchestra concerts, and a growing desire on the part of all sorts and conditions of people to improve themselves, musically and otherwise, and thus increase their enjoyment of life. The public realized the full value of these concerts once they were discontinued. The inquiries made at our New York office for information and tickets by people living in New Jersey and Connecticut lead us to believe that the demand will be unprecedented. Those who buy the ticket booklets are sure of hearing the concerts at a uniform price, while we reserve the privilege of increasing the price of tickets sold at the music hall on occasions when we are offering an exceptional attraction, such as vocal soloists. This is a business-like inducement which we offer, and if we enjoy brisk sales, we will be enabled to do much good both for the music-loving public and for that class of pleasure-seeking people which we have tried to benefit. The benevolent work of the Society is ever upheld by generous hearts and willing hands."

Mr. Johnson folded his pad. "Mrs. Langford. I thank you for your time."

"That is already enough?"

"Oh, more than enough. I have the materials you forwarded to the *Eagle*."

"Then I have surely bored you."

"Oh, not at all. But I have several other stories to file and I am shortly due at Borough Hall.

They both arose.

"It has been a pleasure to meet you, Mr. Johnson, however briefly. Do give my regards to those at the paper who remember me."

* * *

He surveyed the room from the rostrum. Blue and white bunting, and also two large floral pieces in the shape of the letter "S," festooned the walls. The tables were decorated with daisies, buttercups, and—a novelty—wild flowers. The windows were open to the salty air and the breakers' roar. Some two hundred diners, their sherbet dispatched, fastened their attention on his presence.

"Ladies and a few gentlemen!"

The room tittered excitedly. He looked down and started reading in emphatic tones, distorting many vowels and abusing certain consonants.

"Now we are again at work to play good music for good men and women. Those who like only such airs as 'Johnny Get You Gun' find places on this shore very many. We will play only *good* music; we know the people need it, and that this is the cause that the noble ladies of the Seidl Society don't spare the large expenses and the terrible difficult and heavy work to give the good people what they need, and what they must have. The people do not understand it first, but later they will whistle it with more dash and vigor as the rich, who sits in his box and chatters. One of the many good works of the Seidl Society is to give good music for the less rich, for the poor, and at the same time enjoys and educates himself. This is a grand and glorious mission!"

His female listeners, who from the first exchanged expressions of incredulous delight, now erupted in applause, beating their hands rapidly together. The men, far outnumbered, clapped sluggishly but dutifully.

"And a point to which must we direct the eyes of the whole world is that this society works not for money, as the so-called managers of nearly all the musical organizations do, but the noble ladies of this society bring many thousands and thousands of dollars together to enable themselves to give good music for twenty-five cents to the poor and music needing people. This only women can do!"

The audience arose as one, the women applauding, the men laughing good-naturedly. He looked up, expressionless, then returned to his script.

"The men must be astonished before such a grand work! We don't ask for kind criticism of our performances, if you don't like it. But our missionary work is worth your support. And if you remember always that these concerts are popular concerts to make popular good music in the big heart of the American people, then you will find very easy the way in which you take part in this very needed missionary work, and you will say with me: Hats off before these noble women!"

Prolonged applause.

"How Wagner, Beethoven, Schumann, Schubert, Liszt, and all the great men of musical art admired the women and her mission in life and art, you need only to look at the different operas, songs, oratorios, what they have written about women. Take *Fliegende Holländer*, *Tannhäuser*, *Lohengrin*, *Götterdämmerung*, *Fidelio*, *St. Elisabeth*, the various songs of Schumann and Schubert and you will have the ideas of the great men about the eternal woman and her glorification in the musical art—and all these glorious works shall be never heard by the great mass of poor people? That man, who asks for not playing some classical works at the popular concerts, is not a Democrat, is not a Republican, not an *American*. He is a *despot*."

Applause.

"Ladies and gentlemen, I thank you for your attention and give you my good wishes. You may drink each other's healths in wine or any beverage you will, but we can only drink the health of this Society in pure cold water. I give you the prosperity of the Seidl Society."

He raised his water glass. The diners rose, cheered, and drank alike. His formality in public was rarely so discernibly droll. He rejoined Auguste at the lead table. Mrs. Langford's reappearance silenced the buzzing room. She introduced the Society's great friend Mr. Henry Edward Krehbiel. Krehbiel strode to the rostrum, bowed to his host, and mopped his considerable brow.

"Ladies and gentleman, my duties here this evening are akin to those of the pitchman who hawks bottled Indian remedies, except that my merchandise is musical and more worthy of your attention and support. I beg you to indulge my brief appeal. Our great friend and paladin Mr. Seidl has eloquently, and I might add distinctively, with regard to his linguistic achievements …"

Laughter.

"… reminded us why we are here, and what the Seidl Society embodies for the betterment of our musical culture. Especially given the continued absence of German opera at the Metropolitan, the Seidl Society's winter season at the Brooklyn Academy is a vital resource for music-lovers who wish to remain acquainted with the most important developments in music abroad. And this is to say nothing of the remarkable Brighton Beach seasons which will now at last resume. But the chief goal of the Society, zealously pursued by both Mrs. Langford and Mr. Seidl in their planning for the long-term, can only be an annual season of staged opera at the Brooklyn Academy of Music, for there is no other way, no better way, whether in Manhattan or Boston or Chicago or Cincinnati, to ensure that recent progress in the presentation of opera in the United States shall not be squandered and its advantages forever lost. And this progress, moreover, will eventually and inevitably lead to a native foundation for operatic art, with American singers singing American works in their own native language.

"I feel compelled even at this gathering to address the calumnies to which the Seidl Society has sometimes been subjected. It is not true that it aims to glorify the reputation of Mrs. Langford or any other of its members. This objection is jealous and it is petty. It serves to mask and distort the magnitude of the Society's achievements, which can only be understood as being national in significance. The very presence of my distinguished colleagues here today whom I see among us—Mr. Henderson, Mr. Finck, Mr. Aldrich—testifies to that.

"Mainly what I wish to emphasize, however, is that the Seidl Society is democratic and as such stands apart from the individual benefactors who play such a large role in our musical affairs. It does not depend on the generosity of persons of vast wealth to sustain its labors. Rather, it depends on the generosity of persons such as yourselves. Look to your pockets please and study well their contents."

Krehbiel paused to observe that his injunction was in fact being taken up by certain facetious gentlemen. Meanwhile, music could be heard from outside.

"The Huldigungs March tells me that the hour is late and that our concert—doubtless in the hands of one of Mr. Seidl's capable assistants—has already begun. And so I must abbreviate my salesman's pitch and trust to your best intentions. Mrs. Langford, do we now adjourn?"

Mrs. Langford thanked Mr. Krehbiel and released the gathering. Those smoking cigars showed no eagerness to remove themselves. Their wives, however, were importunate.

* * *

The children were wearing their little helmets, yelling at him to go faster. The "horses" pulled the carriage round the drive, in front of the house. Daniela, alongside, was—how old? It was his sixty-fifth birthday, 1878—she would have been eighteen. Her worldly, already far-seeing eyes—their heavy lids and glazed patina—resembled Wagner's when he was *sehr innerlich*. Or Liszt's religious countenance—he was her grandfather after all. Too shy to meet her gaze, I studied her long hands. Aristocratic, like her mother's. That was also the day we sang the scene of *Parsifal* and the swan, to celebrate. Reading from the pages I had copied from his damnable scribbles. If only I had such an able assistant. Most of that monologue Francis scripted is already firm in my ear, but I have no time to write it down. Besides, I am not sure that I approve of it. Am I like today's Germans, a counterfeit Wagner? Dvořák absorbs Schubert, Brahms, Wagner without distorting his own style. Because he is grounded in the music of his homeland. Whereas my homeland is—Hungary? Germany? The New World?

American opera in English. It is our only way forward. In epic music drama. It is a mistake to say that the new forms of music are due wholly to Wagner. Wagner created them, but he was himself the creation of his time. Conditions were ripe for a higher development. Wagner glimpsed unprecedented possibilities for expressing the deepest and noblest sentiments. He developed them as no man before or since has done. He understood that no art deserved the name of art unless it was perfectly rounded; so he made opera, newly understood, his vehicle. There can be no doubt that the future evolution of music will be along the lines he has laid down.

But who among our Americans is remotely ready? Templeton Strong is a heroic symphonist, but only that. MacDowell and Herbert are composing music that will surely endure—in the form of concertos on the German model. Herbert's new cello concerto is an airy departure, as informal as American congenialities; he may be moving in the direction of an American popular art. Dvořák admires it and will write a cello concerto of his own: a major work. But Herbert is all fellowship and good cheer; he lacks a gift for gravitas. No, the American music drama is in the hands of our universal American musical genius Walter Damrosch. Doubtless he will complete his *Scarlet Letter*. Doubtless we will see it staged, and elaborately. The man's capacities are as limitless as his talent is Lilliputian.

When Neumann found that Berlin position for me in 1887, I could not face a second immigration. Gusterl was against it. German opera was flourishing here, I had acquired friends and allies, my troubles at the Met were as yet unbegun. Cosima's offer in May 1886 at Bayreuth—that was quite another thing, when she offered me *Tristan* and *Parsifal* but with Mottl and Levi taking the first performances. As if it were not I whom Wagner chose to tour the *Ring,* as if it were not I who assisted in the composition of *Parsifal.* A spider's web, from which I barely escaped before being devoured. Scarcely had I left than her letter of censure and seduction arrived in pursuit, a letter whose tone and substance contrasted so sharply with the notes of brisk instruction and encouragement from her harried husband. "There are no secondary roles here, no common hierarchy. Foreigners understand this as do our countrymen. By excluding yourself from the cause, you cannot avoid being perceived as discontent and you might thereby hurt yourself severely." Next: "Your nature is too profound—that is why it will weigh on you that you have left our cause behind and denied service to the holy ideal of Art." And then, fondling perceived personal weakness: "But now I would like to talk to you my way, from the heart even though you walked out on me. I took you seriously as a child of the house. I talk to you the same way as I would talk to" — he inwardly shuddered — "my own son." And then, deploying Daniela: "The children are suffering for you like your good angel is suffering for you now, and cannot believe that you are not all ours." Finally, the coup de grâce, paraphrasing Wagner's 1872 appeal to Liszt: "Come back! I dare contend that your better self is calling to you through me!" The entire diabolical performance was a maternal simulacrum, veritably a Kundry seduction masterpiece—except that, no less than Kundry, she carried it a step too far and like Parsifal crying "Amfortas!" I fled and saved myself.

It is no easy thing to replant roots and then rip them asunder. I still prefer American growing pains to centuries of habit and prejudice. The energy here must be grasped and directed. Thomas in Chicago. Higginson in Boston. Damrosch. Mrs.

Thurber. Cultural industrialists. I have founded no permanent orchestra, no touring opera troupe, no summer festival, no conservatory. "Yankee push." Wagner had something like that, of course.

Wagner's *Wahnfried* no longer exists. It is Cosima's now, she decrees the manner in which the *Ring* should be played, she keeps the flame as she sees fit. But Cosima is less than she imagines, less an artist than … an impresario! Underneath her widow's veil she is herself a worldly embodiment of "push." Not so remote from Mrs. Langford, actually.

He picked up the script of his *Rheingold* lecture, as translated by Finck for delivery by Mrs. Langford. It began with a brief excerpt in the brass, which he would conduct. Then she would begin:

> Two years from now, it will be two decades since the first complete performance of Richard Wagner's great *Nibelungen* work was announced with the call you just heard. The great master summoned his audience, which represented the entire artistic and aristocratic world, with fanfare motives specially selected from his new work, blown from a balcony before the start of each act to alert the audience to take their seats. These motives at the same time succinctly represent the core of the drama. The motive you have just heard signifies the shining gold that is carefully guarded in the depths of the Rhine by the three lovely Rhinemaidens, only to be stolen by the treacherous Nibelung, the dwarf king Alberich. Alberich has his unsuspecting brother, Mime, whom he has forced into slavery, forge a ring from this Rhinegold; and this ring gives Alberich immense power …

– a vocation.

Auguste was long asleep. He missed Neilson, missed his dogs, missed his Catskills retreat. The Brighton Beach Hotel had always seemed a lonely and impersonal place at night.

Chapter Ten

November and December 1895: Manhattan and Brooklyn

"Ach, Isolde!
Wie schön bist du!"

Seidl ceased playing the piano and paused. Then he looked up at the tenor, an unreasonably handsome man with golden locks and a fine mustache. "Monsieur de Reszke," he said, "never before has this music been so beautifully sung."

A Pole fluent in many languages, the tenor responded in German: "Herr Seidl, I thank you for this compliment. But is it not *too* beautiful?"

"No," Seidl replied. "But the beauty is not self-sufficient. You must also convey the most extreme fatigue. You are emerging from a period of complete derangement. You have hallucinated the appearance of Isolde's ship. You have collapsed into a coma. You have now awakened. Your mind begins to clear. You begin to remember and understand. You are regaining sanity and even a sense of responsibility for your lover's madness. And yet you cannot possibly rejoin the world. Your fatal glimpse of another realm—of pure being, pure desire—is beyond remedy. And *now* you re-envision

Isolde, your balm, your release, your salvation, sailing toward you across the watery void. And you are also summoning your death."

De Reszke shut his eyes.

"We have already been rehearsing for too long a time, we are growing drunk," Seidl continued. "But once more, please—for me. From 'Wie sie selig.'"

He recommenced conjuring an orchestra's murmuring strings and solo horn, transcendental water-music intimating cosmic mystery and oceanic repose. De Rezske glimpsed all he could of Tristan's longing and Isolde's mirage of healing loveliness; of Tristan's life abandonment and Isolde's complicit love pledge. The intimacy of their dialogue, in a room with drawn curtains and attentive memorabilia, was intoxicating; unwittingly, inadvertently, they themselves became the lovers. The piano's throbbing hypnotic pulsations caressed the singer's song. The love vision mounted toward an expostulation at once ecstatic and forlorn. Seidl interpolated a cadence, stopped, and shut the piano lid. De Reszke retrieved his jacket, hat, and walking stick. He bowed once and departed.

Seven years previous, Niemann had rehearsed Siegfried, from *Götterdämmerung*, in the same room. Like de Rezske rehearsing Tristan, he was learning the part for the first time. Niemann had been an assiduous student. They sat at the table discussing the markings and possible meanings like a pair of rabbis. Seidl waved my arms while Niemann sang. Gusterl was sewing in the corner. Niemann's performance of Siegfried's death was a triumph of histrionic art, his Tristan even more so. Compared to de Reszke, he achieved beauty through his rendering of words and feelings, of subtle gesture and facial nuance. No singer ever said as much with his eyes. And, of course, his physical presence was colossal. Seidl tipped his eyes toward the ceiling. But de Resze *sings* Tristan's delirium; it is something wholly new and bewildering. Perhaps Schnorr von Carolsfeld did the same, Wagner always insisted that Schnorr was the ideal Tristan. "Pure being and pure desire": an abyss; a fatal plunge.

De Reszke was a phenomenon without precedent: the most glamorous of "opera stars," monarch of the French and Italian repertoire as Faust, as Romeo, as Radames, as da Gama—but at the age of forty-five determined to undertake Wagner. Veritably, he was Seidl's deus ex machina, presiding over Grau's agreement to re-admit Wagner, sung in German, after an excruciating four-year hiatus. Or had de Reszke sold his soul, baited by Wagner? He had actually staked his career, his future reputation.

Next: Nordica, the Yankee prima donna. Born Lillian Norton in a Maine farmhouse. No one could ever be as imperious as Lilli as Isolde. But Nordica had the instrument and was not without temperament. And a prodigious worker. He had waited for her voice to grow. Then she ripened quickly: Venus, then Elsa for Bayreuth two summers ago; Cosima was surely surprised that a mere American could so partner her Lohengrin. And after all Isolde has no hallucinations, no clairvoyant visions. "Als für ein fremdes Land"—they would have to rehearse that until it was truly death-directed. Props: they had created a spectacle in a Broadway "department store," spending the better part of an hour choosing Isolde's veil for act two, sampling the various kinds of tulle, testing their properties when vigorously waved at a height …

Seidl had not moved since de Rezske's leave-taking. The piano lid remained closed, the genie in the bottle. Or was it? An existential disequilibrium akin to vertigo suffused his being. Love perfumes pervaded the room. Daniela.

* * *

Of Jean de Reszke's Tristan, with Lillian Nordica as Isolde and Anton Seidl conducting, on October 27, 1895, the *Tribune* had recorded:

> Never before has "Tristan und Isolde" been sung in tune throughout. Never before has there been a Tristan able to sing the declamatory music of the first and last acts with correct intonation, to say nothing of the duet of the second act. Never since Mme. Lehmann left us have we had an Isolde capable of the same feat. But Mme. Nordica and M. de Reszke not only sang in tune, they gave the text with a distinctness of enunciation and a truthfulness of expression that enabled those familiar with the German tongue to follow the play and appreciate its dramatic value and even its philosophical purport. It is wonderful how Mme. Nordica took to the opportunity which Wagner's drama opened to her. As for M. de Reszke, his voice was warm and every note he sang a heart-throb. He will not be more famous with the general public, nor will he be any the greater tenor, for having sung Tristan. It is not essential to greatness to be a Wagnerian artist. But M. De Reszke has proved that by adding a new role to his repertoire—and in a language new to him—he had the insatiable hunger of the genuine artist to achieve the one grand and noble thing that was left to him to achieve.

And yet the circumstances of this performance became controversial, and the controversy pressed Henry Krehbiel into a further, Solomonic critical capacity. At first blush, Anton Seidl's engagement by Maurice Grau, through the intercession of Jean de Rezske, seemed a holy war justly won. An entire German sub-season was planned with German singers and Seidl in the pit for the first time since 1891. At the same moment, Luigi Mancinelli resigned all his New York conducting responsibilities, leaving the field of Mozart, Beethoven, and Wagner at Seidl's command. However, whether by accident or design, the Metropolitan Opera dates assigned to Seidl by Grau conflicted with those in Brooklyn assigned to Seidl by Laura Langford's Seidl Society. As a result, Seidl stood to lose as much as he might gain—and Krehbiel, in his knowledge of all the parties at hand, was tested with weighing the scales.

Krehbiel sympathized with Mrs. Langford. Even in the best of times, her venture excited ridicule and she herself was resented by certain members of the press, most notably the *Musical Courier*'s Otto Floersheim, a composer *manqué* as exacerbated by Krehbiel's intellectual pretentions as Krehbiel was intolerant of Floersheim's creative aspirations. When the Seidl Society beautified the Academy of Music or the Brighton Beach pavilion with flowers and bunting, Mrs. Langford was maligned in the columns of the *Courier* for her femininity. On other occasions, she was ostracized for being too forward and "manly." The exclusion of the press from Seidl Society gatherings, their special railway cars and club rooms, furnished further grounds for objection. She was said to have thrust herself too prominently into the public gaze. The Seidlites were prone to "hysterics" and "Seidolatry." They pursued "personal aggrandizement" and "social supremacy" for a privileged few.

To be sure, Mrs. Langford advertised her authority. Krehbiel knew all that. When in December 1894 Nordica withdrew from a Seidl Society concert because of conflicting assignments at the Metropolitan Opera, Mrs. Langford wrote not to Maurice Grau but to the artist herself and released the letter to the press. "Dear Mme Nordica, it seems impossible to believe that you will consent to break a contract with the Seidl Society," a contract, that is, preceding her operatic engagement. "Until you tell me yourself, I will not withdraw the announcement." And Mrs. Langford requested "reply by bearer of this note." A program note for the concert recorded a contract violation on the part of the scheduled and advertised soloist, requiring a change in the Wagner selections. And this contretemps was not unique. Seidl's withdrawal from the Seidl Society concerts of fall 1895 was therefore the crowning debacle in a series of publicized contractual disputes. Even the *Daily Eagle*, not normally a party to the anti-Langford press, opined that it would be a strange thing if a body of women wholly dedicated to Seidl should maintain their allegiance once he had repudiated his obligations; if they were men Seidl would have already been shown the door. The *Courier* gloated that the Seidl Society had been exposed as a mere tool for a famous conductor's professional advancement. Seidl himself was reported to assert that he would answer no questions. In Krehbiel's summit view, the incident was a tawdry postlude to de Reszke's triumph, inflamed by predatory journalists and a choice opportunity to inflict humiliation.

Not since the Reverend Beecher was accused of a clandestine dalliance with Mrs. Tilton has Brooklyn Heights buzzed with so much malicious gossip abetted by the vultures of the newsroom. If in this the newspapers reflect the taste of their readers, it is a taste which they have instilled and cultivated, for it did not exist before the days of photo-engraving, illustrated supplements, and press agents. Mrs. Langford is challenged to endure a public betrayal. The practical question is: can the Seidl Society survive without Anton Seidl? And if not, what will Laura Langford do? Having tasted the fruit of Wagnerian self-abandon, she is not a likely candidate to return to the parlor séance or to the "Eagle" society desk.

As for Anton Seidl—here Krehbiel rolled his eyes, sighed, and abandoned his bulky typewriter. Seidl's fortunes at the Metropolitan Opera remained precarious. His New York Philharmonic as ever lacked the stable membership and artistic distinction of Colonel Higginson's Boston Symphony Orchestra, or the newer orchestras of Chicago and Cincinnati. Those orchestras are anchored by guarantors whose largesse supports permanent membership and a full season. The same is true, on a somewhat smaller scale, of Damrosch's New York Symphony, inherited from his impressive father Leopold. But the Philharmonic remains what it was from its humble beginnings in 1842: a musician's cooperative that collects and distributes to its musician members the modest ticket revenues of half a dozen concert pairs. No such orchestra can insure the retention of a city's best instrumentalists, whether from rehearsal to concert or from season to season. No such orchestra can ever offer anything like the one hundred programs Colonel Higginson's orchestra presents, in Boston and on tour, from January to December. Seidl is not the man to seek symphonic benefactors or to oversee a commensurate structural reorganization. In fact, he believes that this responsibility should be that of the government. That is a fine opinion, but not an American one.

That Seidl deserves a full-time permanent orchestra is a fact that cannot be doubted. However limited may have been his experience as a symphonic conductor when he came here, he has proven as much a revelation on the concert platform as in the opera pit. Symphonic works which we had known as abstract Classical sonata and variation forms have re-emerged with an opulence of color and descriptive suggestion more akin to the Romantic tone poem, and have acquired a pliability of pulse that can only be termed Wagnerian. The variations ending the *Eroica* Symphony, in Seidl's rendering, become a series of character pieces, whimsical or majestic. In the same composer's Seventh Symphony, Wagner's appellation "apotheosis of the dance" is applied as a Dionysian prescription. The Theodore Thomas tempi for the scherzo and finale are accelerated; every remnant of Classical repose is shattered by the bacchanale. While it may be true that such readings violate the letter or spirit of the score, their cataract effects signal a new age of the performer's art. And when the same approach, Wagnerian in concept, is applied to a Liszt's *Les preludes* or to a Richard Strauss novelty, Seidl's unprecedented popularity among the city's concert-goers is instantaneously explained. Meanwhile, the Philharmonic's ticket receipts have steeply grown, as have the players' dividends and the guest artists' fees. Like Theodore Thomas before him, Seidl contributes part of his own fee to the players' pension fund. Mr. Francis Hyde, the organization's president, is occasionally called upon to add a modest sum to the pot. But no adequate thought is given by our cultural fathers, such as they are, to transforming the orchestra in scale and mission. In plain truth, it has become as much an anachronism as a too easy success.

With Dvořák's resignation from the National Conservatory and return to his native Bohemia, and the unlikelihood of his re-appointment unless Francis Thurber were suddenly to reacquire the fortune he placed at his wife's disposal, Seidl has lost the one composer of genius buoying his New World venture. He retains his faith in Edward MacDowell's Second Piano Concerto, echoing Liszt; he hopes for something more from Victor Herbert than his songful Second Cello Concerto. He continues to offer many dozens of transient symphonic concerts in the Ansonia Rooms and lesser New York venues. He increasingly pursues the dream of an American school of composition that Dvořák here inspired. But if in fact he is to be orphaned from Brooklyn, his American fate is now more than ever fundamentally unsure.

That Anton Seidl is a man of honor cannot be doubted, and the final outcome of his differences with Mrs. Langford cannot be known. The carnival trappings in which they remain wrapped conceal a familial misunderstanding that will be settled, if at all, beyond the precincts of prying eyes and ears. Older observers of New York City's musical affairs remember better times than these.

* * *

Brünnhilde's rage of hurt and betrayal. Her capacity to forgive and arise to wisdom. Can I? Will I?

A lifetime may inhabit other lives to come. It may itself inhabit multiple lives successively endured.

Junius was an instrument of betrayal when I was Laura Vaulx Carter. He inflicted a name I despise and must bequeath to my son. He married without honor and soldiered without courage and escaped from every duty he had vowed to serve.

Blavatsky was an instrument of betrayal when I was Laura Carter Holloway. I succumbed to her magnetic gaze, to her volcano of esoteric learning, to promises of purpose and power only to discover her jealousy and the treachery of forged letters from the Masters. Her human weaknesses sullied her worldly wisdom.

And now Anton Seidl has become an instrument of betrayal and scandal, his name, which I raised, linked ignominiously with that of Mrs. Laura Holloway Langford. Or am I dreaming?

She sat at her desk with paper and pen. Earlier in the day, Edward had recommended a trip abroad—as if she were an invalid, another Brooklyn neurasthenic prostrated by life. He thought his wife delicate, nervous, hypersensitive. And she had had visitors. The Reverend Mr. Abbott consoled and advised. He was a milder variant of his blustery predecessor Mr. Beecher, who effused so when I called strong-minded women their own worst enemies; "the most eloquent lecturer on the subject of the American woman," he called me. Lyman is a friend to the Seidls, a devotee of *Parsifal*. Call on

Mr. Seidl, he said. Or at least call on Auguste. But I cannot risk it. A further disappointment might prove unsupportable. And then Susan called with her Susan B. Anthony severities. At least she did not see fit to remind me of the occasion—the lecture on "Woman's Mission"—when she censured us for supposing that the object of a woman's life is to help a man. Charlotte Brontë achieved success without the ballot, I had notoriously pronounced. Those tempests seem long ago. So am I to shed Seidl and forge onward with my female brethren with some new mission at heart? The suffrage agitation is not for me. Perhaps I remain a child of the South after all.

She discovered herself thinking about her mother. Anne Catherine Vaulx was fourteen when she married a man less pedigreed than herself, twice her age with two infant children. She bred fourteen more while he raced his horses and drank his home-brewed whiskey, sat on the porch spinning tales, sauntered inside to be fed and tended. And he philandered, no doubt. She died of exhaustion, not yet sixty years of age. Her maternal labors spent her spiritual powers. Her piety had no forceful outlet. Her Calvinist propriety, her trusting heart were instruments of self-enslavement. I missed her already while she was alive, a tiny and fragile creature debilitated by childbirth and marriage, broken by civil war and dislocation. No wonder I so often re-encountered her spirit—in a pale chrysanthemum haze: purple, her favorite color. As a fireplace specter she bid us adieu; the telegram arrived the following day. Or her face, her very shape and form would materialize unbidden in twilight to comfort me abroad when I was slandered for allegedly enticing Mr. A. P. Sinnett. I grew to hate the God who made me persevere, working, earning, barely holding on to those I loved. I would sit in my rented Brooklyn room thinking of her by candlelight, alive to her unseen electric presence, scanning the flickered shadows for shapes or signs. Or ride the streetcars for hours into a gathering penumbra of gaslight. Mother counseled me, the living, not to so fret and grieve. "We will grow nearer if you cease your mourning" she would tell me in soft honeyed tones. The ring you wear—my wedding ring—is proof that I am with you. The dead know.

The little rebel Andrew Johnson adored was rebelling against her mother's fate. Fallen gentility: withdrawal and self-pity, honor and rectitude, languor and an enervating midday sun. I spit on those Union soldiers from the hotel porch, feeling proud but in actuality powerless and defeated. I moved on, fled the devastation and heartache none can know, moved the family north, wrote my *Ladies of the White House*, won my reputation. I reinvent myself time and again, I relapse into recurrent attacks of malaise but never will I succumb to mother's hopeless fatigue.

And my own motherhood, what is that? George makes do. I helped him into West Point. But I am no mother really, nor a wife. A midwife is what I became, to Wagner and to Seidl. And now I pause and ponder and cope. "Theodore Thomas," writes the *Eagle*. "The best musician in America." "A man who inspires confidence." "His success would be greater than that of Mr. Seidl." "He has been known longer here and has a larger and better orchestra." Is this all we have achieved? Regression to soldier musicians of an earlier era? No Theodore Thomas Liebestod ever kindled the dormant soul-fires of disused mothers and wives. Is this my fate: to capitulate to the past?

The paper on the desk bore three words: "Dear Mr. Thomas." She now dipped her pen and wrote:

> As you have doubtless read, Mr. Anton Seidl is not available to conduct this season's Seidl Society concerts at the Brooklyn Academy of Music. Given your past association with the Brooklyn Philharmonic Orchestra, and the many friends and admirers you retain in Brooklyn, it occurred to me to inquire if you might be available to take Mr. Seidl's place

She stopped, crumpled the paper, and began again:

> Dear Mr. Thomas:
>
> As you have doubtless read, Mr. Anton Seidl is not available to conduct this season's Seidl Society concerts at the Brooklyn Academy of Music.
>
> Brooklyn warmly remembers your many years of service to the Brooklyn Philharmonic Orchestra. You now have your own splendid Chicago Orchestra, and are infrequently heard on the East Coast. However, as your superb orchestra travels, it occurs to me to inquire if it might be possible to present some of its seasonal New York concerts at the Brooklyn Academy of Music under the auspices of the Brooklyn women's club formerly known as the Seidl Society.
>
> As you may be aware, we have since 1890 acquired a large and loyal following for our symphonic programs. The need for Beethoven and Wagner here is very great, and we do not normally have the privilege of hearing so large and refined an ensemble as the one you now command.
>
> I am not so naïve as to imagine that the Academy dates secured by the Seidl Society will suit you on such short notice. If the idea appeals, perhaps you yourself could propose a series of Brooklyn dates for the present season, possibly in the early spring.
>
> Our financial resources, while not comparable to those of Mr. Damrosch across the river, are not inconsiderable, and if you can offer to Brooklyn programs that are already rehearsed I am optimistic that an adequate fee can be afforded. The Daily Eagle is already agitating for your return, which our Society would be highly privileged to facilitate.

Please believe I am
Yours truly

Without having added her signature, she read the letter and read it again. Then she heard Edward downstairs. She folded the page and placed it in the topmost desk drawer. She listened to Edward amble up the stairs and toward her study. The door opened. She observed his sympathetic eyes and bristled.

Chapter Eleven

May 1896 to March 1897: Brooklyn, Brighton Beach, Manhattan

SEIDL SOCIETY CONCERT

It is alleged of some lovers that they like to quarrel for the joy of making up. There was a quarrel or so in the winter between the Seidl Society and Mr. Seidl and the society declared its independence and said that it never, never would like Mr. Seidl again. It changed its name to the Symphony society and engaged Theodore Thomas for two retributive concerts at our Academy of Music. But it is all over and it was a beautiful sight to see last night how the smoldering affection leaped into flame again when the object of it appeared in his jovian impassiveness and suffered himself to be decorated with wreaths and roses and stayed from his business by applause. In a sense it was he who extended the olive branch, for this was his concert, offered to the society that uses his name, and given for the purpose of raising money to help along the summer music at Brighton Beach. The audience was fair in two senses, and the leader never had a more willing and enthusiastic one. Lillian Nordica, too, had offended the society once, and she, too, received more peace offerings than she could carry out. In brief, the occasion was so full of joy and forgiveness that the Seidl concerts may be looked upon as local permanences henceforth.

Mr. Seidl offered a good programme, though perhaps not so popular a one as he might have devised.

It contained the third "Leonora" overture, "The Preludes," an air from "The Queen of Sheba," the "Siegfried Idyl" and three numbers from "Tristan and Isolde." In "The Preludes" leader and orchestra were at their best. So is the composer. Liszt has never excelled himself as his genius is expressed in "The Preludes." If in some of his other works his gypsy wildness shocks the polite ear, or if in certain other symphonic poems there is an occasional evidence of manufacture, there is nothing of such in this work. It is forcible, yet never feverish, strong, yet never rash. Its sentiment is true, grave and in its expression beautiful. The "Siegfried Idyl," too, was charmingly played. It is one of the few things among the later works of Wagner that is absolutely free from suspicion of pessimism and morbidness. It is as fair and calm as a summer day. Of deeper human import, but perhaps of less worldly account, are the "Tristan and Isolde" selections, the prelude and ending, for here are glooms and despair, uttered, of course, with marvelous art and power, and afflicting the sense with the same pained admiration as do the Greek tragedies. In this the soloist appeared in great advantage. Her voice was never clearer, fuller, more flexible, more bright, more musical, more delightful, and she sang with dramatic force. The blending of the pleading vocal tones with the tones of the instruments was most beautiful.

There were notable offerings, during the night, of wreaths and flowers. Leader and soloist receive immense circles of laurel leaves with flowers and ribbons, and big bunches of roses were passed across the stage. It was pleasant also to see the Academy turned into a garden again by the addition of the palms and flowering plants that are so missed at the concerts of the Boston orchestra, and the tempering of the lights during the music saves many aching eyes and heads. It may be assured that Peace has descended upon the fold and is spreading her bright winds over a space that extends all the way from the Academy of Music to Coney Island.
—*The Brooklyn Daily Eagle*, May 2, 1896

THE SEIDL SOCIETY

Ever eat crow? Like it? Come over here and learn how to cook it, and maybe you will find it not displeasing. Take a crow that has ripened in the ice box, and stuff it with ingyuns, serve it with sauce piquante, have proper drinks and side dishes, the prejudice against this useful bird will be at least partially dispelled. The great lesson in how to eat crow was given at the Academy of Music on Friday night. If you have seen the newspapers you will know that on that evening, Mr. Seidl played there for the Seidl Society, to raise money for a continuation of Seidl Society concerts by the Seidl Orchestra at Brighton Beach. You will also remember that a little while ago there wasn't any Seidl Society. It committed suicide in a huff, and its ashes were reincarnated as the Brooklyn Symphony Society.

Mr. Seidl was applauded with rapture when he appeared on the stage a quarter of an hour late and lightly flushed, but firm and outwardly calm. They wouldn't even let him play until he had allowed the multitude to encore his charming bow two or three times, and it was well that he struck into the third Leonora overture with some precipitation, or the reception might have advanced to hysterics. After the Liszt *Preludes* an usher ran up with a big laurel wreath. At the conclusion of the *Siegfried Idyll* there was another rush and another big wreath, only this time it had roses on it. Mme Lillian Nordica, too, who was freighted in a similar manner, spared one of her bouquets for Mr. Seidl, and put it on his desk, so that when he got into his carriage the director must have felt more like a greenhouse than a crow. And now it is all over, and the crow has been digested.

—*The Musical Courier*, May 6, 1896

* * *

With the passage of time wounds may heal, or may fade but fatigue the spirit.

The failure of Thomas's two Brooklyn concerts of March 1896—many who attended the first shunned the second—paradoxically invigorated Mrs. Langford. As for her differences with Seidl, all was explained and forgiven. Grau had been late in setting his fall dates. Seidl had been misquoted in the *Eagle*. Nordica, her differences with Mrs. Langford also mended, sang her *Tristan* selections for Seidl and the Seidl Society.

But for Seidl the sequence of disappointments beginning with his expulsion from the Metropolitan Opera in 1891 had all too visibly told. The understated grandeur of his presence, his way of dominating a room "through sheer existing," as Huneker once put it, was now streaked with a worldly ennui. It became him, but it added weight where there was already weight enough. In a man not yet fifty, his weary bouts of fatalism were sadly premature. Deprived of sufficient operatic work, he conducted a miscellany of symphonic concerts with punishing frequency. Gusterl observed him eating irregularly, sleeping insufficiently. He suffered from ailments of the stomach.

His morning meeting with Mrs. Langford at the Brighton Beach Hotel a week after the commencement of the summer season, in the paneled offices of the Railway Company, took a new tone. Her briskness of authority was more pronounced than ever.

First on her agenda was the case of Miss Inez Casuri, the orchestra's new harpist, replacing Mr. Cheshire. She had already been featured in the Bach/Gounod *Meditation*. The press observed and approved ("a handsome Italian-American, with the temperament of a woman and the touch of a man"). But she was being paid forty dollars a week, versus Mr. Cheshire's fifty-four. Mr. Bernstein explained that Miss Casuri was not a union member. Which, as a woman, she could not be. Mrs. Langford had (of course) taken up the matter in the press: "The Seidl Society is composed entirely of women; women have worked for it and sustained it, and this woman will be sustained in her position—not because she is a woman, but because she is a musician. She will remain at her post until the season closes." Would Mr. Seidl support her?

"N*atürlich.*"

Item two: the weekly Monday children's matinee. The Railway Company had agreed to free transportation for children and caretakers. Adams & Sons had contributed one thousand pieces of tutti frutti. The orphans' asylums would prepare their children to sing "America." It would be performed by the audience at every such concert. Would Mr. Seidl care to contribute to the children's festival fund?

"For ten dollars you can put me down."

Third: planning for the October concert at the Rink continued apace. An audience of four thousand was expected. The huge space would be adorned with electric lights and with flags. Mr. Fischer was available for Wotan's Farewell. An instrumental soloist was needed. Would Mr. Seidl consider Miss Julie Rive King, swiftly emerging as a significant keyboard artist since her renewed studies with Liszt and Reinecke abroad?

"What would she play?"

"She is offering the Saint-Saëns Concerto in G minor."

"Probably it will a little bit tire her. We will see."

Fourth: The benefit concert for wounded Cuban soldiers on July 28. Have you heard that the Spanish are detaining Havana civilians in "reconcentration camps"? Marti's struggle for independence quickens the pulse of all American patriots. Could Mr. Seidl contribute a fresh novelty piece to the program?

"An orchestration of 'Gallina' by Gottschalk. It will be ready."

Gottschalk. Dvořák had admired him. He might have begun an American school decades ago had Americans been readier for his Caribbean delicacies. They are ready enough for Caribbean carnage today. Schurz foresees a new American imperialism. How powerfully he had detested Blaine and his designs on Cuba, Puerto Rico, and Hawaii …

The thought of Walter Damrosch's late father-in-law froze Seidl's meandering intellect with a fixed image of the would-be conductor, the bland expanse of his face, his dark eyes and facile tongue and strategies of ingratiation, his stolid charm and labored attempts at humor, his paucity of training, his accidental ascendance to authority when at twenty-three he took his late father's place at the Metropolitan. I set him aside but like an elastic band, like a mechanical spring he rebounds again and yet again, gaining ground, plying his concerts, touring his opera troupe, serenading Fifth Avenue drawing rooms, chatting at the piano about the wonders of *Ring*, robbing the pockets of Carnegie, of Schirmer, of Steinway, of Vanderbilt, of Morgan, as affable—as shallow and impersonal—as his blanched readings of Beethoven and Wagner, beating time with his long stick, applying his belated "lessons" with von Bülow like a kitchen maid misremembering a recipe for truffles.

"Have you seen Damrosch's Wagner schedule for the spring?"

"Yes I have," she replied in a new tone.

"He gives the *Ring* with his own company at our Academy of Music. With Lilli, with Emil, with Gadski and Brandt. And also in Manhattan. My own Metropolitan Opera German ensemble, until 1891. And also the *Ring* on tour, in many cities. For the third year."

"I know."

"He got Carnegie to build his Music Hall and then each season to pay the deficit. Even he tours his own imitation Wagner opera *The Scarlet Letter*. And again, does in concert *Parsifal*, the entire work, which is reserved for Bayreuth. Which is not to be stolen by the Damrosches of the New World and like a Wagner circus offered for entertaining."

"There is here a great hunger for German opera. And the Metropolitan will not feed it."

"The Metropolitan gives me sixteen opera performances this season, as a favor. Seven *Lohengrin*s, six *Siegfried*s, two *Tristan*s. One *Carmen*."

"Wagner with de Rezske."

"With de Rezske. And only because of that. Because of him. And for Brünnhilde: *Melba*, for her name. And for Isolde: not even a name."

"We have had our own Wagner festival, here at Brighton Beach—with the novelty of Mr. Williams, singing in English, according to your wishes. We presented Adriano's aria from *Rienzi*, which is not any longer given. Our summer season is our longest ever: nine weeks plus five days, including 196 Wagner performances. The railway is introducing a new elevated line direct from the Brooklyn Bridge. We have incorporated the Society with the intention of acquiring land for a proper Brooklyn opera house. We have discussed inviting Cosima, and also of inviting Siegfried to study with you. I know that Cosima occasionally writes to you. We will build."

"What we need is still away far. Away far even from what Damrosch already can do. I speak not of twelve or sixteen German Opera productions—you would have perhaps three or four new singers, nothing more new than that. We must establish an entire opera season, in German and in French. That is stability."

"You know what happened in 1892 when we planned to stage *Siegfried* and Mr. Stanton reneged on his promise to furnish scenery, scenery which the Metropolitan was not even using."

"We must have our own scenery. We must have our own company. *Damrosch* ..."

"I understand what you are thinking. That in Germany Damrosch would be a mere provincial Kapellmeister ..."

"Damrosch would in Germany be a repetiteur."

"... whereas in the United States he marries the daughter of the leading Republican Party politician and insinuates himself into a world of wealth and power. But you will see that his flame will burn low and die. He enjoys success where there is no competition. We will build more slowly but we will build better. We will build to last."

* * *

The hurricane that lashed the Florida coast in fall 1896 moved north with exceptional force and did not dissipate. On October 12, it struck the southern coast of Brooklyn, New York—the shore known as Coney Island, a four-mile outer barrier beachfront connected to the mainland by landfill.

Western Coney Island was a destination for fun. The aerial slide, Ferris wheel, and roller coaster, shooting galleries and sideshows supplied forms of escape from the stress and bustle of the city. Further east, at Brighton Beach and Manhattan Beach, Coney Island was a different destination, offering a pair of large resort hotels each with its own racetrack, music hall, and private detective force. The beaches and boardwalks connected to cropped lawns and expansive covered porches. John Philip Sousa was the bandmaster at Manhattan Beach and wrote a *Manhattan Beach* March; he also led symphonic classics in his own wind arrangements, his favorite composer being Richard Wagner. At Brighton Beach, Anton Seidl's orchestra chiefly purveyed Wagner and Franz Liszt. Coney Island was a music island.

Through a quirk of fate, the historic October onslaught of wind and water targeted neither the Sea Lion amusement park nor the Manhattan Beach resort. Rather, its fury consolidated in between: Brighton Beach. The hotel itself was relatively safe: nine months previous, six steam locomotives hitched to 112 flatcars had relocated its rooms and turrets more than 500 feet inland. But nothing else was spared the tidal attack. Hundreds of feet of beach were gouged by the storm's vicious undertow. The boardwalk was erased. Sea Breeze Avenue was washed into the race track. Cakes of asphalt five feet square were ripped from Ocean Parkway and tossed asunder. The Music Pavilion, on an outcropping, took the hardest hit. A wall of water demolished the new double bulwark, then the seaward wall it was intended to defend, spreading ruin with stark suddenness and impartiality.

The next day, drizzly and overcast, saw thousands of visitors arrive to survey the damage. Many were tearful women intent on inspecting what was left of Seidl's concert auditorium. They discovered mazes of timber heaped ten feet high, torn bodily from what had once been a circular 3,000-seat structure. Red leather chairs littered the sand amidst trolley poles and sidewalk slabs.

Though rubbish and wreckage hugged its piazza, the hotel survived intact. Enough of the Race Course remained to reconstruct the rest. But the Brighton Beach Music Pavilion, home of Wagner festivals and children's matinees, orphans' excursions and lectures with orchestra, was no more.

* * *

Auguste felt stricken for Mrs. Langford. Her husband, too, had suffered a grievous setback.

But his own reaction was tempered. The tidal wave, a hand of fate, canceled foreseeable Brighton Beach summers. Corbin had invited him to lead symphonic Wagner concerts the following August at Manhattan Beach. Sousa—not a jealous man, like Thomas; not a climber, like Damrosch—had readily agreed. Far more important: Grau wanted him for a summer Wagner season at Covent Garden. And then Cosima, learning he would be abroad, had invited him to conduct *Parsifal*. What is more: the Covent Garden and Bayreuth offers were compatible if he would submit to a period of travel between London and Bavaria. He would agree to do both.

The prospect of returning to Europe after an eleven-year absence, of returning to Bayreuth, canceled his accustomed preoccupations: Mrs. Langford's incessant triumphs and travails, the Philharmonic's more desultory impetus, his sporadic attentions to *Manabozo*. The day after Cosima's cable arrived, he celebrated at the Lotus Club. He pounded out the *Meistersinger* Prelude. Ysaÿe and Gregorovitch produced their violins. Joseffy played Chopin. Around midnight, Neilson arrived from the Garrick Theatre, where he was appearing in *Secret Service*. He improvised a speech. "Our friend Seidl has wandered the world, plying the *Ring*, acquiring the Wisdom of Experience. Coping with beleaguered impresarios, with nervous prima donnas and above all with overtaxed tenors assaying Tristan, he equally has attained the summit of *Parsifal*-like fellow-feeling: *Mitleid*. And now he undertakes the test supreme—as Kundry's siren song once imperiled Wagner's hero, Cosima beckons from afar and our friend must heed her call. Will our friend, our hero, succumb? Or will he like Parsifal heal the sinner and emerge stronger and more whole? She awaits him with her knights and retainers on high alert.

Can Seidl handle it? Will he regress to infancy? Or will he grow up at last?" While Seidl roared with laughter, Scharwenka pushed him off the piano bench and commenced the Entrance of the Guests from *Tannhäuser*. Fischer led the singing with Herbert conducting. Stamping feet and gyrating arms punctuated the performance.

Neilson had never before seen Seidl giddy. He had been looking worn. Seidl himself was overcome by an urge to undertake the long view: a conversation with Wotan was in order. Anyway, it was past three and time to go home.

Notwithstanding the late hour, his dog greeted him with interest. They proceeded to the upstairs study with a box of crackers and a handful of cigars. "You will have to vacation in the Catskills without me this summer," he began aloud. The rest of what he had to say he kept to himself. That *Parsifal* is my destiny is inescapable and just. It was only the arrangement with Ludwig—the engagement of his Munich orchestra, chorus, and conductor at Bayreuth—that required Levi in 1882. And Levi conducted *Parsifal* skillfully. But otherwise, Wagner would have entrusted it to me, he told me that more than once. The Festspielhaus is above all a *Parsifal* house. Nowhere else can I or will I lead a staged *Parsifal* performance and not merely because of Cosima's ban. The invisible orchestra, the cathedral acoustic, the alchemy of the Prelude emanating in a void: *Parsifal* conditions. My destiny might have been a homecoming had he lived. But Bayreuth is Cosima's now, a tribal community ruled by a high priestess as remote and formal as Wagner had been histrionic and inventive.

Of Cosima, he now had no fixed impression. Serving Wagner, she had supported the elation or indignation that daily buoyed or embroiled the household. She was pious, humble, and self-sacrificing. She also shrewdly managed the

Master's business affairs and social obligations. She had tolerated "friend Seidl" and other satellites according to their utility and the Master's whims. She was at least as uprooted as Wagner or Seidl, as Siegmund or Parsifal. Her parents never wed. Her mother was no mother. Her father Liszt had engaged a venerable madame—the choice of his new mistress—to indoctrinate Cosima in aristocratic manners and anachronistic beliefs she could not possibly sustain. Both her siblings died young. She married von Bülow at the age of twenty—too young—and six years later discovered herself in love with the musical genius most revered by her husband; her father, who equally recognized Wagner's greatness, disapproved. But Bülow and Liszt in their different ways—the one a hypersensitive masochist, the other a serene and worldly moralist—tolerated an infamous ménage à trois condemned by the King, the court, and the press. These were the conditions under which she and Wagner had raised two daughters—Daniela and Blandine—indisputably Bülow's; a third—Isolde—probably Wagner's; and two further offspring—Eva and Siegfried—fathered by Wagner (though out of wedlock). Siegfried was heir and did no wrong. Isolde and Eva she educated as she could. Blandine married badly: Count Gravina; "Count Zero," Bülow called him.

Daniela, with her precocious eyes, the one blue, the other brown—what had become of her? Cosima repressed and admonished her vivacious oldest child; alone among the five offspring Daniela bore the stigmata of her mother's guilt. She was to write to Bülow, to visit Bülow, to comfort Bülow as his onetime wife could not, as no one ever could or would. A plan was hatched to marry Daniela to Brandt, who managed the technical side of the Festspielhaus productions. Bülow intervened and Brandt withdrew. And now she has somehow wed Herr Henry Thode, the Heidelberg art historian and ardent Wagnerite. Cosima was enchanted by his lineage and erudition. Liszt obeyed the summons to Bayreuth. Bülow for once held his tongue. But Seidl had heard nothing good about the marriage. Her formidable pianistic gift squandered, Daniela was reportedly sinking into a malaise of insomnia, exhaustion, and splayed nerves. She remained the victim of severity and neglect, of Bülow's instability, of Cosima's veil of suffering, guilt, and renunciation. More than ever did she seem fated to endure her mother's religious complex. Wagner would tease Cosima for her "Catholic expression," deflating her exaltation and ecstasies of pity and self-reproach. For him, for the family, she had in Bayreuth converted to Protestantism, evading censorious Catholic priests and her father's Catholic scruples. But the Jesuit in her was as ineradicable as her sham marriage and adultery, or Liszt's carnal charm, or Wagner's continued infidelities, or the King's blatant homosexuality and incipient derangement. The sinner in her and the saint, real and counterfeit, occupied a world of religious theater in which the transcendent religious opera *Parsifal* was born.

Seidl tried to imagine re-encountering Cosima Wagner. She would now be sixty years old versus his forty-seven, a grande dame and worldly autocrat in mourning. Having sat clutching and caressing her dead spouse, having climbed into his open grave, having refused food or company or medical counsel, she had been thought by some a candidate for permanent seclusion if not suicide. But over time she descended widowed but erect from Wahnfried's upper realm to implement the Master's wishes as she saw fit. His spectacles and other personal effects—the sofas on which he sat, the pictures he hung, the books he collected—were not to be disturbed; the house, with its backyard mausoleum, was office, residence, museum. Wagner's ribaldries were silenced, his perfumes extinguished, his luxurious costumery discarded.

Only two weeks after Wagner's death she had Daniela write to Lilli—and many others, no doubt—asking that any letters in her own hand be returned so they could be properly incinerated. Cosima was to assume Wagner's posthumous identity. Lilli said no of course. She said many things. Last summer she announced her intention to leave Bayreuth for good. She reported that Cosima had scant respect for the 1876 *Ring*, with exceptions made for—of all things—Schefsky's miserable Sieglinde. How Cosima's Rhinemaidens and Valkyries were so poorly blended. How Lilli's own counsel—she who had supervised the Rhinemaidens and Valkyries for Wagner himself—was never invited. How the singers were treated as dolls made to stand in profile, palms cupped. How movements of the eyes, even of individual fingers, were specified according to ostensible memories of the Master's instructions (always with Siegfried's assent). At rehearsals, Cosima sat in a black-curtained booth to the side of the stage, observing through slits. She neither spoke nor was spoken to. What she had to impart was conveyed to the artists on slips of paper delivered by her assistants. She had also established a school to train singers in the proper Bayreuth style, stressing diction and verbal expression: words. Nothing wrong with that, Wagner thought no differently. But did Bayreuth produce artists who could sing as beautifully as de Reszke or Plancon? That Cosima would take charge of such matters had been no forgone conclusion. Some Wagner Vereine objected, and even sent emissaries to Bayreuth to complain; Cosima refused to receive them. With Levi retiring her preferred conductor would be Mottl, who submitted to her guidance and preferred turgid tempos. She tolerated Richter. As of 1896, Siegfried (naturally) joined the conducting staff.

Neilson enjoyed sharing the acidic reviews of George Bernard Shaw, who experienced Bayreuth through the eyes of a playwright. "Reeks of tradition," Shaw wrote. "The law of death: do what was done the last time." Krehbiel, Huneker, Finck—they all went and came back attesting that his conducting made Richter and Mottl seem tame and dull. But Cosima had her champions. No less than Wagner she had erased the histrionics that passed for operatic acting. Like Wagner, she could read the librettos aloud with transporting conviction. And he knew her to be no mean musician. As a child, she had not shrunk from her father's most diabolical exercises in keyboard wizardry. He used to hear her play Haydn and Mozart symphonies with Wagner as piano duets. That seemed like only yesterday. No, it seemed even more than eleven years ago: their last, calamitous Bayreuth meeting. He would journey into his past. It could determine his future. "Time and space are one," says Gurnemanz, spiriting Parsifal to the sanctum of Monsalvat.

Seidl sighed aloud and addressed the dog: "We will see." Wotan glanced upward, repositioned his hind legs, and went back to sleep. The tidal wave that destroyed the Brighton Beach pavilion had propelled him—a Seidl Society splinter; a particle of Coney Island sand—toward Cosima's lair. Or into her lap. He would ask Neilson to join him. And Neilson only.

Chapter Twelve
July and August 1897: Bayreuth, Germany

Two men walked up a gentle incline flanked by lawns and greenery. One, with flowing raven hair and a distracted manner, gazing aloft or at his feet, wore a black suit and carried, underarm, a large bound score and tiny baton case. The other, in brown, was younger and more animated. It was early afternoon and hot. Strolling in the opposite direction were small groups of women. Some, upon passing, froze in startling displays of reverence.

At the crest of the hill, in front of a large wooden theater oddly attached to an undersized brick façade, were a mother and son. The mother stood tall, gaunt, and erect. The son, shapeless and ungainly, about thirty, began to advance downward. Smiling, he shook hands with the older man and said, "Welcome home." Then he shook hands with the younger and said "Siegfried Wagner."

"Francis Neilson."

"Welcome to Bayreuth. Mother wishes to greet you."

All three now proceeded toward the immobile apparition silhouetted, statue-like, against a cloudless sky. Cosima wore a long black dress. She far more resembled her father than before. Her large, long nose, her large mouth, her long narrow face had turned androgynous. She was very tall; her neck, her arms were long and thin. Removing a green shade, she disclosed wide gray eyes, clouded but keen, under flaring eyebrows. Her hair, now wholly white, flowed abundantly to the sides, softening the masculine severity of her visage. Withholding facial movement or expression, she offered an aristocratic hand, looked down from her superior height, and said in a deep and musical voice: "Friend Seidl."

"Madame Wagner," he replied and looked to his right. "Francis Neilson."

"Welcome to Bayreuth."

Neilson nodded.

"We had hoped you would both stay with us in Wahnfried."

"We received your offer. It is quieter for us in Graben."

"You will visit us, of course."

"We will see."

"My daughters are eager to see you."

Each had now observed complementary changes in the other. Both seemed older than their years. Both, absent Wagner, had formidably absorbed his posthumous authority—but differently, according to their different readings of husband, teacher, thinker, surrogate father. They were disciples in common and also rival disciples. Each knew the other understood this and more.

"You arrived yesterday from London?"

"Mr. Neilson had a theatrical engagement there, at the Adelphi Theatre. I conducted at Covent Garden. *Lohengrin, Die Walküre, Siegfried, Tristan*. And I return there in July."

"For further *Siegfried* performances."

"Correct."

"I trust your accommodations here are at least comfortable."

"Comfortable and calm."

"You will find Bayreuth calmer than in 1876. We have grown and stabilized."

"I am sure."

"And how is America?"

"Also growing. Never stable."

"The Metropolitan Opera?"

"I now have de Reszke for Tristan and Siegfried. Also in London. Last week."

"How is his German?"

"He is a complete artist."

"He once worked on Tristan here with Kneise. I am attempting to secure him and his brother. It is not simple. You should hear our new Wotan, Von Rooy. You *are* attending the *Ring*?"

"Yes. But it is for *Parsifal* that I have come."

"Then let us proceed."

She led the way toward the Festspielhaus. "Nothing has changed here. Or almost nothing. Your orchestra comprises 107 men. Many played *Parsifal* for Levi. Some were here in eighty-three when Wagner himself conducted the third act. How is your orchestra in New York?"

"New York has many orchestras. The standard is high. But we often lack adequate rehearsal."

"That is not an issue here. And we maintain an ensemble. We maintain a style." She paused. "Is it true that *Parsifal* has been given in New York?"

"I have conducted extensive excerpts in concert. But I would never conduct *Parsifal* in its entirety anywhere but here. Walter Damrosch has given *Parsifal*, complete, in concert. Twice in New York. Also in Boston."

"This was unknown here until Frau Lehmann informed me. We are not happy about it."

"Damrosch is a New World phenomenon. A law unto himself."

"Did he not study conducting with Bülow some years ago in Frankfurt am Main?"

"It had no benefit."

She turned to Neilson, who was walking silently alongside Siegfried. "Do you speak German?"

"Nein—afraid not."

"French?"

"Non. Sorry."

"Well here we are."

They entered the building. In the relative darkness, she relied on Siegfried's guidance, a hand on his shoulder. That her eyesight was weak humanized her; the magnitude of her task registered. By her own lights, she was supremely selfless, having bequeathed her ego to a nexus of living memory that she cherished and guarded, hoarded and shared.

"You know the way. Siegfried will introduce you. Mr. Neilson can come with me." And she was gone.

He entered the pit closely observed by the musicians, but saw nothing. Climbing with Siegfried toward the high podium, he was overwhelmed by the vacuum of Wagner's absence. Or did he rather sense Wagner's presence? Not the gnomic specter who used to visit, lurking in some corner of the steep chasm of bodies, chairs, and instruments. Rather, with *Parsifal* already in his ear, Seidl sensed a different Wagner spirit suffusing the dark sequestered space with a painful warmth. Siegfried said something, that a Grail Knight was returning home—a banal conceit. The orchestra applauded. Seidl removed his jacket and hung it on his conductor's chair. He sat and placed the closed score on his desk. He looked at the men's faces.

"Have you tuned?"

They had. He sighed, paused, and stood. Then he closed his eyes and cued the sad unison chant of strings, clarinets, and bassoons, reinforced by an English horn as it slowly crested. He dropped his arms and waited for the music to stop.

"Much more weight on the G, please."

They rebegan. A world of grief and consecration, an aureole of strings and palpitating winds, flooded the underground space. He opened his eyes to cue the trumpet and oboes, whose rising song pierced a billowing carpet of euphony, then fell to a hush, then a silence. The sequence repeated in C minor, acquiring a tragic cast. Next from the sunken understage depths—singularly, the pit plunged at an even steeper rake than the steeply raked auditorium—horns and trombones pealed a fanfare abruptly interrupted by loud knocking. Incredulous, he stopped, turned, and discovered Cosima, barely discernible in the dark hall, briskly tapping a parasol. She was accustomed to Mottl's slower tempo. He winced and said: "If you will wait, you will know."

Gradually distended, the sequence of fanfares described an expanding portal of experience. Cosima's parasol was not heard again.

* * *

The subtraction of Wagner from Bayreuth, for Seidl, not only subtracted the living force that had conceived operas of a new kind, and a new kind of theater in which to present them; Wagner had embodied a divine insanity, a spirit of disturbance. His mercurial moods and contradictory habits were as endemic and inescapable as the Bayreuth weather.

Cosima esteemed "stability." Yes, there was now a sufficiency of food and accommodations. But the town seemed paradoxically smaller and more contained. And more fashionable: in Wagner's day, no such surfeit of German, Russian, Italian, French, and British royalty set the tone. There were now, as well, generals, diplomats, politicians, and heads of state in profusion: a bustle of refined social activity masking a condition of trance-like stasis. Coney Island had its aerial slide and Brighton Beach. Manhattan had its immigrant masses and Park Avenue mansions. America had its Boston and Chicago, Negros and Indians, Western peaks and wastelands. How the New World recontextualized the Old.

Shunning Wahnfried, he had found rooms above a tannery in Graben, the hamlet in which he had lived during his apprentice years. His visitors already included the King of Württemberg, the Princess de Polignac, and the young American Arthur Farwell, who vowed to "take up Dvořák's challenge," exploring Indian chant as a basis for new rhythms and harmonies. Meanwhile, Neilson stayed with him for ten days. He had earlier joined Seidl in London, having ingeniously persuaded Frohman and Gillette to transplant *Secret Service* from New York—and then quit the London production (not without controversy) in time to cross the channel for Seidl's *Parsifal.*

Neilson was ever an engrossing companion, in whom a gift for histrionic diversion combined with practical intelligence and a fund of knowledge about history, politics, and world events. As his experience of the theater already encompassed both acting and playwriting, he was a keenly professional observer of the operatic stage. He found fault with many technical details of the Bayreuth *Ring*. The steam curtains were sometimes late. The backcloths caught. The swimming machines and dragon required improvement. Covent Garden and the Metropolitan Opera, in his opinion, also failed in these departments. Seidl and Neilson had Kranich, the chief machinist, demonstrate the capacities of the Festspielhaus stage. They learned that Cosima insisted that nothing new be attempted. Kranich was frustrated.

Subsequent to the first *Parsifal* rehearsal—on a Monday without rehearsals or performances—Seidl and Neilson undertook a pair of Bayreuth excursions: one to a theater, the other to a cemetery. When Wagner first visited Bayreuth in 1871, he inspected the Margrave's Opera House—notable for its lavish encrustation of pastel Baroque ornament—as a possible festival venue. Though the stage was vast, neither the pit nor the seating capacity was adequate for Wagner's needs. But it was at the Margrave's Opera House that Seidl had first heard Wagner conduct. The occasion was the laying of the foundation stone for the Festspielhaus on a rain-soaked May afternoon in 1872—a ceremony followed, down the hill, by a performance of Beethoven's Ninth Symphony. Seidl, barely twenty-two years old, attended from Leipzig with his teacher Richter. Wagner spoke from the stage of a rebirth of the German spirit in which he continued to place his faith, notwithstanding many a disappointment. At 5 p.m. he faced a select orchestra assembled for a single performance and cued Beethoven's quivering sonic void. Wagner's rendition was less symphonic than dramatic. The plasticity of shape, the extremes of tempo and dynamics were wholly new in Seidl's experience. In the finale, the vocal soloists had been coached to sing words, almost as in a play. Niemann, his colossal physical presence trembling with excitement, enflamed Beethoven's invocation to Joy. Wagner drove the movement to ever greater heights of exaltation. The day's epochal events were consummated.

Revisiting the old opera house with Neilson renewed Seidl's earlier impressions of gratuitous opulence and disproportionate intimacy. But it was a disused space untouched by

Cosima's new regime; he could luxuriate in memories. He recalled to Neilson how on the vacant green hill, in the pouring rain, Wagner had struck the foundation stone three times with a hammer and turned away, tearful and pale. How Niemann strode forward like a Nordic god to do the same. How the stone was lowered along with a metal casket containing a telegram from Ludwig. How en route to the opera house Wagner shared his carriage with the young Nietzsche. How Cosima and the children were invited on stage before Wagner's speech. How after hearing the Beethoven performance, he resolved that he would find his way to Wagner at any cost. How during his years with Wagner he often conducted here, in the same incongruous eighteenth-century setting.

"Wagner would come always, also for my rehearsals. He would sit ..." — Seidl pointed to a chair on the aisle a dozen rows back — "... and *run* to the stage to tell me it was wrong. He taught me: follow an idea, a concept, without fear. Beethoven's Seventh Symphony—'Apotheosis of the Dance.' Dionysian rhythm—except for movement two: Apollonian ritual. For Bach, for Mozart, for Schubert: unbottle the demons. No mentions of baton technique; that I got from Richter. To see Wagner conduct, with a very long baton—the men would at first complain. They could not follow. Nothing was predictable. Wagner would become impatient. Then he would show the men with his face, with his eyes, glittering, glowing, an electric current. He would not beat time; he felt the phrase, the expression. He was the greatest of actors, you see."

Neilson surveyed the royal box, festooned with flights of angels. "A bizarre space. What's the point?"

"Baroque opera," Seidl replied with whimsical eyes. "The big stage for costumes, effects, display. The small pit for strings, harpsichord, a few winds. The boxes for aristocrats, to show off. Very few seats because the public does not matter.

Eighteenth-century opera, one century before Wagner. But Wagner here made music. I made music."

"You learned to project feeling fearlessly."

"With conviction. Great confidence."

They paced the stage looking for ghosts. But the past remained inert. "Now the cemetery." Seidl said. They would visit Liszt's grave. He had never seen it, Liszt having died in Bayreuth in July 1886, when Seidl was already based in New York. Liszt's relationship to Bayreuth, to Cosima, to Bülow, to his grand-daughters Daniela and Blandine—it was all unfathomable. That Cosima resented her father's absence and inattention during her childhood, that she had felt frustrated by his loyalty to Bülow and ambivalence toward her re-marriage was understandable to a degree, Seidl said. But Cosima never sufficiently esteemed the artist in Liszt; in this she was a victim of her anger and resentment. Liszt had arrived at the festival in 1886 ill, tired, frail. He was seventy-five. He took rooms next to Wahnfried. He succumbed to pneumonia. Cosima was busy with festival affairs. Liszt swiftly declined and died. His body began to decompose before being transferred in a handcart to Wahnfried. The memorial service omitted any music of his own. There was no memorial concert. Cosima hosted a dinner party the day of the funeral.

Seidl and Neilson arrived mid-afternoon at an old cemetery crowded with tombstones. There were few visitors. Liszt's grave was housed in a tiny structure resembling a church. Inside they found a plaque and a cross. "He was my countryman, of course. But Hungarian he spoke barely. His life was Paris, Weimar, Italy, travel. He helped many. He helped Wagner. The first *Lohengrin*—he conducted, at Weimar. We owe to him the symphonic poem and also a new Romantic sacred music. His *Faust* Symphony, the *Legende von der Heiligen Elisabeth* are original, nothing like them came before. And then he composed Hungarian Rhapsodies, Hungarian Fantasy, Rakoczy March—the Hungarian gypsy style and the virtuoso style in Liszt, they connected. He would visit the gypsy camps, you see, study the violin playing …"

"He's out of place here," Neilson said. "A grave among many. Was any thought given to burying him elsewhere?"

"The Grand Duke of Saxe-Weimar wanted for him a Weimar grave. The Hungarians, the Order of St. Francis, wanted him in Budapest, of course. Big graves, big memorials. But who says where Liszt belongs? Cosima said he wanted here, in Bayreuth. He had no home, really. No wife, no family. Daniela and Blandine—the other children—they both died young. And Cosima, she went her way. Liszt and Wagner were old, old friends. Not always friends, perhaps. But never enemies. Each knew the other—what he really was."

"And where shall we bury you when the time comes, I wonder?"

"New York. Cremated. You won't have my corpse to smell."

"We could always ship the ashes to Bayreuth, to Budapest, anywhere you please."

"Bayreuth—now I am an outsider. Like Liszt. Another displaced Hungarian. Well, our pilgrimage to the grave of Liszt we have made. I do not come here again."

They returned to Graben to discover an envelope from Daniela Thode. Seidl blushed when he read its contents and disappeared into his room. Some time later he opened the door and invited Neilson to enter and sit. He said that he had been invited to a reception and could not decide whether to accept.

"I will tell you why. It is something you do not know, that few know. You see, when I was with Wagner, Daniela was already a beautiful young lady, eighteen years old. We were together. Often." Seidl locked his gaze so that Neilson held his breath. "We fell in love. We fell in love and Cosima did not approve. Maybe Wagner, too, I never knew. But it was arranged for me to leave, that I would go to Neumann. Perhaps a coincidence, perhaps a plan, but with that it was over. But later there came more. Gusterl—you know this—after our marriage, she went to America first. And then in Munich I discovered Daniela—this was 1885 fall, so she was twenty-five. She was supposed to marry Brandt, who did here what Kranich now does. But Bülow, her father—she suffers all her life from this relationship; Bülow was always tormented, always alone, a difficult man, difficult to himself and to all others. Bülow knew Brandt very well—and told him that he must not marry Daniela, that the Wagner family was a cursed family. He saw in this marriage Cosima's hand; he could not bear. And meanwhile Cosima was always telling to Daniela—visit your father, visit Bülow, write to him. I saw how Daniela was suffering, how she was trapped. And I thought that I can save her, you see, that I can rescue her. Probably I could not, probably no one could, because—you see yourself Cosima's power. You see Blandine's marriage—a disaster. You see Siegfried's weakness. And Daniela, she is vulnerable. She was becoming a nervous person, pulled in many directions. Which she was not before, she was an artist, a pianist even. A person of great qualities—you can read her eyes. So we still had feelings, from many years before. And then I realized: I must get away—to America. To flee."

Neilson's actor's face, with its high mobile features and lantern jaw, was drained of affect.

"Will you go?" he asked.

"Probably I should."

He had to ascertain what of Bayreuth remained within him, and what to do with it.

* * *

A thread of sound—a chant of sorrow and redemption—materialized in a void. It ceased, recommenced, dissipated aloft. The curtains parted to disclose a forest clearing. Suddenly a woman was seen riding the sky. She entered spasmodically, wildly attired, her black hair disheveled, her eyes burning or indolent. Lunging forward, she produced a vial—an Arabian potion for the infirm—and collapsed.

Of the many Americans who had come for Seidl's *Parsifal*, Natalie enjoyed the closest personal relationship. She had first attended Bayreuth at the age of fifteen in 1891—the same summer as Schurz and also Mark Twain, a family acquaintance. In the upcoming fall, she would study at Bayreuth, taking part in Kneise's classes. She revered Lilli Lehmann for her Isolde and as Kundry at the Seidl Society's *Parsifal* Entertainment. Lehmann's Kundry had trailed regal vestiges of a previous persona. Maria Brema, the Bayreuth Kundry whom Natalie now observed, was a personage more obscure, more purely deranged.

The elderly Gurnemanz told a story: how Klingsor, a fallen knight now a eunuch, had stolen a Holy Spear when Amfortas was bewitched by a sorceress. The knights, a celibate order led by Amfortas, retained a second relic—a Grail cup, like the Spear associated with the Redeemer. Wielding the Spear, Klingsor had dealt Amfortas a chronic wound. In a vision, Amfortas had learned that only a holy fool, made wise through compassion, could cure him and refresh the brotherhood.

A commotion interrupted his narrative: a swan had been slain. A young man with a bow was brought in. He felt no remorse. He had no name, no father. He vaguely recalled his mother. Kundry brusquely announced: "Your mother is dead." The young man attacked her and was subdued. She ran to fetch him some water. "I long only for rest," she said. She began to tremble violently, then sank into slumber. Gurnemanz led the boy to a ceremonial hall where Amfortas was enjoined to uncover the Grail. He resisted, then acceded, raising the cup in blessing. Wine and bread were distributed. Amfortas's wound bled anew. The ritual ended, Gurnemanz upbraided the youth: "In future, leave the swans in peace; a gander should seek a goose!" The scene was animated by music from the underground orchestra and from choral groups at a height. The song of the Prelude—the trumpet's chant of compassion—returned when Amfortas lifted the Grail cup. Natalie here surrendered self-awareness. She sobbed quietly until the curtains closed. There was no applause. She and her mother spoke little during the hour-long interval.

Act two showed a castle tower. Klingsor summoned Kundry: Nameless one, primeval witch, Gundryggia, Herodias. Aroused from long slumber, she screamed, wailed, whimpered. She yearned for nothingness, for death. Klingsor ridiculed her for serving the knights—they treated her as a beast, he said—as if she could atone for seducing Amfortas (for it was she who had bewitched him). Now she was to entice an intruder shielded by innocence. "I will not!" she shouted. Veering from hysterical laughter to savage groans, she mocked Klingsor's impotence. But castration, self-inflicted, had rendered him immune to her predations. Helplessly submissive, beauteously adorned, she called out to the youth: "Parsifal!" The young man froze: in dreams, his mother had so named him. Kundry now told him that his mother had died of neglect—"Did you fear her kisses?" She urged that he find solace in mother-love. She curled her body around his and pressed a long kiss on his lips. A coiled erotic variant of Klingsor's theme enwrapped the couple. Parsifal leapt to his feet and exclaimed: "Amfortas!" Reeling, he assumed the other man's blood wound. He fell to his knees and to the Prelude's piercing trumpet chant pleaded: "Redeemer! Rescue me!" For this turning point in the drama, Ernest van Dyck strained every nerve of his being. Natalie fought to retain consciousness. Kundry, stupefied, regrouping, recounted her own miserable history. As Mary Magdalene, she had mocked the Redeemer. She cunningly appealed for compassion, for salvation. Parsifal thrust her away. "Relent for an hour of bliss," she desperately begged, but to no avail. Klingsor appeared and hurled the Spear. Parsifal caught it and made the sign of the cross. Klingsor and his castle crumbled to dust. Parsifal turned to Kundry and said, "You know where you can find me"—and was gone.

The Festspielhaus audience again silently dispersed. Outside, it was early evening. Natalie's mother asked her what theosophy taught about Kundry. She was Parsifal's lower self. She represented the irrational soul of man, his animal nature, which must be reabsorbed as higher realms are attained. She had already lived many lives—but her quest would soon be over. Lehmann's Kundry had been imperious. Brema more evinced the victim: enslaved to a world of men, an instrument of service or temptation. Driven, fatigued, eternally disquiet, she dragged her long past behind her. What is woman? Natalie asked herself.

In act three, Parsifal found his way to the forest of Monsalvat—the domain of the Grail knights—after having wandered the world for years untold. Gurnemanz recognized the Spear and intuited all. Parsifal shed his armor. Kundry bathed Parsifal's feet. It was Good Friday: an undulating melody, begun by an oboe, bathed the forest meadows. As in act one, Parsifal was escorted to the hall housing the Grail. The knights were failing and discontent: Amfortas could no longer endure the

Grail ceremony. Wielding his spear, Parsifal healed Amfortas. Then he raised the Grail aloft. As its red glow suffused the vaulted chamber, the chant of the Prelude resumed and lifted to closure. Kundry, her long journey ended, expired.

Natalie and her mother found a bench near the stage door; they would await Seidl there. To her mother, Natalie said little. To herself, she described her quest to come. She would not marry. She would apply her musical gifts to understanding herself. Inspired by Dvořák, who had shared his search for America, inspired by Busoni, for whom America, apart from its ersatz cities and symphonies, was primeval, she would undertake to know the Red Man. Of Busoni's many tales recounting his encounters with indigenous Americans while touring the West, she most remembered that he once met an Indian whose brother was a violinist in New York; she wished to create "earth music" by stretching a string around the edges of a deep hole in the ground. For Wagner, myth and wisdom, philosophic and occult, were Nordic or Germanic, Christian or Asian. An American seeking points of origin could not evade the sacred song and ritual of the first Americans, now a scant minority facing extinction. She would escape her mother's world of housebound service and malaise, escape Kundry's syndrome of self-contradiction, a driven condition whose only remedy was nothingness.

The two women observed a slow procession of departure. Emma Calvé, famous in New York for her Carmen, emerged barely ambulatory, supported on both sides by companions. A somnambulistic quiescence pervaded the night air. At last, Seidl appeared, walking slowly, steadily, his gaze vacant yet composed. The mother and daughter did not stir. They watched him pass and proceed toward a younger man, heavyset, square-jawed. Without visible greeting, Seidl and Neilson descended the green hill and disappeared.

***

A room was found in which to sit and talk privately while the others entertained one another.

"How is America for you?" she asked.

"I am an American citizen. We have our brownstone apartment on East Sixty-second Street, our summer home in the Catskill Mountains. We have many friends, even the music critics. New York is full of Germans, you see. There are challenges. The government pays for nothing—the music conservatories, the opera, the orchestras must obtain support from the very rich. Music education is a problem. But the opportunities are big. Everything is big—the opera houses and concert halls, the mansions, the hotels, the rivers …"

Daniela had changed greatly since 1885. Her large, lidded eyes were worn and thirsty.

"At first, it came easily," he continued. "The Metropolitan Opera, when I arrived, was a German house. We had Lehmann, Brandt, Emil Fischer. Later Niemann. He even sang Siegfried, in *Götterdämmerung*, which he had never done before. Excellent orchestra, excellent chorus. And for the audiences it was all fresh—the first American *Tristan*, the first American *Meistersinger*, *Rheingold*, *Siegfried*, *Götterdämmerung*. But the boxholders are the owners, you see. They wanted *Faust* by Gounod. So, we were thrown out. That was in ninety-one. Now German opera has resumed, alongside French and Italian. We will see. And I conduct symphonies—Mozart, Beethoven, Tchaikovsky, Dvořák. In America there are orchestras that give one hundred concerts—'symphony orchestras,' they call them, they play no opera. Boston, Chicago, Cincinnati have orchestras of this kind. In New York, there are various part-time orchestras, including my New York Philharmonic which must grow if it is to become a great orchestra like Boston's. And then there is Brooklyn. This is a part of New York City with two million people. In Brooklyn I conduct concerts throughout the year. I am here this summer because our summer Music Pavilion was destroyed in a hurricane—it sat on the ocean. Many things can happen in Brooklyn. There is actually a 'Seidl Society' composed entirely of women. Its leader is our Cosima—Mrs. Langford. An unstoppable force."

"And Auguste?"

"We have many guests. We have our dogs. She no longer sings—you know that. She worries about my health and whether I have remembered my umbrella ... Yourself?"

"My marriage is no marriage. This is no secret. Henry and mother remain great friends. Also, Henry and Siegfried—he lived with us in Frankfurt, you know, during his university years. Henry writes his articles about Dürer, about Böcklin, about Wagner. I am married to Bayreuth. There are worse fates than this. And I am needed here. Much has changed. My father's death in eighty-four—that was really difficult. We were never close. But I tried. Mother wanted that; she carried a heavy burden of guilt. She honored Bülow for what he was. He was simply never intended to be a husband. Or a father. Anyway, his final days were very hard. In Egypt, which he was told might have a salutary climate. Siegfried and I attended the funeral, representing the family. Then, two years later, Liszt died. He came to Bayreuth for my marriage only a few weeks before. It was unfortunate that his final illness occurred here. Mother was conflicted and did not handle it well. But the biggest change of course is that Wagner is gone. Not just his genius, but his personality. On the floor with Siegfried, teasing us for our perfect French and impeccable manners. He teased Cosima for her earnestness. At mealtimes she would have to leave the table. He would stick his finger up his nose and described the 'stalactites,' for the children. You know all this. It is a paradox—we honor him daily, that is our purpose. But at times I feel that his spirit is wholly absent."

"I cannot find it here. I have looked."

"Cosima is a completely different personality. It happens in marriages, even in the most successful marriages. Many are harsh on her. But her task is difficult. It is actually heroic. There is both the festival and the family to deal with. Gravina suffers from a severe depression, we fear for his life. Siegfried remains unmarried, there is no male heir. And yet the festival thrives. Mother commands all. She can and does. The future of Bayreuth was by no means assured—Wagner left no structure, no institutional establishment. Then Levi, whose relations with mother were never easy—he has now retired. Richter came on board—and has his own ideas. Mottl has been a bulwark. Siegfried is conducting now. Mother has to sort it all out. And it is she, of course, who has brought *Tristan* to Bayreuth, and *Die Meistersinger* and *Lohengrin* and *Tannhäuser*—repertoire not everyone has welcomed. And then there is the school she began with Kneise in1892. We are training important singers: Gulbranson, Burgstaller. Natalie Curtis is one of our students. In fact, she has become a dear family friend, she very often comes with her mother to Wahnfried. They joined us at Christmas, for the New Year, for Siegfried's last birthday. *Fräulein* Curtis will make something of herself, I am sure. You know her."

"Yes, I know the family. Is she here now?"

"She already attended your *Parsifal*—and was going to greet you afterward. But your head was elsewhere—as ever … Do you think of the old days? The Wahnfried years?"

"I carry many memories. I carry memories of you."

"You never even noticed me until I turned eighteen." She suddenly smiled and he felt the once familiar tingle of her warmth and intellect. "You had your own world."

"That is not entirely true." His heart had begun to pound.

"But I noticed you years before that. I noticed and knew many things, while you were buried in music with Wagner. Do you remember when he turned sixty-five and we gave him a carriage? We wheeled the children in circles in front of the house."

"They were wearing their little helmets."

"Helmets and capes. And then he had Cosima summon you inside. I followed and eavesdropped. The two of you sang *Parsifal* act one, the scene with the swan. He teased you and called you a 'homeless hero.' Then you said that Wahnfried was your home. And he grew serious—as only he could—and said you were his 'better half.' I heard everything. Every word. He often called you his Parsifal. Sometimes he would call you a 'goose'—when he was being Gurnemanz. Life and art were all the same for him."

"I was shy."

"He loved you like a son."

"Daniela …"

She braced herself. "Do you imagine you will return to Bayreuth? Mother will invite you, I am sure."

He exhaled heavily. "We will see."

"She will consider you disloyal if you do not come."

"I know."

"Whatever you decide, I will understand. But I will miss you, Anton."

He stood, fumbled with her hand, and drew it quickly to his lips. He turned and walked toward the door. He stopped, turned again, and said, "I will cherish the memory of this meeting."

Slowly, carefully, he closed the door behind him.

Chapter Thirteen
January 1898: Brooklyn and Manhattan

As the Wall Street pier receded, he stepped onto the ferry deck to be blasted by the winter rawness. It invigorated his stocky body, now swiftly aging. It gruffly stroked his long black hair. He gazed upriver at the gigantic suspension bridge, ever a source of wonderment, a sight elsewhere unimagined and unknown. Its twin towers of limestone and granite glistened in the stark mid-day sun. Its cables, an intricate web as graceful as the towers with their peaked arched passageways were ponderously Gothic, sloped majestically to the roadbed and thence high upwards once more toward the clear, chill sky. A train—a dark silent mass—traversed the bridge's river-breadth from west to east; then a second crossed in the direction opposite. A dozen hearty gulls bobbed aloft in the ferry's wake. The water traffic, near and far, included boats for pleasure or oceanic transport, barges of all sizes, tugboats whose billowing plumes streaked the freezing element. Far downriver, astride the Statue of Liberty, an ocean liner in silhouette crawled toward the Battery. The departing Manhattan shore bristled with piers and vertical windowed slabs. Trinity's black spire pierced the crowded skyline. On the Brooklyn side another city loomed whose residential grandeur, churches and cemeteries limned more reposeful, more aesthetic habits of mind and heart.

But ferment and flux, perpetual and unrelentingly, would swiftly refeature and configure both cities, he knew, for he knew this to be the New World, whose landmarks unless bridges of astonishing girth and mass were transient and replaceable. Who any more remembered when the Academy of Music signified grand opera and the Philharmonic's splendid auditorium was Steinway Hall? The Metropolitan Opera House, a dozen years old, had already lived three lives; tomorrow, it would like the Brighton Beach Music Pavilion become a place newly forgotten, wholly erased.

Cosima, dragging weighty dynasties of barnacled history and tradition—she was older than even the most aged American. The lordly Liszt, the neurotic von Bülow, the mercurial world genius Richard Wagner; Madame Patersi, her brittle French governess, who had prescribed an encyclopedia of *ancien régime* manners and modes of belief; her five children from two husbands, who had proved variously wayward or submissive—each had separately possessed and redirected her. She was like a time traveler whose centuries of luggage invaded every precinct of the Bavarian hamlet become a staging ground of martyrdom and musty myth. Her avenues of self-contradiction were of such legendary dimension—could it actually have been that Wagner was partly thinking of his multifarious second wife when he created Kundry? That a creature so guilty and tormented should at the same time be an autocratic tool with the dead Wagner her Klingsor, laying her snares—could the resemblance be coincidental? And to be, withal, a victim—of historic circumstance, of personal travail; was she not a living creation as pathetic and yet tragic as any operatic fiction?

Mrs. Langford, too, had her Kundry aspects: of servitude

and dominance in contradiction. But for her Kundry's was a fate to be avoided. She had erased her Tennessee past and begun again—and yet again, if necessary. No matter that her autonomy was controversial, that she was envied and resented by some; freedom, re-invention—it was the American way. And it had become his way as well: he was becoming an American musician. Look at Victor Herbert, born in Ireland, schooled in Stuttgart: an American composer, finding his *métier* in Broadway operettas.

Montague Street. He boarded a cable car, open to the cold, and commenced the steep ascent to the Heights. MacDowell's Second Piano Concerto at the Brooklyn Academy last week. America's leading composer: a complicated case, high-strung and introverted—which his music, oddly, was not. The concerto was acquiring popularity. Its poetry and pomp were Lisztian. And Liszt had encouraged MacDowell, in Germany. Of course, in Liszt's hands the finale would have been heroic, not cheerful; MacDowell played at profundity. The Dirge from his *Indian* Suite was MacDowell's Wagner opus, Siegfried's funeral relocated to the North American forest primeval. MacDowell adapted Indian tunes in that piece. Then, a month ago, Seidl premiered August Walther's *Hiawatha's Wooing and Wedding* in Brooklyn. No Indian tunes, just forests murmuring "Minnehaha" and Pau-Puk-Keewis performing his whirling wedding dance—not to be compared with Dvořák's version.

The Academy of Music and the Art Association marked his terminus. He would brave the elements and walk the rest of the way—needed to exercise more, Gusterl said. His own music for *Manabozo* now infiltrated his sonic mindstream: the West Wind's climactic departure 'midst thunder and lightning; the storm's dissipation, disclosing bewildered Dakotahs awed by the spectacle of Manabozo's ritual suicide. He had heightened and knitted the motifs, modulating toward an apotheosis. Manabozo fell dead. The Star of Morning evaporated into space. The sun bathed the dawn. As Nature, prophetic, sang "Hiawatha!", the vacillating chromatics of Manabozo's theme—that Iroquois tune from Krehbiel—transformed into a culminating E-flat major transfiguration. Had Neilson's libretto led him Icarus-like too near *Götterdämmerung*? He needed to take his scribblings and turn them into a decipherable score. He needed the manner of assistance that he had rendered Wagner. Neilson did not even read music—and was still in London anyway. Gusterl believed in *Manazobo*. Well, of course …

181 Schermerhorn. He had walked barely half an hour, and as always deliberately, but was winded. He knocked once and the door opened. "Good day, Mrs. Langford."

"Mr. Seidl, you must be freezing! You're all red with cold."

He stomped his feet and rubbed his hands. She took his coat.

"Let me get you something hot to drink. Coffee? Tea?"

"… A cup of coffee please."

"Your head is elsewhere, I can see. Do sit down."

He entered the parlor and found a chair. "Yes, it is true. I am thinking of many things. How to be an American."

The Hiawatha theme was itself superb. Memorable. And the Manabozo theme was properly malleable. The transformation of one to the other was no more contrived than the motivic mechanics of Liszt's sonata. But the "American" coloring—was it a pastry topping or a national identity?

"How to be an American. Do you mean like Mr. MacDowell?"

"We must believe in Mr. MacDowell."

"We will. We do. In Brooklyn we are making a statement. We are presenting American works with American soloists."

"Mr. Tidden played very well the MacDowell concerto. Not so well as MacDowell himself, but good. Mr. Brockway's Ballade—it shows some talent. Mr. Walther's Hiawatha symphony, too—it has weaknesses, but the public was pleased."

"And now, in February, we have Mr. Dudley Buck—his *Marmion*. Mr. Buck assures us that he will bring the members of his Apollo Club to the Academy. And we must do Mr. Huss—his piano concerto—and Mr. Arnold, Mr. Shelley, more of Mr. Herbert. It is not true that American music is not popular with audiences. It needs proper exposure."

"A composer must hear his music. This is part of training. Musical education in the United States—it is not adequate. What if Dvořák had no stipend from Vienna, so he could study? What is there at Mrs. Thurber's conservatory without Dvořák? Without scholarships? Where is our government? All the money goes to the pockets of our friend Mr. Damrosch, who now visits Brooklyn with *Tannhäuser*, in our own Academy of Music, with our own Emil Fischer—and Gadski, and Bispham who I just had in London. And brings with him a full production—the Metropolitan Opera scenery and costumes. Meanwhile, there is this season no Metropolitan Opera, only Damrosch. So, I conduct not a single opera. Nothing."

He noticed his coffee. It warmed his throat.

"The Seidl Society is attempting to raise funds for a Brooklyn opera house, you know that. We have incorporated. We have conferred with three architects."

"Before I die, just one time, I would like to give opera as it should be given. To rehearse the chorus the summer before. To choose with care the stage manager. To create the correct *mise-en-scène*. At least we have our *Parsifal* Concert in April."

Mrs. Langford shifted her body. "This is chiefly what I wanted to talk with you about today. There is a problem. It seems that we cannot obtain Lilli Lehmann for Kundry. She is not singing in New York this spring. As you know, she has barely appeared at the Metropolitan Opera since 1892. This means we also cannot have Mr. Kalisch. Even getting Mr. Fischer for Gurnemanz may present a problem."

"We are since September rehearsing the chorus."

"Yes, of course, I know that. And I am not saying that we cannot proceed. But we would need to do so with different soloists. Might we be able to secure at least some of your Bayreuth cast? Frau Brema? Mr. Van Dyck?"

"This is the last thing Cosima would allow. She reserves *Parsifal* for Bayreuth."

"But we are doing excerpts in concert."

"It is not likely."

"Could we not invite Frau Wagner and her son to Brooklyn? We have talked about this before. Perhaps …"

"They do not need us. We do not need them. I do not need them."

"I had thought that their presence could impart a special validity to our *Parsifal* enterprise."

The conversation halted awkwardly. She felt impelled to ask him a question she had only dared to ask herself.

"Mr. Seidl—may I be so bold as to inquire about your own plans? We all know of the offers you received abroad—from London, from Hamburg."

"I do not wish it. But I must conduct. I require an orchestra. Our thirty-eight strings—it is not enough. New York must have what Boston has, what Chicago has, what even Cincinnati has—a permanent orchestra. Instead, I must conduct now at Carnegie, now at the Astoria Hotel, now at Chickering Hall, now at the Brooklyn Academy, often with just one rehearsal. And no opera. Without opera, I cannot breathe."

Mrs. Langford's face fell.

"We will see."

She tried to gauge the inflection of Seidl's utterance, but could hear none.

***

If American composition on good lines is to be encouraged, if our best musicians put the claims of art above the claims of self, if conductors and managers but open their eyes to the merits of home productions, if the public be made to recognize the fact that a foreign label is not necessarily a proof of excellence or a native label of inferiority, it will not be long before the musician will arise who will compel the attention of the world, and furnish the example whose imitation will speedily develop an American school of composition. We are not hoping for an American school in a year or even or in a decade. But some day the strong, successful creator will come and the school will follow. I do not hold that it be essential that it should have a flavor wholly distinct from all the music produced elsewhere. It will be enough if we bring it to pass that the productions of native composers in the field of music shall receive the same respect and attention as the productions of native writers in the field of literature do.

When some seasons ago Mr. Theodore Thomas presented the premiere of Tchaikovsky's Fifth Symphony, he produced on the same New York program the Piano Concerto No. 2 of Mr. Edward MacDowell with the composer himself as soloist. I confess to having derived keener pleasure from the work of the young American than from the experienced and famous Russian. This concerto, most recently heard at a Seidl Society concert in Brooklyn, affords a delight of no mean order. It is so full of poetry, so full of vigor, as to tempt the assertion that it must be placed at the head of all works for soloist and orchestra produced by either a native or adopted citizen of America. Is Mr. MacDowell already the awaited paladin for American music? He is in certain respects an unlikely standard bearer. His works are in part frankly German, in part frankly "Keltic." He has said that he admires the "manly and free rudeness" of the American Indian, and has produced sundry miniatures evoking the forest and wigwam. But he disavows "purely national music" generally, and most specifically the Negro melodies so beloved of Dvořák when the latter composed the most famous and esteemed symphonic work yet conceived on American soil, the "Symphony from the New World."

Last night's New York Philharmonic concert, again conducted by Mr. Seidl, offered a valuable opportunity to audition Mr. MacDowell's "Indian" Suite, a work concurrent with the Dvořák symphony, having been composed in 1892. Scored for large orchestra, it is fully half an hour in length and comprises five movements, each a vignette of Indian life and lore. Of these the most striking, a "Dirge," is also strikingly Wagnerian, Siegfried's Funeral Music having served as an evident source of inspiration. The fateful tread and pang of world sorrow are the same. The pronounced pentatonic inflection, from Indian sources, is Mr. MacDowell's. Whether Mr. MacDowell's Indian lament advances an American school, or advances Mr. MacDowell's candidacy to become a catalyst that all others will follow, remains …

Krehbiel set down his busy pen and scanned the newsroom. That the Philharmonic had featured the MacDowell composition was, alas, as notable as the composition itself. In four programs to date for the current season, featuring thirteen composers, MacDowell's was the sole American name. This neglect did not mirror Seidl's propensities—elsewhere in New York, his advocacy of American works was ever more pronounced. Rather, venerable Philharmonic traditions preferred known European imports to fresh native efforts. But the wheel of time was churning fast and the Philharmonic and its traditions would soon suffer a juggernaut of change. While public disclosure remained some weeks distant, many already knew what the future likely held.

In the wake of Seidl's summer triumphs in London and Bayreuth, faced with the possibility of losing him to Berlin, Hamburg, or some other European musical capital, a committee had been hastily assembled to amass funding for a Permanent Seidl Orchestra.

Ingersoll and Finck were among the first to sound the alarm bell and each assembled a galaxy of wealth. The lists were then consolidated, creating a guarantee fund for five years commencing the first of May of the present year. Many of the city's great names, from disparate fields of endeavor, had subscribed, including W. Bayard Cutting, Richard Watson Gilder, Charles F. McKim, Henry W. Poor, Whitelaw Reid, and Gustav Schwab. As in Boston, Chicago, and Cincinnati, the new orchestra would enjoy a full season and a stable roster. Damrosch's New York Symphony, it is true, had for some time achieved a comparable status, but never a comparable pedigree. Seidl's concertmaster would be no less a violin master than Eugene Ysaÿe, who would also sometimes conduct. Even more remarkable was that Grau, having witnessed the London Wagner season galvanized by Seidl's leadership, had agreed to make the Seidl Orchestra his Metropolitan Opera orchestra. It would also give a dozen seasonal concerts of symphonic works at the Opera House.

Seidl's friends had of late observed a precipitous decline in his physical wellbeing. He had previously endured a severe bout of pneumonia in 1896. His relentless summer in London and Bayreuth had required six channel crossings; he had returned with a worrisome cold, having barely eaten for nearly two weeks. His current New York schedule imposed sixty and more concerts with a variety of bands in a variety of venues, a calendar he maintained in order to maintain income even when the artistic result risked disappointment. Bernstein, his contractor, did what he could to keep intact a core "Seidl orchestra," but the men whom he contracted took whatever additional work they could even at the cost of missing rehearsals for concerts where no second rehearsal was possible. That Seidl wished to remain in America could not be doubted; his affinity for his adopted homeland, its habits and freedoms, was clinched. That he would in fact do so had become more doubtful than at any time since his arrival in 1885. Though his remote manner bespoke composure, a nervous artistic constitution seethed beneath. His travails had not hardened his disposition, but he was plainly worn. And so, he straddled the horns of a dilemma, unable to mutually satisfy personal desires and professional requirements. The Permanent Orchestra plan materialized not a day too soon. London, Berlin, Munich, Budapest were vying for his services. The de Reszke brothers wanted him for St. Petersburg. Hamburg was inviting him to make his own terms of engagement. All these posts promised a formidable salary and a reliable pension. But Seidl had yielded not—the fresh New York opportunity mattered the most. His mood had lifted; the old buoyancy looked to return if it could.

It was a pathetic commentary on the vagaries of New York's musical culture, vagaries born of dependence upon fickle personal largesse, that it had required the threat of Seidl's desertion to mobilize an effort to furnish him with opportunities his benefactions had long deserved. Whether New York would receive further such benefactions, or rather choose to squander them, hung in the balance still.

* * *

They had met in 1891 when Damrosch brought Tchaikovsky to New York for the opening of Carnegie's Music Hall. Tchaikovsky conducted stiffly and self-consciously. He was made to endure an onslaught of admiration, including social obligations like the dinner party at Schirmer's, where they were first introduced. He impressed Seidl as one of the shyest, most private artists he had ever encountered, painfully concealing or helplessly disclosing his nervous fragility. His thinning white hair and worried eyes made him seem at least a decade older than his fifty-one years. Miss Ivy Ross of the *Journal*, who knew how to do such things, had Tchaikovsky write a little article deploring the "Wagner cult" and also asserting that Wagner had misapplied his great gift: he should have composed symphonies rather than operas. Seidl had responded with a little article of his own, courteously composed, testifying that there were no Wagnerites who did not also follow Bach, Mozart, and Beethoven. Then the lonely Tchaikovsky returned to Russia, to his friends and colleagues, and composed his masterpiece in which the operatic art of musical characterization and evocation, and the symphonic art of musical structure and argument, were conjoined in a sorrowful autobiographical narrative. Violating every precedent, his *Pathétique* Symphony climaxed with a slow finale, an "Adagio lamentoso" with religious overtones; he stared at his own grave and saw only blackness and extinction. Tchaikovsky conducted the premiere in St. Petersburg and died nine days later. Rumors ensued—as if the symphony, with its dire terminus, had been a suicide note.

That was some four years ago. The *Pathétique* was already widely performed—not least by Seidl in New York. He read it as a reminiscence of life at death's door. Its preface—a grieving bassoon swathed in darkness—was the sepulcher framing a series of fraught memories. The activity of life—its solitary turmoil or ballroom frivolity—was shadowed by ennui, a disaffection for earthly pursuits, given supreme expression by the first movement's long sighing song for violins and violas. The pervasive falling motion of innumerable kindred phrases mapped an existential descent punctuated by episodes of enforced gaiety or cataclysmic vertigo. An unstable and evanescent waltz—the second movement—was interrupted by throbbing heartache and mortality. The third movement's life-march was an empty hope hijacked by Mephisto. The finale's gong stroke summoned from a side-stage the reaper who watched and heard it all. For Tchaikovsky, the stages of man comprised a tale of anguish, tenderness, and march-like determination filtered through a film of regret, a patina of resignation, mediated by the distance of loss.

Wagner, at the end of his life, had planned a series of one-movement programmatic symphonies. Had he lived to compose them, his soulmates would have included Dvořák and Tchaikovsky. With its ripping energies and elegiac landscapes, its sorrow songs, its Indian dance and sunset leave-taking, Dvořák's "New World" was the personalized portrait of a nation. Tchaikovsky's Fourth, Fifth, and Sixth Symphonies were self-portraits, a quest for solace yielding instead a manifesto of futility. Notwithstanding the redemptive messages of *Die Meistersinger* and *Parsifal*, even of *Götterdämmerung*, Seidl had discovered in himself a fathomless affinity for Tchaikovsky's fatalism. The *Pathétique* had become as much his signature as the *Ring*. He had most recently plunged into its darkest crevices at Chickering Hall. The stoic immobility of his black mane and sturdy torso, visible to fifteen hundred transfixed listeners, concealed the pale and tear-stained countenance to which his musicians responded in hypnotic accord.

At home, at the piano, Seidl would tirelessly explore Tchaikovsky's Adagio. Slowing it down, rebalancing the textures, fingering latent nuances, he discovered new worlds of sadness, personal and impersonal, until one day Gusterl could stand it no longer.

"Tony! Can't you play something else?"

He ceased and turned his head. She had stopped knitting. "What would you like to hear?"

"Anything. Anything at all. Something uplifting."

"Up*lift*ing." He rolled his eyes and pursed his lips. He played a euphonious ascent. "*Tod und Verklärung* by Herr Richard Strauss. But only the *Verklärung* theme, of course."

He closed his eyes, shook his mane, and cocked his head skyward. "Counterfeit Wagner. A reasonably adroit facsimile."

The theme modulated upward, growing in amplitude and volume. Seidl's left hand pounded the striding bass. His right hand superimposed climbing tremolos. "Marching to heaven!" he roared, and began to stamp his feet.

Mime, being the most musical of the dogs, barked in protest. All the dachshunds joined in. Wotan and Auguste arose as one and left the room.

CHAPTER FOURTEEN
March 1898: Manhattan

Auguste woke him up in time for his late morning rehearsal with Henry Huss. The coffee did some good. She reminded him that the dinner party could still be postponed. No, he said, Pugno leaves for Europe tomorrow, we must host him this evening with Ysaÿe and the others. And you have a strenuous morning rehearsal tomorrow—the chorus for Beethoven's Ninth, she said. His mind was elsewhere. He knew Huss well—an American Romantic, not be to be confused with Chadwick or Foote in Boston. A vigorous man, trim and erect, with a finely molded black mustache. Unlike Strong, who doubted himself, or MacDowell, who was withdrawn.

Huss arrived with Madame de Vere bearing a present: a Beethoven fragment he had realized as a Lied—"Heidenröslein"—at Krehbiel's request. Seidl glanced through it, beginning to end, with patient interest. How much was Huss's? The accompaniment and harmonization, wholly. The tune was extrapolated from a series of Beethoven's sketches. Seidl set it aside and the three of them plunged forthwith into *Cleopatra's Death*, a "dramatic fragment" for soprano and orchestra setting Shakespeare. Seidl admired its fervor and largesse. For the culminating exclamation—"I come, O

Antony, I come!"—Huss had composed a vocal line climbing by degrees, then by ecstatic leaps, to a high D-flat. The passage was prepared in the orchestra by a lengthy chromatic descent followed by a strategic pause. Sitting at his piano, Seidl showed Huss where to thin the scoring so as not to cover the singer. With de Vere marking her part, he tried a variety of tactics to pace the ending for maximum effect. When, finally, he invited her to sing at full voice, his excitement took over; his right arm waved and drove, his left hand alone fingered the keys. That was enough, no need to over-prepare. Huss's piano concerto, with de Ohe, also needed playing—at the Brooklyn Academy certainly, and also with the new permanent orchestra, we will not neglect American repertoire. And the violin concerto, with Maude Powell—Huss must remember to trim the first movement tuttis.

The visitors departed. Auguste served lunch: shad roe. Seidl's energy suddenly ebbed, but as Auguste noted his appetite was better than usual. She found de Vere's top voice shrill, but no matter. He would take the streetcar to Fleischmann's for some social refreshment, then return home by 6 p.m. for Pugno and Ysaÿe.

"Good day Professor;" he tipped his hat to the motorman and took a seat. The permanent orchestra was already scheduled for thirty spring concerts; he needed to make programs. Huss's piano concerto, definitely. And Strong's *Sintram* Symphony, unperformed since he gave the premiere with the Philharmonic: a priority. The American Composers Concerts had done a job but MacDowell was right about not coddling the best American works—let them stand alongside the new music of Brahms, Dvořák, Tchaikovsky, Strauss. And then another summer Wagner season for Grau at Covent Garden, including a *Ring* cycle for which full attention to stage detail was promised; and another set of *Parsifal* performances at Bayreuth. He had discovered that he could not say no to Cosima after all. The second time would be easier; he might even consent to visit Wahnfried. For Wagner, turning and twisting in his grave, powerless to command his posthumous fate. Next, at the Metropolitan in 1898-1899, Grau had engaged Lehmann and Van Dyck and von Rooy and Gadski alongside the de Reszke brothers—Wagner in German as it had not been purveyed in New York since 1891, with his own Seidl orchestra in the pit, it was the oasis that he had hoped and longed for during his desert years, making do with Mrs. Langford, watching from the wings while Mancinelli Italianized *Lohengrin* and *Die Meistersinger* …

Union Square, Professor.

He strolled to Tenth, nodding when acknowledged, enjoying the spring weather. At Fleischmann's, violating his daily custom, he sat down outdoors under the festive awning. He ordered a coffee and began to peruse the German papers. Herbert and Nahan Franko turned up soon after. Herbert's mood was exceptional. In the fall he would acquire an orchestra, in Pittsburgh. Yes, yes, there would be plenty of Wagner. But he would retain his regimental band, with which he had recently performed some especially splendid marches of his own. So next Friday and Saturday would mark his last Philharmonic concerts as principal cellist. The Henry Huss piece? It would make a strong impression, Seidl opined. Alongside Beethoven's Ninth? Even so, said Seidl. But Franko was disconsolate. With the Metropolitan Opera in abeyance, he had been serving as concertmaster for Damrosch. And the new Metropolitan season next fall would install Seidl's orchestra with Ysaÿe in the concertmaster's chair. Not invariably, Seidl said. There would be an abundance of performances. And Ysaÿe would not abandon his solo career. They puffed their cigars in silence for a period of time. Seidl announced his intention to visit Sam Bernstein. Franko joined him for the short walk uptown to East Nineteenth.

No sooner had Seidl arrived at Bernstein's flat than he was felled by acute stomach pain. He lay down in a virtual faint and harbored blurred thoughts about his wife's future wellbeing. Their savings were scant. The permanent orchestra would furnish—would have furnished?—a pension. He permitted Bernstein to pour some whiskey down his throat. He vomited and lost consciousness. He awoke to the sound of Bernstein's voice, instructing his brother to summon a doctor. Bernstein had a meeting that afternoon with some of the men he regularly contracted for Seidl. Seidl turned his head, barely raised his right hand, and softly instructed: "Sam, you'll have to go." It was the last sentence he would utter.

* * *

Ysaÿe was explaining to Pugno and Gerardi that he foresaw curtailing his activities as a touring virtuoso. As was well-known, he suffered from a hand ailment. Violinists in any event did not enjoy the performing longevity of pianists—the arms and hands were more stressed than at a keyboard. Having attained the age of forty, he was eager to compose more. And to conduct. What better training than to become concertmaster of Seidl's new orchestra—the best possible baton lessons. Yes, of course, he had done it before, in Berlin, playing under Bilse, but that was quite another thing—Bilse had been no Seidl—and long ago. It was also a way of keeping abreast of the latest compositional developments in Europe and America. A mixed blessing for a composer, Pugno remarked. Look at Mahler in Vienna, whose conducting exposed him to such a range of contemporary influences that his own music lacked a consolidated personal style. The point was pondered.

The table was meanwhile set. Seidl was late. At 6:15 the doorbell rang. "That must be Tony now," Auguste said. But Bertha announced the arrival of Sam Bernstein's brother. He told Mrs. Seidl that her husband, at Sam's house, had experienced a serious gastric disturbance, had vomited and lost consciousness. But he was now feeling better and had asked that the dinner begin without him. He would come shortly. He was not in any danger. Auguste had Bertha summon a cab. She would fetch Tony herself, and quickly.

The Fourth Avenue traffic seemed abnormally heavy, the horse unnaturally slow. Seated silently alongside a relative stranger who said little, she could only pray. If she feared the worst, nothing could surprise her—and so she did. Tony's health was precarious. The summer, shuttling between London and Bayreuth—she had never been in favor of it. And now he would do it again. I should have been firmer. But I did not wish to appear selfish. He so wanted to conduct Wagner at Covent Garden. And *Parsifal* at Bayreuth, how could she possibly have stood in the way? If this should prove a warning, a precautionary scare, he must reconsider. At least a holiday, a month upstate …

She froze with fear to discover dozens of women outside Bernstein's brownstone. Mounting the steps, she recognized two or three; they were weeping. She was ushered to a room in which Tony lay with his eyes shut. He was breathing calmly. Sam, a balding man with sorrowful Semitic eyes, was standing alongside. A doctor—Moscovitch, he called himself—told her no, there was no apoplexy, Mr. Seidl's heartbeat was regular. He could slowly move his hands and feet. Retaining her cab, she sent a message to Doctor Langmann to come immediately. Then she waited helplessly for him to arrive. All her earlier thoughts were numbed by the blunt actuality of the motionless body lying face up on Bernstein's bed. Her frantic eyes scrutinized the subtle motion of his chest.

Langmann entered swiftly but noiselessly. He surmised ptomaine poisoning—a rare effect of food not obviously tainted. He sent Moscovitch for a stomach pump. Before Moscovich could return, Seidl's condition deteriorated. Langmann was challenged to sustain his patient's breathing. Blood-letting was tried but in vain. Death was pronounced at 10:15 p.m.

Bernstein spoke first. "Mrs. Seidl: in truth I had for some time believed that your husband was not long for this world. That he had not been wholly well for at least two years. There was his pneumonia, his severe exhaustion this fall … I felt that his body could no longer tolerate the pace of his professional activities."

"Did he realize? Do you think he …"

"It is impossible to say. You know how he was, so strong-willed. He would never acknowledge weakness. Never."

"And better this, Mrs. Seidl, than a lingering death. For such a man …"

The body must be removed to East Sixty-second Street, Langmann finally said, gently grasping Auguste's hand. Bernstein asked Auguste if he should come as well.

"No, I want to be alone with Tony." Bernstein and Langmann left the room. They would return at midnight.

She sat beside the body and studied her husband's face. The dead pallor of his skin refuted the living blackness of his raven hair. She took a comb and with trembling fingers stroked the tangles out. His chiseled features, ever her pride, were puffy with age, and now the more flaccid. Shut to the world, his eyes surrendered their accustomed whimsy, authority, or affection. Familiar still, he had become an object of bewildering and wholly unfamiliar pathos.

Midnight came swiftly, and with it the Bernstein brothers

and Langmann. Outside the house, the late hour notwithstanding, the crowd of mourners now overflowed the sidewalk onto the street. At the sight of the stretcher, and of the shrouded corpse, cries and expostulations broke the silence of the night. The widow, blinded by her grief, neither saw nor heard.

* * *

Anton Seidl In Memoriam

The sudden death of Anton Seidl fills the music-lovers of New York with dismay. His death leaves a gap in the operatic forces of the Metropolitan Opera House, New York, and Covent Garden, London; robs the Philharmonic Society of New York of a conductor under whom it enjoyed six seasons of unexampled prosperity; deprives the borough of Brooklyn of its leading musical factor; weakens the artistic props of the Wagner festival of Bayreuth, which has been more and more in need of fortification as the enterprise has gained in worldly wealth; and orphans numerous additional undertakings including the imminent prospect of a permanent New York orchestra to rival those of Boston and Chicago, Leipzig or Berlin. When he died, he was within a step of the attainment of a position without parallel in the history of musical conductors in respect of the scope and influence which would have been opened to his labors on both sides of the Atlantic Ocean, and this it is that makes his death seem so utterly grievous and disastrous. It is a loss not to one community, but to many; not to a single artistic institution, but to art itself.

Mr. Seidl's activities in New York compassed twelve seasons. He came in the fall of 1885, to be the first conductor of the German opera, then domiciled at the Metropolitan Opera House, and he remained at the head of that notable institution until Messrs. Abbey & Grau and their Italian cohorts overthrew the German regime in 1891. When his labors ended at the opera, they began with the Philharmonic Society. He did not revisit the director's desk in the Opera House pit till German was added to the official operatic languages, in the fall of 1895. Then he again became a Metropolitan Opera conductor, and so remained, extending his labors to London in the late spring of 1897, and to Bayreuth in the summer of the same year. During the entire period of his American residence, he conducted the majority of the orchestral concerts of this city given under other auspices than those of the institutions mentioned, and he was extending his activities more and more widely with each year in both the Manhattan and Brooklyn boroughs, not to mention his enduring reputation in such cities as Boston, Cincinnati, and Philadelphia.

What manner of man and musician was he? More distinctively than any of his colleagues, even those whose training was like unto his, Mr. Seidl was a product of the tendencies given to the reproductive art by Richard Wagner. He represented those tendencies in all their aspects, positive and negative, creative and destructive, progressive and regressive. In all things where in his greatness lay, he was the embodiment of an authority which asked no justification and brooked no denial. Outside his specific field—conducting a range of earlier music, beginning with Bach—he was an empiric. He had no patience with theories, but a wondrous love for experiences. In him, impulse dominated reflection, emotion shamed logic. It was much to his advantage that he came among an impressionable people with the prestige of a Wagnerian oracle and archon, and much to the advantage of the cult to which he was devoted that he made that people "experience" the lyric dramas of his master in the same sense that a good Methodist "experiences" religion.

It was not given to Mr. Seidl's friends to observe traces of his academic training except as they may have been preserved in his skill at the pianoforte. He was, by open confession, what the Germans call a Naturalist. His branch of musical practice was the reproductive, and he believed conducting to be an art which in its truest estate could be acquired only by plenary inspiration. It is commonly said that he was first a pupil of Hans Richter in the art, but he never said so himself. On the contrary, he said publicly that Richter had become a conductor without lessons, and that, though he had made earnest studies of Beethoven and Wagner with Richter, he had never troubled himself with technical practice in the manipulation of the baton. What he learned in this direction he learned chiefly by standing at the side of Wagner, listening for him, and noting the methods which Wagner employed to make his players one with him in understanding, feeling, and aim. The first essential in conducting he held to be complete devotion to the music in hand. The conductor must penetrate to the heart of the composition and be set aglow by its flames. That done, he must make his proclamation big and vital, full of red blood, sincere and assertive—assertive even, as was the case in certain lighter compositions by Mozart and Beethoven, in misconception. He had no room in his convictions for mere refinement of nuance or precision of execution. Too much elaboration of detail he thought injurious to the general effect. None of his confrères of Bayreuthian antecedents can work so directly, so elementally, upon an audience as did he. With him in the chair, it was only the most case-hardened critic who could think of comparative tempi and discriminate between means of effect. As for the rest, professional and layman, dilettante and ignorant, their souls were his to play with.

And now for some purely personal and individual impressions of the man. Anton Seidl was one of those strong characters that give an interesting tinge to all manner of incidents with which they chance to be associated, even though they be of themselves commonplace. Like Moltke he could hold his tongue in seven languages, but singularly enough his habitual taciturnity never made his company any the less interesting. Moreover, when the mood was on him he could talk "an hour by his dial"; and then his reminiscences of the years spent in the household of Wagner, or the story of his experiences while carrying the gospel of the poet-composer through Europe were full of fascination. But the talkative mood seldom came upon him when surrounded by a crowd. He was indifferent to the many and fond of the few, and so his circle of really intimate friends never grew large in spite of the multitudes who sought and obtained his acquaintance. No combination of circumstances could disturb his self-possession, yet he seemed to be most contented and comfortable when seated quietly "under four eyes," as the Germans say. Even under such circumstances he would sometimes sit for minutes at a time without speaking himself or expecting a word from his companion, yet never show a sign of weariness or ennui. Mr. Seidl's hero, Wagner, was his antipode in this respect, and there is a story which indicates that he must frequently have been amused at his pupil's reticence. Coming to a rehearsal he found that Seidl had contracted a cold that had robbed him of every vestige of voice. Wagner laughed immoderately and with mock seriousness upbraided him for his bad habit of talking too much which had now brought him to the pass that he could not talk at all.

His epistolary habits were like his conversation. He wrote as seldom as he talked, but as the talking fit sometimes seized him so did the writing fit. Then he could devote hours to a letter which had the dimensions and sometimes also the style of a formal literary essay. In this kind of writing, he was so prone to drop into a pulpit manner that I once taxed him with it and jokingly asked for an explanation. He paused for a moment then smilingly made a half confession that he had once been destined for the priesthood. His fondness for Scriptural illustrations and his "preachy" manner were habits which had clung to him from that early day. They were the only academic relics about him, however. I doubt if any of his friends ever heard him discuss a question in the theory or history of music. How far his exact knowledge in the art went I shall not undertake to determine; one thing is certain, it embraced every measure of Wagner's greater works.

As an evidence of his reticence touching his thoughts, feelings and intentions, I wish, in conclusion, to offer a story, though it has a personal bearing. Fully three years ago I discovered that he had developed a desire to compose. For that department of music, I did not think he possessed any large measure of qualification. I was therefore not a little surprised to have him, after several hours of general conversation, ask me for a libretto. I told him of a book of words that I had planned on a subject drawn from Norse mythology, but I declined the costly and difficult undertaking of assembling an opera book. Long afterward I learned, but not from him, that he had turned his thoughts to an aboriginal American subject, and wanted to assay what he described as an "American Nibelungenlied" based upon the Iroquois legend of Hiawatha—not that treated by Longfellow, but the story which has a basis of history and connects Hiawatha with the foundation of the Confederacy of the Five Nations. He appealed to Francis Neilson, who wrote the book for him. All this without a hint of his intentions to me. In the fall of 1897 we met in Cleveland, he being on a concert, I on a lecture tour. He asked for some specimens of Indian music, and I sent him a large number selected because of their illustration of the characteristic elements of Indian melody and rhythm. We talked them over afterward, but he gave no sign of the fact that he was working on an Indian opera. It now transpires that at the time of his death the opera was mainly composed, retained in his brain and fingers, but never set down for others to read or perform. This further loss enlarges the tragedy now befallen the world of music.

– H. E. K.

Epilogue

Manhattan and Brooklyn: March 31 and May 1898

The doors to the three-story brownstone opened at 12:30. The coffin emerged shouldered by a dozen pallbearers, with Carl Schurz in the lead. The others, all hatless in the gray drizzle, all recognizable to some two hundred mourners assembled on the sidewalk and street, included the music critics Henry T. Finck, Henry Edward Krehbiel, and Albert Steinberg, the composers Edward MacDowell and Xavier Scharwenka, the pianist Rafael Joseffy, the violinist Eugene Ysaÿe, the magazine editor Richard Watson Gilder, the banker James Speyer, and the physician William H. Draper. The casket bore a silver plate reading:

> ANTON SEIDL
> Born May 7, 1850
> Died March 28, 1898

It was lowered into a horsedrawn hearse. The first carriage was occupied by the widow, her maid, and her physician. The cortège proceeded to Fifth Avenue and turned south astride Central Park. At Fortieth Street it was joined by a hundred-piece band led by Victor Herbert and Nahan Franko.

The massed winds and muffled drums delivered and redelivered a funeral march by Beethoven. Its heavy impersonal tread redoubled the sad weather. Thronged mourners gathered on either side.

The picturesque route embellished the requiem moment. The Metropolitan Club, a white marble palazzo, had hosted many a musicale enjoyed by the deceased. The Savoy and New Netherlands Hotels, at Fifty-ninth Street, testified to the gargantuan scale of the New World's urban aspirations. Vanderbilt Row, with its gaudy turreted mansions, brandished the prerogatives of New World wealth, whose favors were financial and political, social and cultural. The towering, tapered spires of St. Patrick's Cathedral proclaimed a young nation's propensities or pretentions toward uplift. The forty-four-foot granite walls of the Croton Reservoir imposed their Egyptian solemnity. All this prefaced the prosaic enormity of a building whose barren façade fronted a towering horseshoe auditorium vaster than any such abroad.

The vestibule of the Metropolitan Opera House, a plain and puny antechamber, held in check a mass of humanity whose suffocating unrest was helplessly observed by dozens of patrolmen. Some who fainted were nearly trampled. Outside, a far larger deluge, equally dense, swept a mounted policeman from his horse. Once the clogged doors were opened, seething multitudes with arms interlocked forced their way in. Within ten minutes the downstairs seats were filled with women outnumbering men twenty to one. Surging upstairs, an army of determined faces and pounding feet crammed every box and balcony until the standees massed five and six rows deep. More than four thousand persons managed to fit in a space designed for 3,600. Fifteen thousand had applied for tickets.

The stage was set for the cathedral scene of Gounod's

Faust, streaked by shadows cast by tall candelabras. An orchestra—the Philharmonic—was eventually joined by the cortège band; a male chorus stood to either side. Atop the pit, which was floored over and carpeted, was a tall catafalque swathed in an American flag. At its head, a music stand of white roses and violets bore an open score with portraits of Richard Wagner and the departed, with the inscription "Vereint auf ewig." Masses of flowers surrounded this centerpiece. Jean and Eduard de Rezske had sent a wreath of four thousand violets. Lillian Nordica's rose wreath quoted Isolde: "Gebrochen der Blick! Still das Herz! Nicht eines Atems flücht'ge Wehn! Muss sie nun jammernd vor dir stehn." The Seidl Society contributed a large double "S" of red carnations united by a bow of pink silk, the Philharmonic a tall lyre in red and white. The Liederkranz Society, the Arion Society, the Maurice Grau Opera Company, the Metropolitan Opera Orchestra, the Musicians' Protective Union, the German Press Club, the Steinway Brothers, Robert Ingersoll, Lilli Lehmann all contributed to the floral tributes.

At 1:15, signaling the arrival of the coffin, the band resumed its inexorable dirge. All rose with a sudden rustle of fabric and furniture. The bier was slowly conveyed down the left aisle and set upon the waiting catafalque. The audience and the musicians sat. The male chorus sang "Wenn zwei Freunde scheiden." Led by its concertmaster, Richard Arnold, the orchestra performed the Adagio Lamentoso from Tchaikovsky's *Pathétique* Symphony. A "Helden Requiem," by Heinrich Zoellner, was sung under the composer's direction. All this was absorbed in heavy silence.

As Seidl, born a Catholic, was not a traditional believer, the presiding clergyman was a Unitarian minister: the Reverend Merle St. Croix Wright. He spoke without notes. "We honor a man who first honored himself, us, our city, and our country, by making America a worthy member of the international fraternity of art," he said. "We honor him as a leader with the courage and capacity to give music a new birth in America. This magnificent and unsolicited assemblage, gathered to do him honor who has done them and humanity honor, is a testimony to his worth. Today he receives a silent tribute from every humane soul, every lover of the arts. He was a foreigner, but of that class of foreigners who make a newfound country native to their souls—a citizen preferring America and by America preferred." He also said: "The soul staggers in this material world and here lies one who has soothed and caressed it. He has conferred on us individually and as a nation an unforgettable and imperishable boon. And so we mourn Anton Seidl. His influence is imperishable."

Though the printed program listed Carl Schurz as the designated eulogist, Reverend Wright's place on the lip of the stage was now taken by Henry Krehbiel; Schurz had found himself unable to speak. The clergyman's professional composure contrasted with the critic's shambling gait, quavering voice, and tear-stained countenance. Intermingling robust bursts of oratory with restorative pauses, he read a script prepared by Robert Ingersoll, who could not be present. "In the noon and zenith of his career, in the flush and glory of success, Anton Seidl, the greatest orchestral leader of all time, the perfect interpreter of Wagner, of all his subtlety and sympathy, his heroism and grandeur, his wondrous harmonies that touch the longings and the hopes of every heart, has passed from the shores of sound to the realm of silence," Krehbiel began. But Ingersoll's striving rhetoric could not compete with the greater pathos and sorrow of the speaker's bearing and voice. The huge space throbbed with sobbing and cries of incredulous pain. Gaining momentum from this desperate response, Krehbiel hurled a final invocation into the darkened room. "Anton Seidl is dead. Play the great funeral march! Envelop him in *music*! That will express our sorrow—that will voice our love, our hope, and that will tell of the life, the triumph, the genius, the death of Anton Seidl."

While Krehbiel fumbled with his papers, Henry Schmitt mounted the podium. With the dolorous timpani taps commencing Siegfried's Funeral Music, the house arose as one. The music—a dead-march punctuating songs of plaintive remembrance—animated the building with a proud and despondent combustion of energies. In an instant, it stirred the ghost of the deceased and propelled to living memory his doomed triumphs and early end. A long and insistent crescendo drove Wagner's dirge toward heights of gravitas and grief, yielding a plateau of thundering heroic declamation in brass and drums. Gauging every musical vicissitude, the hall's ambience rose and fell in communal waves of high feeling. The march dissipated, drawing with it in a downward spiral of conscious recognition the limp reality of the actual funeral at hand. The musicians onstage sat with bowed heads. The bewildered listeners remained standing. The band reassembled and proceeded up the left aisle. The pallbearers retrieved the coffin and joined this second processional. The Beethoven dirge resumed, its strains fading to silence as it vacated the chamber. The community of grief now disassembled, leaving each individual member uninstructed.

The ceremonies recommenced at 4:30 with the arrival of fifteen carriages at a crematorium in Fresh Pond, Long Island. Many hundreds who had left the Opera House took trains or trolleys to witness this final mourning event. An organist played Siegfried's dirge and Elsa's Prayer. The body was removed and swathed in a sheet saturated with alum. Time was permitted for a final uncovering of the face. The incineration was quickly performed. Several women scrambled to secure flowers from the casket. Two hours later, the ashes of Anton Seidl were taken from the retort and placed in a tin canister, to be scattered over the waters of Long Island Sound.

* * *

Though Mrs. Langford's health had been robust for years, her nervous disposition was generally taut and there were periods when the vicissitudes of her postbellum odyssey had subverted her high energies. But never had she been prostrated as by Anton's death. Though neurasthenia was diagnosed, it was a condition so elusive that some experts prescribed exercise and others rest. In any event, she spent many a waking hour in bed or otherwise inactive. Edward had never witnessed his wife in any such condition. His alarm was mitigated by certain knowledge of its cause. That Seidl and Wagner anchored her being was evident to all. Minus Seidl, Wagner ceased to direct the missionary proclivity that drove her public persona. And yet the needs of the moment were undeflectable. If the Seidl Society were to consecrate Seidl's passing, a venue had to be found, a program chosen, an orchestra booked, soloists and a conductor engaged. Also, a memorial statue was being urged. The *Eagle* envisioned a novel Brighton Beach monument at sea—a pile of rough stone, suitably stabilized, with a smooth face for an inscription. A proper project for the Seidl Society, the newspaper had said. And so it was, especially with the Music Pavilion gone, perhaps forever.

All her adult life, negotiating migrant allegiances and shifting identities, she had kept faith in herself. She had turned obstacles into opportunities and throttled occasions for envy. Her marriage to Junius: blotted out. Her betrayal by Blavatsky: expunged from the narrative of her London adventure. In

Ladies of the White House, her ticket to Brooklyn Heights celebrity, she had extolled Lucy Hayes as an exemplar of Christian duty, visiting reform schools and orphanages, eschewing diamonds and short sleeves, courageously enforcing temperance as hostess of the President's House. It was another lifetime: she had long surpassed Lucy's modest activism. At the *Eagle* she found a world of men to which she could sometimes belong. But nothing was ever enough. Driven by her acutely pious upbringing, her ceaseless quest for stability, her sins of self-misrepresentation, she had acquired theosophy until it turned upon her with grotesque accusations. Then she found her haven and became the Seidl Society. Daily, indefatigably, it enveloped her activity and belief. When her bravado bred resistance, her activity and belief accelerated and deepened. Now, suddenly and irremediably, the vacuum of Seidl's passing unmasked her autonomy as the merest illusion. She had in fact acquired a dependency so complete that no future life was visible: she could not make concerts because there was no one to lead them, could not host orphans because there was no place to take them. The revelation of lost independence was a naked and humiliating reality, not least to her enemies. And what intimate friends did she have? Her relations with Edward originated in a business opportunity; she had never transcended her ambivalence toward marriage and the marriage bed. Auguste, her sworn "dearest friend," would soon be gone. In fact, like a nun married to the Holy Virgin, she had wedded the Wagner spirit embodied in ritual by the holiness of Parsifal and manifest on earth in the ineffable person of Anton Seidl. And now a single existential calamity had destroyed it all as swiftly as a Hindu sage declaring the world a mirage. Had she not once given Seidl a copy of the Vedanta? "Interesting," he had said, smiling with his eyes alone, a typical communication, confiding and yet everlastingly remote.

Only one element of the pending concert had come easily. Of the vocalists Seidl had engaged under Seidl Society auspices, Emil Fischer was the most popular and—with Lehmann, now abroad and hence unavailable—the most loyal. He quickly volunteered to sing Wotan's Farewell. But Fischer had decided to retire to Germany and was about to depart the United States. Mrs. Langford managed to book the Academy of Music for May 2 with Fischer's consent to stay and sing that day, but not a day later. Mr. Bernstein, meanwhile, was unable to assemble the usual Seidl Orchestra. Mrs. Langford was too weak to importune. Nor could she find a solo pianist or violinist of great reputation. Richard Burmester agreed to perform on condition that he play his own concerto arrangement of Liszt's *Concerto Pathétique* for solo piano. Mrs. Langford consented. For a conductor, she settled for Franz Kaltenborn, a Seidl Orchestra violinist who led a string quartet but was untested on the podium. A program was created with two Wagner selections additional to Fischer's *Die Walküre* solo: the *Meistersinger* Prelude, to begin the evening, and—of course—Siegfried's Funeral Music to end it. The ersatz Liszt piano concerto was coupled with *Les préludes.* Humperdinck's *Hänsel und Gretel* dream music was coupled with a short number Seidl had composed for children's chorus: "Good Night," to words by Edna Dean Proctor:

> Good-night! Good-night!
> The morn will light
> The east before the dawn
> And stars arise to gem the skies
> When these have westward gone,
> Good-night! And sweet be thy repose
> Through all their shining way,
> Till darkness goes, and bird and rose,

With rapture greet the day –
Good-night!

The result entirely lacked the trajectory of the Metropolitan Opera memorial one month prior. The orchestra's strings were ragged. The Liszt selections proved incongruous. The Reverend Lyman Abbott offered a brief eulogy whose theme—that the artist never dies, nor would the society bearing his name—was recklessly prophetic. Mrs. Langford had not intended to speak. But, awkwardly, Fischer's imminent ocean departure required that he sing earlier in the evening than announced—and so it fell to her to share this information with as much dignity as she could. She was warmly applauded, but less so than Fischer himself. What in fact most poignantly evoked the memory of Anton Seidl was his little lullaby, sweetly rendered by the choirboys of the Church of Heavenly Rest. Otherwise, he seemed an already distant presence: a fallen star.

In the weeks that followed, the Seidl Society ceased to exist. No Seidl monument was planned. The Seidl permanent orchestra did not materialize. But Henry Finck was able to launch the smaller project of a Seidl memorial book with contributions by himself, Krehbiel, Huneker, Herbert, Huss, Lehmann, Nordica, the de Rezskes, and various others. Cosima Wagner was invited to submit an encomium—and declined. Auguste agreed that in collaboration with Finck she would furnish a substantial memoir once she had relocated permanently to the Catskills. This flight into seclusion, partnered only by the grieving dogs, became her primary object. But preliminary to that she insisted upon composing acknowledgements for every note of condolence. The last of these, and the hardest to write, read:

New York City
May 19, 1898

Dear Frau Thode,

Please forgive my tardiness in acknowledging your exceptional letter—and also the beautiful obituary notice in the Bayreuther Blätter (for I realize that it was probably you who wrote it), and the stipend for Mr. Farwell so he can transcribe some of Anton's Wagner arrangements into full score.

I feel that I must tell you that I have long been aware that many years before our wedding, you and Anton considered a marriage opposed by your mother, and that your affections for one another remained strong. I have always respected the nobility of your restraint.

At the same time, I feel the need to confide that I most probably played a role in Tony's long absence from Europe. The Wagner household was in some ways the most profound home that he ever knew and I dreaded the power it might exert were he to go abroad to conduct. I will never forget the impact of Richard Wagner's death on my dear husband—who was not yet my husband—when we were in Aix. He came back from the funeral an older man. I think the weight of that event never wholly lifted for him. Though he did not tire of talking about his relations with Wagner at Wahnfried, New York in some ways kept at bay the emotions those memories might have aroused were he to have regularly returned to Bayreuth—and to you.

During our years in New York, I struggled with feelings of guilt and selfishness, recognizing the opportunities Tony would have enjoyed in German lands. At the same time, we both became proud Americans, and he died at the very moment that he would have acquired an American calling as stable as the appointments he was offered in London, Hamburg, and Berlin.

These are thoughts and feelings I did not want to conceal from you, my dear Frau Thode—even if they matter no longer.

Very truly yours,
Auguste Seidl-Kraus

A Brief Note on Sources

When Anton Seidl died in 1898, it was assumed that statues would be erected in his memory, that he would long be memorialized. But no statues were forthcoming, and Henry Finck's 1899 memorial volume had no successors. When four decades later Arthur Farwell remembered Seidl in the *The Musical Quarterly* ("America's Gain from a Bayreuth Romance: The Mystery of Anton Seidl," October 1944), he endeavored—fruitlessly—to retrieve a forgotten icon. Meanwhile, the two archives at Columbia University and the Brooklyn Historical Society were uncatalogued and unused. And under-utilized they remain.

The Columbia archive, left by Seidl's widow, comprises letters, clippings and memorabilia, Seidl's occasional writings (both published and not), and musical scores. Of the scores, among the most notable are what may be his sole surviving composition, the children's chorus "Good Night," composed for Brighton Beach; and a symphonic synthesis of *Siegfried*, act two, elegantly copied by Arthur Farwell. I presented the first performance of the former in more than a century in Washington, D.C., in 2014 (it may be found on YouTube); curating a New Jersey Symphony Wagner festival in 1999, I had occasion to revive the latter (of which an archival recording was made). The archived letters include Cosima's tenacious 1886 effort to lure Seidl back to Bayreuth (in chapter nine of my novel). The writings include Seidl's unpublished lecture on *Das Rheingold* (also chapter nine).

The Seidl Society Archive at the Brooklyn Historical Society includes programs, letters, clippings, scrapbooks, and memorabilia. Among its treasures are speeches in English composed by Seidl and set down in his hand. As Seidl's surviving English-language letters are mainly notes of instruction, the speeches furnish our best evidence of what Seidl's game but fractured English sounded liked. In my novel, Seidl usually speaks in German (rendered as grammatically correct English). Where he speaks in English, I have attempted to render a less ambitious, more grammatical version of the laboriously elaborate English-language style preserved in the speeches.

Both archives of course inform *The Disciple* as do my books *Wagner Nights: An American History* (1994), *Moral Fire: Musical Portraits from America's Fin-de-Siècle* (2012), and *Classical Music in America: A History of its Rise and Fall* (2005). *Wagner Nights* is mainly about Seidl. *Moral Fire* includes long chapters on Henry Krehbiel and Laura Langford. *Classical Music in America* deals in some detail with Dvořák in New York. I have also produced a pertinent documentary film available on DVD from Naxos: *The "New World" Symphony: A Lens on the American Experience of Race* (2021) and two pertinent Naxos CDs: "Dvořák and America" (2014) and "Arthur Farwell: America's Neglected Composer" (2022). The Dvořák CD includes a 35-minute *Hiawatha* Melodrama I composed with the music historian Michael Beckerman; it mates Longfellow's *The Song of Hiawatha* to Dvořák's *New World* Symphony and *American* Suite. Both CDs include compositions by Farwell, "the first composer to take up Dvořák's challenge"; he ignited the Indianist movement in American music. He also knew and championed Seidl.

Though it remains forgotten that Coney Island once hosted Seidl's twice-daily concerts, this feature of New York City's musical life was once sufficiently prominent that Broadway's first electric sign—1,500 lights colored green, white, red, blue, and yellow—thus advertised Coney Island:

> SWEPT BY OCEAN BREEZES
> THREE GREAT HOTELS
> PAIN'S FIREWORKS
> SOUSA'S BEST
> SEIDL'S GREAT ORCHESTRA
> THE RACES

And so Seidl's activities were copiously recorded by the city's newspapers and magazines: a trove. Seidl in Brooklyn was comprehensively observed by the *Brooklyn Eagle*. When Susan Anthony lectured for the Seidl Society, when Colonel Olcott failed to turn up for a Seidl Society lecture, when Howard Orphan Asylum children were regaled by the Society, when Laura Langford lectured on Wagner with Seidl conducting a full orchestra, the *Eagle* was there.

There is (alas) no biography of Henry Krehbiel. The fullest extant treatment of his life and protean achievements is my chapter in *Moral Fire*. But Krehbiel left many interesting books, of which the most pertinent to *The Disciple* are *Studies in the Wagnerian Drama* (1891) and *Chapters of Opera* (1908).

Diane Sasson's biography *Yearning for the New Age: Laura Holloway-Langford and Late Victorian Spirituality* (2012) is much more about the theosophist than the Wagnerite. Of Langford's own books, the most important (and pertinent to *The Disciple*) is *Ladies of the White House* (1880). Exceptionally informative—in addition to mainstream literature on theosophy and Madame Blavatsky—are the articles about Olcott (October 1915) and Blavatsky (December 1915) published in the theosophical journal *The Word.*

On Dvořák in New York, an essential source is Michael Beckerman's *New Worlds of* Dvořák: *Searching in America for the Composer's Inner Life* (2003); it includes a detailed perusal of extra-musical references to *The Song of Hiawatha* in the *New World* Symphony.

Post-Seidl, Francis Neilson pursued a distinguished career in the theater and politics. Though Seidl never set down the music, Neilson's libretto for *Manabozo* was published and is the source for the excerpts I cull. His libretto for Victor Herbert's *Prince Ananias* is also a published work (chapter eight). His two volumes of reminiscence—*My Life in Two Worlds* (1952)—includes "A Dear Memory" of accompanying Seidl abroad.

Of the many biographies I consulted, Lilli Lehmann's *My Path Through Life* (1914) includes especially telling insights about Anton Seidl.

As in my novel *The Marriage*, few of the incidents in *The Disciple* are wholly invented. For instance: The Bayreuth vignette beginning my book derives from Cosima's diaries, volume 2, May 22, 1878. Wagner's rant, in the same Prologue, is partly based on things he actually wrote or said. A valuable source for Wagner's view of the United States is the two-part "The Work and Mission of My Life" in *North American Review* (1879)—attributed to Wagner but probably written by his disciple Hans von Wolzogen. As in *The Marriage*, my renderings of Krehbiel's reviews and essays (including his Seidl obituary) liberally intermingle actual Krehbiel writings with passages and paragraphs I have invented based on my knowledge of what Krehbiel thought and believed. (I have acquired Krehbiel's distinctive prose style sufficiently that I myself can no longer tell which sentences are mine.)

There exist a few versions of the romantic relationship between Seidl and Daniela Thode. Confusingly, in New York City he was at least once termed "not a lady's man"—a shorthand for homosexuality. His observed companionship with Francis Neilson was pronounced. Neilson later married. In any event, it seems certain that Seidl and Daniela were mutually attracted, and that they re-encountered one another in Bayreuth in 1897. The letter by Mrs. Seidl with which I end *The Disciple* is my own. But Daniela's stipend for Farwell and the Seidl tribute in *Bayreuther Blätter*, here referenced by Auguste, were both real.

Glossary of Names

Dankmar Adler (1844-1900), German-born American architect and civil engineer. He is best known for his fifteen-year partnership with Louis Sullivan, during which they designed influential skyscrapers including the Auditorium Building, completed in 1890 and in its day the tallest building in Chicago and the largest building in the United States.

Helena Blavatsky (1831-1891), Russian-born spiritualist who claimed to have studied with Hindu gurus in Indian and Tibet. In 1873 she moved to New York City, where she became closely associated with Colonel Henry Steel Olcott; they jointly founded the Theosophical Society in 1875. Theosophy impacted widely in the US in the late nineteenth century. Blavatsky's far-flung travels eventually landed her in London, where she died.

Hans von Bülow (1830-1894), eminent German conductor and pianist. He was the first husband of Cosima Liszt, prior to her marriage with Richard Wagner. He influentially championed both Wagner and Liszt, and also Johannes Brahms. His historic tours of the United States propagated the Germanic repertoire.

Harry Thacker Burleigh (1866-1949), Dvořák's assistant at New York's National Conservatory of Music. Born in Erie, Pennsylvania, he acquired the sorrows songs from his blind grandfather, a former slave. After Dvořák death, he played a pivotal role in turning spirituals into art songs, beginning in 1913 with his inspired settings of "Deep River." He also pursued a notable career as a baritone recitalist.

Ferruccio Busoni (1866-1924), Italian/German pianist/composer. A musician of supreme artistic and intellectual gifts, he was based in Berlin but both toured and taught in the United States. His antipathy toward the New World was married to fascinated admiration for Native Americans. He composed an *Indian* Fantasy for piano and orchestra, and two shorter *Indian Notebooks*.

Ludwig Schnorr von Carolsfeld (1836-1865), German operatic tenor admired by Wagner for his artistry and intellect. He created the role of Tristan at the 1865 premiere of *Tristan und Isolde* in Munich. He sang three more performances, took part in *The Flying Dutchman*, and suddenly expired. The cause of his death remains mysterious. A drafty stage was blamed by some, the exertions of learning and performing Tristan was thought causal by others.

James Creelman (1859-1905), Canadian-American journalist identified with "Yellow Journalism," an American species of reportage characterized by sensational scoops and the desire to influence events. His employers included Joseph Pulitzer's *New York World* and William Randolph Hearst's *New York Journal*. Jeannette Thurber engaged him as a publicist for her National Conservatory. Hearst once said: "The beauty about Creelman is the fact that whatever you give him to do instantly becomes in his mind the most important assignment ever given any writer … He thinks that the very fact of the job being given him means that it's a task of surpassing importance, else it would not have been given to so great a man as he."

Natalie Curtis (1875-1912), American ethnomusicologist. With Alice Fletcher and Frances Densmore, she was a pioneering figure in transcribing and preserving Native American song. She also published a collection of African-American music. Her teachers included Ferruccio Busoni; she also crossed paths with Anton Seidl and Antonin Dvořák, and with Cosima and Siegfried Wagner in Bayreuth.

Walter Damrosch (1862-1950), German-born American conductor. As Damrosch owed his considerable eminence and influence not to talent but to impeccable financial and political connections, he may be considered a distinctive product of the New World. He engaged Mahler to guest-conduct his lavishly bankrolled New York Symphony. But Mahler became chief conductor of the rival New York Philharmonic. When the two orchestras merged, Damrosch undertook a second career as an avuncular radio pedagogue via the "Music Appreciation Hour."

Eugene Debs (1855-1926), charismatic American Socialist. In 1894, he led a nation-wide strike against the Pullman Palace Car Company, ended by federal troops sent by President Grover Cleveland. Debs was convicted of defying a court injunction and spent six months in prison. He ran for President five times between 1900 and 1920.

Andreas Dippel (1866-1932), German-born operatic tenor and impresario. Long a stalwart member of the Metropolitan Opera's German casts, beginning in 1890 under Anton Seidl. He became joint manager of the Met, with Giulio Gatti-Casazza, in 1908. Mahler looked to Dippel to safeguard his interests. But the Italians proved unstoppable and Dippel left the Met in 1910.

Antonin Dvořák (1841-1904), Czech composer. As director of New York City's National Conservatory of Music from 1892 to 1895, he exerted a momentous influence on American music, espousing "Negro melodies," and Native American lore and chant, as likely sources of an "American school" of concert music and opera. His own *New World* Symphony (1893), embedding both influences, remains the best-known, most beloved symphonic composition composed on American soil.

Arthur Farwell (1872-1952), American composer and music journalist. He called himself the first composer "to take up Dvořák's challenge," spearheading the Indianist movement in American classical music. Such impressive early Farwell compositions as the astringent *Navajo War Dance* No. 2 for piano (1904) evoke Bartók. Farwell was also a significant musical journalist, whose review of Mahler's performance of Schubert's Symphony No. 9 with the New York Philharmonic (*Musical America*, Nov. 5, 1910) may be the most vividly detailed description of what Mahler's Philharmonic performances sounded like. For more: Joseph Horowitz. *Dvořák's Prophecy and the Vexed Fate of American Classical Music* (2021).

Henry T. Finck (1854-1926), *New York Evening Post* music critic. A confirmed Wagnerite, he reviewed the first Bayreuth festival in 1876. His many enthusiastic books include *Wagner and His Works* (1893). He edited *Anton Seidl: A Memorial by his Friends* (1894).

Philip Hale (1854-1934), eminent Boston music critic. A blue-blooded product of Exeter and Yale, and of subsequent musical instruction in Germany and France, he became a Boston critic in 1889 and also wrote program notes for the Boston Symphony. His tastes were those of a Francophile aesthete. His prose was notable for its worldliness and breezy aplomb. He eloquently embodied Brahmin Boston.

Victor Herbert (1854-1924), American composer and cellist. Though born in Guernsey, he mistakenly thought himself a native of Ireland. A German resident from 1867, he graduated from the Stuttgart Conservatory. He was already a prominent composer and solo cellist when in 1886 he relocated to the US with his wife, Therese Förster; at Anton Seidl's Metropolitan Opera, he became the company's principal cellist and she a principal soprano. A Seidl protégé, he sometimes (as at Brighton Beach) served as Seidl's assistant conductor. In 1894, Seidl premiered Herbert's Cello Concerto No. 2—today, his best-known symphonic composition—with the composer as soloist. Though Herbert led the Pittsburgh Orchestra from 1898 to 1904 (programing a lot of Wagner), he eventually became associated with lighter repertoire and with operetta. His best-known stage works were and are *Babes in Toyland* (1903), *Mlle. Modiste* (1905), and *The Red Mill* (1906). He also composed an ambitious Indianist grand opera, *Natoma* (1911). His genial personality was widely known and admired.

Henry Lee Higginson (1834-1919), orchestra inventor. A colossal figure in the history of American classical music, he amassed a sufficient fortune in banking to realize his dream of creating a world-class concert orchestra for Boston. This was the Boston Symphony Orchestra, founded in 1881 with Higginson as sole owner and operator (there was no board). He built Symphony Hall, still the orchestra's home, in 1900. For more: Joseph Horowitz, *Moral Fire: Musical Portraits from America's Fin-de-Siècle* (2012).

James Gibbon Huneker (1857-1921), American arts critic and journalist. Of the "Old Guard" New York City music critics, a turn-of-the-century critical community unsurpassed before or after, Huneker was the prophet of modernism—an antipode to his good friend Henry Krehbiel. Krehbiel's prose was tangled and dense; Huneker was a virtuoso hyper-stylist. He was also a public celebrity, swilling his libations, launching his orations, banging the "Marsellaise" and the "International" on smoke-stained pianos with rattling keys. H.L. Mencken, a Huneker protégé, recorded in detail a five-hour Huneker monologue, a "veritable geyser of unfamiliar names, shocking epigrams in strange tongues, unearthly philosophies out of the backwaters of Scandinavia, Transylvania, Bulgaria, the Basque country, the Ukraine." "I have never encountered a man who was further removed from dullness; it seemed a literal impossibility for him to open his mouth without discharging some word or phrase that arrested the attention and stuck in the memory." The prodigious Huneker rant recorded by Mencken spanned the topography of Liszt's warts, Shaw's struggle to throw off Presbyterianism, what Cezanne thought of his disciples, what George Moore said about German bathrooms, D'Annunzio's affair with Duse, and the last words of Whitman.

Henry Holden Huss (1862-1953), American composer and pianist. A native of Newark, New Jersey, the son of German immigrants, Huss was a graduate of Munich's Royal Conservatory. He was one of a number of American Romantics whose music enjoyed a brief degree of prominence during the late nineteenth century.

Robert Ingersoll (1833-1899), possibly the most famous American orator of his day. He was dubbed "the great agnostic" by Henry Ward Beecher in 1880. His causes included Wagnerism.

Sissieretta Jones (1868/1869—1933), celebrated African American soprano. The highest paid Black performer of her time, she was known as "the Black Patti"—referencing the Italian diva Adelina Patti. She sang for four Presidents and the British royal family, and toured widely with her Black Patti Troubadours. Though her soprano was highly trained, and her repertoire included some operatic selections, Black vocalists of her generation could not appear on American operatic stages.

Josef Jan Kovářík (1870-1951), violinist/violist born to Czech emigrants in the United States. He met Dvořák while studying in Prague and accompanied him to America in 1892. In New York, he became Dvořák's amanuensis. It was at Kovářík's invitation that Dvořák and his family summered in 1893 in Kovářík's hometown: Spillville, Iowa. Kovářík later became a member of the New York Philharmonic and of the Dannreuther Quartet. He regarded his years with Dvořák as the happiest of his life.

Lilli Lehmann (1848-1929), German operatic soprano. She was the leading soprano at the Metropolitan Opera during Anton Seidl's Wagner seasons. Her regal presence textured her high artistry. Her social persona was impressively forward and frank. When she was in her late twenties, Richard Wagner took a shine to her at Bayreuth. Later, in New York, she intermingled with male colleagues at Luchow's and other drinking establishments mainly frequented by men. In retirement, she became an important pedagogue whose pupils included Olive Fremstad. For more: Joseph Horowitz, *Wagner Nights: An American History* (1994).

Henry Wadsworth Longfellow (1807-1882), the most popular American poet of his time. He was known as a "fireside" poet because his works were read aloud by families. His verse epic *The Song of Hiawatha* (1855) narrates the adventures of the Ojibwe warrior Hiawatha and his tragic love for Minnehaha, a Dakota woman. It is based on Native American oral traditions and on the writings of Henry Rowe Schoolcraft. Longfellow had originally planned to follow Schoolcraft in calling his hero Manabozho. He wrote in an 1854 journal entry: "Work at 'Manabozho;' or, as I think I shall call it, 'Hiawatha'—that being another name for the same personage." But he was mistaken in thinking the names synonymous.

Francis Neilson (1867-1961), distinguished actor, playwright, stage and opera director, and politician. Born in Britain, he moved to New York City at the age of eighteen and there became Anton Seidl's inseparable companion. The *Manabozo* libretto he wrote for Seidl was published in 1899 but never set. The *Prince Ananias* libretto he wrote for Victor Herbert became Herbert's first operetta; it opened at the Broadway

Theatre on November 20, 1894. Subsequent to accompanying Seidl to Bayreuth and London in 1897, Neilson resumed residency in England, becoming a Member of Parliament in 1910. His radical political views were greatly influenced by the writings of Henry George in the United States. A pacifist, he resigned from Parliament in 1916. Returning to the US, he became an American citizen in 1921. His second wife, Halen Swift Neilson, was a notable American writer and art collector. He authored more than sixty books.

Albert Niemann (1831-1917), German operatic tenor. For Wagner (with whom he had a consequential personal and professional relationship), he created the role of Siegmund in 1876. He arrived at Seidl's Metropolitan Opera in 1886, at the twilight of a long and eminent career. His towering physical presence, expressive face, artistic intelligence, and seething emotional veracity (especially as Tristan) instantly made an overwhelming impression. For more see *Wagner Nights: An American History* (1994).

Lillian Nordica (1857-1914), American operatic soprano. Born Lillian Allen Norton in Maine, she pursued a prominent international career as a dramatic soprano. She sang leading roles at the Metropolitan Opera from 1891to 1909. In New York, Anton Seidl coached her as Elsa (in *Lohengrin*), Venus (in *Tannhäuser*), and Isolde (in *Tristan und Isolde*). She was the first American to sing at Bayreuth: Elsa in 1894.

Henry Steel Olcott (1832-1907), American journalist, lawyer, and theosophical leader. Having met Helena Blavatsky in 1894, he was co-founder and first president of the Theosophical Society, formed in 1897 in New York City; its headquarters were moved to India (where Olcott died) a year later. He was the first American of European ancestry to formally convert to Buddhism.

Emil Paur (1855-1932), Austrian conductor. As conductor of the Boston Symphony from 1893 to 1898, he did not enjoy success comparable to that of Wilhelm Gericke, Arthur Nikisch, or Karl Muck. He later conducted the New York Philharmonic (1898-1902) and Pittsburgh Symphony (1904-1910), and at the Berlin State Opera.

Jean de Reszke (1850-1925), Polish operatic tenor. The pre-eminent dramatic tenor of his time, he was equally appreciated for his glamour and integrity. He first sang at the Metropolitan Opera in 1891 as a master singer renowned in French and Italian roles. After assaying *Lohengrin* and *Die Meistersinger* in Italian at the Met, he successfully campaigned (with his brother, the baritone Edouard de Reszke) for the return of German opera under Anton Seidl. For Seidl, he acquired and sang his first Tristan in 1895, and his first Siegfried (in the opera *Siegfried*) in 1897. Subsequent to Seidl's death, he added the *Götterdämmerung* Siegfried to his repertoire. His late acquisition of these Heldentenor roles was instantly legendary.

Carl Schurz (1829-1906), German-born statesman, journalist, reformer. A pre-eminent German American, he fled his homeland after the revolutions of 1848-49. After service as a Civil War general, he was a U.S. Senator from Missouri and Secretary of the Interior. A literate musician, he was a Wagnerite.

Auguste Seidl-Krauss (1853-1939), Austrian American soprano. She married Anton Seidl in 1884 and accompanied him to the New World. At the Metropolitan Opera, her repertoire included five Wagner roles: Elisabeth, Elsa, Sieglinde, Gutrune, and Eva. She last sang at the Met in 1888 and subsequently retired from the stage; New York weather was said not to agree with her. After her husband's death she moved permanently to their summer home in Kingston, New York. Her memorabilia (including scores, letters, and clippings) became the Seidl Collection at Columbia University.

Louis Sullivan (1886-1929), pre-eminent American architect. In an initial stage of his illustrious career, he partnered Dankmar Adler as a theater architect; their culminating achievement was Chicago's Auditorium Building (1886-1890), which incorporated a 4,200-seat theater, a hotel, and a seventeen-story office tower. He later mentored Frank Lloyd Wright.

Daniela Thode (1860-1940). Born Daniela Senta von Bülow Liszt, she was the daughter of Hans von Bülow and Cosima Liszt. Following Cosima's alliance with Richard Wagner, she became Wagner's stepdaughter and part of the Wahnfried household. She married Henry Thode in 1886. Following their divorce, she settled permanently in Bayreuth, where she worked as a costume designer for the festival. She was also a highly trained pianist.

Theodore Thomas (1835-1905), German American conductor. A dominating personality, he was the individual most responsible for spreading symphonic culture nationally in the United States; his credo was "A symphony orchestra shows the culture of the community, not opera." Born in Germany, he toured as Master Theodore Thomas, the prodigy violinist, from an early age. In 1850, he settled in New York City and began to study conducting. His world-class Thomas Orchestra toured nationally beginning in the 1860s. He was conductor of the New York Philharmonic (1877-1878, 1879-1891) and of Jeannette Thurber's American Opera Company (1886-1887) before becoming founding music director of the Chicago Orchestra (later the Chicago Symphony) in 1905. Artistically, he was the antithesis of Anton Seidl; he shunned the Romantic use of *rubatos* and extreme tempos of the Wagnerian school. Beethoven was his lodestar.

Jeannette Thurber (1835-1905), visionary American music educator. A graduate of the Paris Conservatory, she founded the National Conservatory of Music, in New York City, in 1886. Her intention was to keep gifted young American musicians from studying abroad, with the ultimate goal of furthering a distinctive American school of composition. Bankrolled by her husband, and endowed with formidable powers of persuasion, she lured Antonin Dvořák to the New World to become the conservatory's director in 1892. Concomitantly, she offered full scholarships to gifted African Americans—like Dvořák, Henry Krehbiel, and various others, she believed that Black America would shape a future American music. The Panic of 1893 undermined her financial resources and led to Dvořák's departure in 1895. Her American Opera Company, a kindred initiative, began touring opera in English in 1886 but expired a year later.

Cosima Wagner (1837-1930), the daughter of Franz Liszt and the writer Marie d'Agoult. Her first marriage, in 1857, was to Hans von Bülow. Her relationship with Richard Wagner began in 1863; she married him in 1870. After his death, she took over the Bayreuth Festival and insured its survival. Her controversial tenure, lasting until 1907, was tenacious, resourceful, and conservative.

Richard Wagner (1813-1883), German composer and conductor. Wagner's relationship with Anton Seidl began in 1872 when he moved to Bayreuth and Seidl joined him there. Wahnfried, the Wagner family home, was finished in 1874. The first Bayreuth Festival followed two years later; Hans Richter conducted the *Ring* cycle three times. Following this landmark summer, Wagner commenced work on *Parsifal*, finishing in 1882. The 1882 Bayreuth Festival premiered the new work—after which the Wagners moved to Venice for the winter. Wagner died there on February 13. Seidl took part in the funeral procession on the Grand Canal, after which Wagner was buried at Bayreuth in the Wahfried garden.

Eugene Ysaÿe (1858-1931), famous Belgian violinist, composer, and conductor. As an instrumentalist, he was admired for his virtuosity, individuality, and tonal ravishments. Declining health directed him toward composing and conducting. His compositional output includes an important set of solo violin sonatas. He was to become the concertmaster of the Seidl Orchestra—a post that would have also included conducting responsibilities. When Seidl died, he turned down the directorship of the New York Philharmonic. He was music director of the Cincinnati Symphony from 1918 to 1922.

ABOUT THE AUTHOR

Joseph Horowitz is a cultural historian and concert producer. His thirteen previous books include a sequel to *The Disciple*: the novel *The Marriage: The Mahlers in New York (2023)*—which he turned into a play (premiered in 2026). *Dvořák's Prophecy and the Vexed Fate of Black Classical Music* (2022) links to six "Dvořák's Prophecy" documentary films Horowitz produced for Naxos, exploring topics in American music. He regularly produces "More than Music" documentaries for National Public Radio (via the daily newsmagazine *1A*). As an artistic consultant for orchestras in all parts of the US, he has produced nearly 100 thematic festivals. He was a *New York Times* music critic (1976–1980) and, subsequently, executive director of two orchestras: the Brooklyn Philharmonic and PostClassical Ensemble. As a performer, he is increasingly active as a vocal accompanist. His website is www.josephhorowitz.com. His blog, *The Unanswered Question*, is www.artsjournal.com/uq.

By the same author

Conversations with Arrau (1982)

Understanding Toscanini: How He Became an American Culture-God and Helped Create a New Audience for Old Music (1987)

The Ivory Trade (1990)

Wagner Nights: An American History (1994)

The Post-Classical Predicament (1995)

Dvořák in America (for young readers, 2003)

Classical Music in America: A History of Its Rise and Fall (2005)

Artists in Exile: How Refugees from Twentieth Century War and Revolution Transformed the American Performing Arts (2008)

Moral Fire: Musical Portraits from America's Fin-de-Siecle (2012)

"On My Way"—Rouben Mamoulian, George Gershwin, and "Porgy and Bess" (2013)

Dvořák's Prophecy and the Vexed Fate of Black Classical Music (2021)

The Marriage: The Mahlers in New York (a novel, 2023)

The Propaganda of Freedom: JFK, Shostakovich, Stravinsky, and the Cultural Cold War (2023)

The Marriage: The Mahlers in New York (a play, 2026)

Bearing Witness: The American Odyssey of Leonard Bernstein (in preparation)

Why Ives? – A Celebration of Cultural Memory (in preparation)